Going Off the Rails

Richard S. Brown

Black Rose Writing | Texas

First printing

This is a work of fiction. Names, characters, businesses, places, events, and incidents are either the products of the author's imagination or used in a fictitious manner. Any resemblance to actual persons, living or dead, or actual events is purely coincidental.

ISBN: 978-1-68433-630-2
PUBLISHED BY BLACK ROSE WRITING
www.blackrosewriting.com

Printed in the United States of America
Suggested Retail Price (SRP) $18.95

Going Off the Rails is printed in Gentium Basic

*As a planet-friendly publisher, Black Rose Writing does its best to eliminate unnecessary waste to reduce paper usage and energy costs, while never compromising the reading experience. As a result, the final word count vs. page count may not meet common expectations.

To Stephanie and Amy

ACKNOWLEDGEMENTS

I chose south central Wisconsin as the setting for this story, because it's the place where I spent most of my early years, and it still feels a part of me. The characters and the events depicted in this story are fictional. However, the names of towns and villages are real. The Sparta Herald is the actual name of the Sparta newspaper that published for more than a hundred years until it merged with another paper in 2001 and became the Monroe County Herald. Current managing editor, Pat Mulroney, kindly concurred in my use of the Sparta Herald name as a center piece for my story.

There are many people I have to thank for helping me through the process of writing this book. Foremost among them are members of my writing group that provided invaluable chapter critiques as part of our monthly meetings. They include Marlis Brodhead, Adam Sales, Charlotte Henderson, Gregg Coonrod, Joyce Brown, Kent Moore, Shawn Parkison, and Tim Brown. In addition, Frank Cook was particularly helpful in editing the complete final manuscript. Bill Pollard and Tom Pollard, both with long careers in law enforcement, provided useful input for prison and sheriff office scenes. Finally, my wife, Sung Hi, gave invaluable support to keep pushing me through the tough spots, reading over every chapter and giving pointed suggestions to make my characters' emotions and behaviors as true to real life as possible.

The Monroe County Historical Society maintains an excellent website with many period pictures that I used as a guide in my description of Sparta. *Northwestern Lines*, the official magazine of the Chicago and Northwestern Historical Society likewise provided useful photos and stories pertaining to railroading in the 1950s. In fact, a story I read in the first quarter 2016 issue of the magazine was about a 1959 train derailment thirty miles northwest of Eau Claire. Although no one died in that accident, and to my knowledge, no one went to prison because of it, that article gave me the idea to write this fictional story revolving around a train derailment in Wisconsin.

Going Off the Rails

CHAPTER 1

September 1958

Stan Ellis sat hunched over his typewriter, struggling to find the right words to wrap up his story on last night's boring city council meeting. He'd been at it for a half-hour and was hoping for a distraction when his phone rang.

"Sparta Herald, news desk."

A woman's faint voice, almost a whisper, came over the line. "I'm calling for Mr. Ellis. Is he there?"

"Speaking. What can I do for you?"

"Are you the reporter who wrote about that train accident a few years ago where three people died?"

He didn't have to think hard to recall it. It was less than a year after he started working at the Herald. His first big story—bigger than anything he'd covered since. Normally Irv would have taken the assignment, but he was on vacation up north, and Ed Malloy let him handle it. The accident and trial afterwards attracted papers from all over the state. It wasn't often you saw something like that in Monroe County.

"Yes, I covered the accident," he said. "What about it?"

Stan noticed a slight tremble in the caller's voice. "George didn't do what they said he did. He wasn't responsible for what happened, and he shouldn't be in prison. I was hoping you could find some way to help him. He's not well."

"Why are you calling me?"

"Because you're a newspaper reporter, and I think I can trust you. You may not remember me, but I talked to you once during the trial, and you seemed sympathetic to George's situation."

"You're talking about the engineer who was convicted?"

"Yes, George Cashman."

"You think someone else was responsible?"

"Yes, I'm sure someone else caused that train wreck. It wasn't George."

"Why don't you go to the police?"

"If I do that, then he'll know I told them, and I'll be in big trouble. I can't do that."

"Can we meet someplace and talk about this? What's your name?"

The line seemed to go dead for a moment. "I... I can't get involved anymore. I shouldn't have called. I'm sorry." Click.

Stan rocked back in his chair. Lord yes, he remembered the accident. The railroads had been an integral part of the Wisconsin landscape for a long time. Sparta had two of them running through the center of town—the Chicago & Northwestern and the Milwaukee Road. Like any big industry, accidents happened from time to time. But three passengers died in that accident. It was a big deal.

Stan felt bad for whoever was on the phone, but what could he do? He went back to his typewriter, and after putting the final period to his piece, he got up, walked over to Irv Sloan's desk, and handed him the council article.

Irv had been a newspaperman his entire life, working at the Herald for most of that time. He was in his late fifties, but looked older. With droopy eyes, a curved back, and a wobbly gait, he reminded Stan of an old basset hound on his last legs. Nevertheless, he had always treated Stan well, and had given him expert advice when he first started on the paper five years ago, just out of college. Back then, Irv was the senior reporter, but he took over as the news editor when John Ingram retired last year. He still covered some stories, but now, unless there was something that piqued his interest, he let Stan do the local news and sports.

Pushing his glasses up onto his bald pate, Irv looked up. "Any fireworks at the meeting last night?"

Stan shook his head. "Nope. Nothing out of the ordinary. Pretty dull stuff."

"Too bad. We could use a good lead story. We haven't had anything to stir up the readers since last month when Kastner's furniture store burned down."

"Can't help you, Irv. Sorry."

Irv didn't respond, but started reading over the piece. Stan turned and went back to his desk.

That night as he lay in bed, Stan kept thinking about the anonymous caller. He tried to picture some woman he might have talked to during the trial. Although Irv had covered most of the trial himself, Stan found time to sit in on the first two sessions. As he let his mind wander, he recalled standing in the hallway during a break. A young woman came up to him, and they started talking. She looked about twenty-five—just a little thing in a modest dark blue dress with a buttoned top. With her short honey-blonde hair and pretty smile, he thought she looked a lot like Debbie Reynolds. It hadn't occurred to him she might be related to the defendant who reminded him of Ernest Borgnine, the guy who played the heavy in *From Here to Eternity*.

He remembered he told her he had covered the accident and wrote the initial story, and she'd asked him what he thought of the trial. He told her he didn't see enough evidence to convict, and she seemed happy about that. His opinion had changed though, later in the trial, when the fingerprint evidence came out.

Stan closed his eyes and tried to sleep, but thoughts kept rolling through his mind. If he could find that woman and talk to her, maybe there'd be a story he could dig into. If she had information that showed George Cashman was innocent, a story like that could go statewide or even get picked up by the wires.

CHAPTER 2

Stan hadn't slept well and had a lot on his mind as he walked into the Herald's lobby the next morning. Sid Hunter, the circulation manager, gave a cheerful wave, but he passed by without responding. Esther, who took care of advertising and bookkeeping chores, called out 'good morning' twice before he heard her and waved a half-hearted hello. When he got to the newsroom, he headed straight for his desk. Rose Woodley, who wrote the "personals" gossip column and a weekly column on women's issues, raised her coffee in greeting, and held it in the air until he noticed her. He finally looked up and said. "Oh, hi Rose. Sorry, I had something on my mind. Where's Irv?"

"He said he'd be a little late this morning. Had to take his mother to the doctor."

After checking through his in-box and finding nothing of importance, he told Rose he was going downstairs to look at some files. "If Irv comes in and is looking for me, I'll be in the basement."

He smiled to himself as he passed by Mr. Malloy's office. His boss sat at his desk with his head down, engrossed in reading something, that signature cigar sticking out the corner of his mouth. When he opened the double doors to the press room, he was met by a blast of hot air and the pungent smell of ink. The stairs to the basement were near the rear of the press room. Cal Loomis was sitting at a Linotype, playing it as if it were a piano, and as Stan walked by, he gave him a friendly pat on the back. Cal acknowledged with a wave while keeping his eyes on the keyboard.

As Stan started down the stairs to the basement, he wished he'd kept his notes from the train wreck. Lesson learned, he thought. At least the office kept copies of its newspapers. When he got to the bottom, Jim Carbody, the office's janitor, supply man, and unofficial archivist, popped his head out from his office cubbyhole hidden behind shelves stacked with office supplies and spare equipment. "Hey Stan. What brings you down here to the dungeon?"

"I've got a little research to do. I'm looking for what we have on a train wreck that happened in 1954."

He pointed to a small table next to rolls of newsprint stacked up six-feet high along the wall. "Have a seat there. I'll go pull the book for you."

Stan took a notepad and pen from his shirt pocket, laid them on the table, and began doodling while he waited.

After two or three minutes, Carbody brought over two over-sized books and plunked them down in front of him. "Here you go. Let me know if you need anything else."

Stan thanked him and began paging through the top book covering the first six months of 1954. After several minutes he came to June 21, and his eyes caught the headline:

> **Three Killed in Train Derailment.** Yesterday at about 10:00 a.m. a Chicago & Northwestern passenger train derailed between Wilton and Kendall, resulting in the deaths of three persons and over fifty injured. The train was en route to Chicago from St. Paul, Minnesota. The accident occurred a mile south of Tunnel Number 2.
>
> Two of the train's seven passenger cars overturned and slid down a twenty-foot embankment along the Kickapoo River. Inspectors from the railroad and members of the Monroe County Sheriff's Office were on the scene of the accident and were looking into the cause. Volunteer fire department rescue units from Wilton, Norwalk, and Kendall attended the injured who were transported to area hospitals.
>
> Train engineer, George Cashman was among the injured. According to Sheriff Leo Bascom, Cashman could not be immediately interviewed because of his condition...

After reading through the article, Stan paged ahead to the next date's front page follow-up. That's what he was looking for—the names and hometowns of the deceased, along with a list of all the injured passengers and hometowns. Among them was George Cashman, age 43, listed as a resident of Elroy, a railway junction town about forty miles south of Sparta. After writing down Cashman's information along with the names of several other passengers who showed a hometown within a hundred-mile radius, he put aside that book and opened the second. He came to July 28 and stopped.

Train Engineer Charged with Negligent Homicide. George Cashman, the engineer of the ill-fated Chicago & Northwestern train that derailed near Wilton on June 20, was arrested yesterday afternoon by Monroe County authorities. Court documents issued by Judge Clement Hershey reveal that Cashman is accused of criminal negligent homicide resulting in the deaths of three of his passengers.

The official cause of the accident, as reported by the Chicago & Northwestern Railroad investigating team, was excessive speed. In addition, they identified alcohol consumption as a contributing factor. The investigative report issued by railroad authorities concluded that at the point of derailment the train was going at least 25 miles an hour over the recommended safe speed of 40 miles an hour.

Stan kept turning pages until he came to October 28, where a brief story about the opening of the trial jumped out at him. He flipped more pages until he reached November 3 and stopped. Bold headlines announced the trial's end.

Cashman Convicted of Negligent Homicide. A twelve-person jury yesterday handed down a guilty verdict in the trial of George Cashman, the engineer who operated the Chicago & Northwestern train that derailed near Wilton on June 20, killing three passengers. Cashman was found guilty of negligent homicide while under the influence of alcohol.

The conviction carries a maximum sentence of twenty-five years in prison.

District Attorney John Hamilton said the key evidence in the trial was the nearly empty bottle of whiskey that was found the day after the crash in a tool drawer in the engine cab. He said lab tests revealed Cashman's fingerprints on the bottle.

Sentencing is to occur on November 16. Cashman's attorney, Anson Puller, says that his client maintains his innocence, and he will appeal...

Stan closed the back-issue book, tucked the notepad back in his pocket, and yelled out, "I'm finished, Jim. You want me to put these away?"

Carbody yelled back, "No. I'll take care of it."

As he went back upstairs to the newsroom, Stan thought about what he'd just read. The investigators had found a liquor bottle, but the articles didn't say anything about them doing a blood test. If they didn't, then there was no proof he was drunk. If Cashman was drinking so heavily, why would the bottle have been tucked away safely in the toolbox before the accident occurred? Something seemed amiss, and he needed to find out what it was. That mystery caller was the key to getting any answers, but before doing anything more, he needed to clear it with the boss.

•   •   •   •   •

Ed Malloy was the sixty-two-year-old publisher and editor in chief of the Herald. The paper had been owned by the Malloy family for more than fifty years, and Ed took over when his father died some twenty years ago. Stan expected the old man would work there until he died too, since the paper was his life. He knocked on the window, and Ed, the thick cigar still in his mouth, looked up and waved him in. "What d'ya got?"

"I think I got a lead on a story about an old criminal case. Remember the train wreck near Wilton where three people were killed about four years ago?"

He scratched his head. "Yeah, I do."

"The train engineer—his name was George Cashman—was sent to prison, and that seemed to be the end of it," said Stan. "Yesterday I got a call from a woman who claimed someone else was responsible, but she wouldn't give me her name. I want to find her and see what she has to say. It could lead to something really big—maybe get the state to look at the case again."

Ed took the cigar out of his mouth and leaned back in his chair. "From what I remember the guy was convicted of being drunk while operating the train. You want to defend a guy like that? Don't you have enough to keep you busy?"

"Well, yes, I have plenty to do, but this could be an important story. I was just looking through the back issues, and I think there's a possibility the guy wasn't actually drunk. Maybe somebody set him up. That's why I need to find this woman."

Malloy peered over the top of his glasses. "I think you'd be chasing an imaginary rabbit down an empty hole.

"If I can't find this woman, or find her and learn that there's nothing to it, I'll drop it."

Malloy took a puff on his cigar and then laid it in the ashtray. "It might not be a bad idea to do a 'look-back' story, but I'm not sure about trying to overturn something that's already been put to rest. It might upset some people around town."

"I understand that. I wouldn't write anything that wasn't based on facts, but I think it's part of our job to print what's important—and this could be important."

Malloy sniffed and picked up his cigar again. "If I go along with your little investigative project, where would you start?"

"I'll do a background story first, maybe interview some of the passengers on the train who were injured. Maybe talk to the district attorney to get his thoughts on the trial. Of course, I want to find this mystery woman and interview her, and then go interview the train engineer to get his side of the story. I'm not sure where he is now, but I'll find out. Then I'll see where it all leads."

Malloy nodded his head slowly. "Okay, I'll give you a shot at this. When can you get the first piece done?

"I can get the background article by the first of next week."

Malloy maintained a serious look on his face. "Just because I let you take on this story doesn't mean you can forget about your regular assignments—city council, local accidents, high school games, and what not."

Stan let out a sigh. "I understand. Thanks for letting me do this. Since I'll have to be on the road for some interviews, any problem with me getting travel pay?"

Malloy looked reluctant. "See what you can get by phone first. You can put in a voucher for day trips, but no overnights without checking with me. Oh... and if you want to go see an inmate in one of the state prisons, you need to talk to Irv. He's done a couple of prison interviews in the past. He can tell you what to do."

"Okay. I will."

Just as Stan got back to his desk he saw Irv scuffling into the office with a preoccupied look on his face.

"Hey Irv. Can I talk to you?"

He looked up. "Huh? What? Oh, sure."

"Ed gave me the okay to work on a feature story about that train wreck that happened a few years ago between Kendall and Wilton."

"I remember. What's to write about?"

"I got an anonymous call from some woman who said she had information that Cashman, the engineer, wasn't responsible for the accident. I need to find her and talk to her."

Irv offered a skeptical smile. "He was operating the train, wasn't he? Who else was responsible? I think someone's pulling your leg."

Stan grimaced. "You may be right, but that woman's call got under my skin. I'd like to get some answers. Not sure where to start, but I plan on interviewing the train engineer to see if he can identify her."

Irv raised his eyes to the ceiling and nodded, "I can see where you're coming from. It seems like a long shot, but where there's a chance for a good story... If I was younger I might do the same thing."

Stan smiled. "Do you know where Cashman went to prison? I need to call them about setting up an appointment."

Irv thought a moment. "No, I can't recall. You can find that out from court records. Or it might be quicker to call Cashman's attorney. I think he was local. Don't remember his name."

"I saw the attorney's name in one of the articles I just read," said Stan. "I wrote his name down. I'll give him a call. Maybe he can give me an address where he used to live. I know Cashman was living in Elroy, but don't have a street address."

"He may or may not give you that."

Stan nodded. "By the way, Ed said you've done interviews at prisons before, and I should ask you about the process."

"Yeah, it's been a while. What I did was contact the prison's admin office and told them what I wanted to do. They verified that the person I wanted to talk to was there, and they sent me some forms to fill out. The prison warden has to approve any press interviews."

"How long did it take to get the approval?"

Irv paused. "It took a little over a week from when I mailed in the forms."

Stan shook his head. "I was hoping to interview Cashman this week. It looks like it won't be until next week at least. Maybe I can find out something about that woman who called while I'm waiting for the approval."

Irv nodded with a smile. "Let me know if you need my help."

"Thanks. I think I've got everything under control for now."

Stan went back to his desk and looked through the notes until he found the attorney's name—Anson Puller. Seeing he had an office in Sparta, he went back to the phone directory, found Puller in the business section, and dialed the number.

A woman answered the phone. "Office of Puller and Kline. Can I help you?"

"My name is Stan Ellis. I'm a reporter with the Sparta Herald. I'd like to speak to Mr. Puller please."

There was a brief pause. "He's not available right now. Can you tell me what you're calling about?"

"Yes. I'm working on a story concerning a man Mr. Puller represented a few years ago in connection with the big train wreck that happened near Wilton."

"I see. If you'll leave me your phone number, I'll pass your message to Mr. Puller."

After giving her the number and hanging up, he began working on another story. Fifteen minutes later his phone rang.

"Stan Ellis. Sparta Herald news desk."

"This is Anson Puller. I got your message about someone I represented."

"Thank you for returning my call. The person I'm inquiring about is George Cashman, the engineer who was involved in the train derailment near Wilton. Do you remember?"

"Yes, of course. But I no longer represent Mr. Cashman."

"I understand sir, but I'm trying to get the address where he used to live. I want to get in touch with his family, and I don't have a street address. I thought I might get that from you."

"Mr. Ellis, I can't release any private information on my clients or their family members. You should know that."

"Yes sir, I just thought you might—"

"I'm curious though. Why are you interested in doing a story on that case? It's more than three years old.

"A couple days ago I got an anonymous call from a woman. She said she knew Cashman was innocent, and she was asking for my help. I asked her why she didn't go to the police, and she just said she couldn't because she was afraid whoever was responsible would do something to her. She sounded terrified. I think it was probably Cashman's wife—or maybe a daughter."

"Hmm—interesting. As I said, I can't give out any information on client family members. Haven't been in touch with Cashman since the court rejected our appeal. However... I will tell you I don't believe he had a daughter—if that's any help."

Stan jerked to attention. "That's a big help, Mr. Puller. Thanks. Can you tell me where he went to prison so I can try to go interview him?"

"He was sent to Waupon. I don't know anything about his current status, but if you uncover anything new, let me know."

"I will," said Stan. "You've given me a place to start and I appreciate your help."

After finishing his conversation, Stan went over to the bookcase where various telephone and reference books were kept. After locating the number for the Waupon Prison, he dialed the number and was transferred three times before reaching a woman who could help him. She confirmed that George Cashman was still at Waupon and told him she would mail him the forms for requesting an interview. When he asked her if there was anywhere he could get the forms locally, she said, "Try the sheriff's office."

After hanging up, he grabbed his jacket and flat cap and hollered out to Irv, "I'm headed over to the sheriff's office. Be back in a half-hour."

CHAPTER 3

The sheriff's office was located behind the courthouse building, just three blocks from the Herald. Stan decided to walk rather than take his car, and as he headed down Oak Street, he heard the whistle of a train. It made him think of the time last summer he and Patty took the Hiawatha into Milwaukee to see an afternoon Braves game. It was a relaxing trip. He didn't have to worry about driving back late at night on dark twisting roads. Then he thought of those passengers in that train wreck four years ago. How shocked and terrified they must have been when everything went flying.

He entered the lobby of the sheriff's office and saw Debbie Crable at the reception desk. He'd interviewed her for a story last year when she was sworn in as the first female deputy on the force, and they'd developed a good rapport ever since.

"Hi Debbie. I'm doing a story on someone who was sent up to Waupon a few years ago. I want to go there to interview him, and I was told you may have visitor request forms here."

She frowned. "I'm not sure. We've got a drawer of forms here in the desk. I'll check." She got off her stool and bent down to open a lower drawer in the desk. After sorting through several files, she raised up with a sheet in her hands. "Here it is. The instructions are attached to the form."

"Thanks Debbie." He took the form, but just as he started to leave, a thought struck him. The sheriff's office should have some record of Cashman's old address. If they'd give him that information, he could save a lot of time and go looking for his mystery caller right away. He turned back to Debbie. "Is Sheriff Bascom in? There's something I'd like to ask him."

"Haven't seen him since early this morning. But you're welcome to check with his secretary. Just sign in on this sheet first."

After signing in, Debbie directed him to the sheriff's office down an open hallway to his right. The sheriff's secretary, busy filing her nails, looked up when he approached her desk. "Can I help you?"

Stan took off his cap and held it to his side. "I'm with the Sparta Herald and I'd like to see Sheriff Bascom."

The secretary put down her nail file. "I'm sorry. The sheriff went out of town for a conference, and I don't expect him back until Friday. If you'd like to make an appointment for next week..."

Stan shook his head. "No, I needed to talk with him today. Thanks just the same."

He turned, head down, and walked back out the way he came. Just as he passed the reception desk, he saw Glen Horner emerge from a door at the rear of the lobby. Stan stopped and spread his arms wide. "Am I glad to see you!"

Glen was a deputy in the sheriff's office, and Stan considered him his best friend—other than Patty. If anyone could help him get the information he needed, Glen would be that person. Stan had known him since their teens when they both ran track at Tomah High. After high school, they went their separate ways and lost touch. Stan went off to college to study journalism, and Glen went into the army. They reconnected a few months after Stan returned to Sparta to take the job at the Herald. He credited Glen with being responsible for his meeting Patty, who was a close friend of Glen's wife.

"Hey Stan. What brings you here? Working on something?"

"As a matter-of-fact, I am. Maybe you could help me with it."

"Glad to, but I'm kind of in a rush right now. I have these warrants I have to go serve."

"I just need a couple minutes. Let's sit over there away from these people so we can talk." He took Glen's elbow and led him over to a line of empty chairs set against the wall.

"So what's up?" asked Glen.

"I'm working on a story about the guy who was sentenced to prison as a result of that train crash a few years back. His name is George Cashman. I thought you might have a case file on him."

"We probably do. What exactly are you looking for?"

"I need to get the guy's last known address, and his wife's first name."

"For what purpose?"

"I got a call from a woman who said she had information that Cashman was wrongly convicted, and she said she knew who was responsible. But when I asked to meet her about it, she got cold feet and hung up. I think it might have been his wife. I know they lived in Elroy, but I don't know the specific address. Since your office arrested him, you should have that information on file."

"You should go through Bascom."

"That's what I tried to do, but the secretary said he's out the rest of this week. I'd like to find that woman tomorrow, if I can. I suppose I could just go there and ask around at the businesses if anyone knows them, but it'd be a lot easier if I had the address."

"You want me go under the radar to look through the files?"

Stan nodded sheepishly. "Yep. That's what I'm asking."

"What's the rush? Why not write to Cashman or just go to the prison and talk to him? He should be able to tell you where his wife is."

Stan held up the form. "That's what I'm going to do. Cashman is in Waupon and I'm going to mail out this visitor request today. But it'll take a week to get approved, and I don't want to wait to start looking for the woman who called. I've got this story I have to finish, and I need to get a jump on it. Besides, the woman could be in some danger."

Glen cocked his head to one side. "Going around the sheriff could get me in hot water, but if you say it's that important... I'll see what I can do after I take care of these warrants. You going to be home tonight?"

"Patty invited me for supper. I'll probably be at her place until late. She's finally off night shift."

"Okay, if I find something I'll call you there."

.   .   .   .   .

After leaving Glen, Stan went back to his office and called to set up an interview with John Hamilton, the county district attorney, for next week. Then he dug out the list of injured passengers that he'd copied down and was able to track down two of them for interviews. By the time he finished writing a quick pre-game story for Friday's high school football game, it was almost six o'clock, and he'd told Patty he'd be at her place at six. He covered his typewriter, grabbed his jacket and cap, and rushed out the door. Before reaching Patty's, he made a quick stop at Grover's Liquor and picked up a bottle of wine.

Glen's wife, Carol, who worked with Patty at Memorial Hospital, had introduced the two of them three years before, but they hadn't started dating until last year. Patty, at twenty-five, was a year younger than Stan and had grown up in Sparta. After attending nursing school in Milwaukee, she came back to her hometown and went to work at the hospital. They didn't hit it off immediately, and if appearances were any guide, they couldn't have been more different.

Stan was a gangly six-foot-one, thin as a rail, with a longish face, a hawk-like nose, and a normally laid-back temperament. His arms almost reached to his knees, and he had a habit, when he got excited, of flapping them like an albatross trying to take flight. Patty was about a half-foot shorter, with a sturdy athletic body, a tomboyish freckled face with full lips, upturned nose, short straw-colored hair, and a quick temper.

After a rough start—she nagged at him often about his arm flapping, and he complained she was too uptight—they came to realize they had a lot in common. They discovered they both cared enormously about other people, loved animals, enjoyed all kinds of sports, and were avid fans of the Packers and Braves. Stan had grown up on a farm just outside Tomah, a small town fifteen miles down the road from Sparta. He'd been a standout miler on his high school track team, and after high school he went to Eau Claire State where he ran the mile and 800 yard relay on their track team. He still enjoyed running for exercise, and after he started dating Patty, he'd taken up tennis as well. Although Patty had never done competitive running, she had played tennis since her early teens, continued to compete in regional tournaments, and had several trophies at home to show for her efforts.

As he parked his car, a gray 53 Ford coupe, in front of the white clapboard house where Patty rented an upstairs apartment, he thought about how much he missed seeing her. She'd been working nights for the past two weeks and there'd been no opportunity to get together. He was looking forward to the lasagna that she'd promised him over the phone earlier in the day. He went up the outside stairs to her apartment—a place she'd shared with her friend Carol until earlier in the year when Carol married Glen and moved out. Now Patty just shared it with the little terrier-mix dog she'd brought home six months ago from the local animal shelter. He could hear Jessie barking as he waited for Patty to answer. When she didn't, he opened the door and went in. Jessie jumped up and sniffed at him playfully for a few seconds before skittering away.

From the entryway, Stan called out, "It's me, Clark Kent, star reporter for the Daily Planet. Are you here Lois Lane?"

From the kitchen she hollered back. "Lois is out, but Patty's here, and you're late."

He walked into the kitchen and saw her standing at the counter brushing garlic butter onto slices of French bread. He set the wine bottle on the counter, put his arms around her, and gave her a peck on the back of her neck. She twisted her neck to look up at him and smiled. "You hungry?"

"Very. The lasagna smells great. Can't wait to taste it. I had an interesting week. A lot to talk to you about."

"Good. We can talk while we eat. You can help set the table while I put the salad together. Everything will be ready in just a few minutes."

When they sat down, Stan filled their wine glasses while Patty doled out a large piece of lasagna for Stan and took a smaller one for herself. She took a sip of the wine and asked, "So what was so special about your week that you wanted to tell me?"

Stan swallowed his first lasagna bite and laid down his fork. "You remember the train wreck about four years ago where three people were killed, and the engineer went to jail?"

"Yes, of course. We took in a lot of the injured. How could I forget?"

"Well, I got an anonymous call from a woman who said the engineer was innocent of any wrongdoing and shouldn't be in jail. She said someone else was responsible for the accident. At first I didn't give it much thought, but then I started reviewing our back issues. I decided it might be worth exploring. Problem is, I don't know who the woman is, and I've got to find her."

Patty took a sip of her wine. "You think this woman might really know something new? She's not just a kook?"

"No, I don't think she's a kook."

"What could she say that didn't come out at the trial?"

"Maybe nothing," said Stan. "But I attended some of the trial, and I never could quite buy into the idea that the engineer who had years of experience with no problems all of a sudden would get drunk and wreck his train like that. The jury bought it, but I thought there was room for reasonable doubt."

"Who do you think this mystery woman is?"

Stan took a bite of garlic bread. "Probably his wife. The guy—his name's Cashman—is in prison at Waupon and I plan on interviewing him, but it'll take a few days to get approval. In the meantime, I'm going to Elroy tomorrow to see if I can dig up anything on him or his wife. I found in a newspaper article that he used to live in Elroy, but it didn't have an address. Today I asked Glen if he could find his street address in the case file, and he said he'd check and call me tonight if he's able to find anything. I told him I'd be here."

After they finished eating, Stan helped clean up the dishes, and then he went into the living room while she remained in the kitchen putting away things. Turning on the television, he called out, "Groucho's on at eight. What channel is it?"

Patty came into the living room wiping her hands with a towel. "Channel 3 I think. Sometimes I think you want to come over just to see my twenty-one inch TV."

He turned the channel dial. "That's not true. I'd come here even if you had a thirteen inch set."

She shook her head, and they settled down on the couch together to watch the show. Jessie jumped up and snuggled in between them. Just as Groucho was about to award one of his guests a hundred dollars for saying the "secret word," the phone rang. Patty got up and answered it. "It's Glen." She held out the phone, and Stan got up to take the call.

While listening, he picked up a pen from the counter and started scribbling on the wall calendar. As he hung up the phone he had a triumphant look on his face. "I got the address, and the wife's name is Lucille. Hopefully, tomorrow I'll find her."

He went back to the couch, and they watched another of his favorites, the new Perry Mason show. When it ended, she rose from the couch and turned off the TV. "Okay, it's time for me to get to bed. I have to work tomorrow."

Stan looked up at her and lifted his arms expectantly. "Is that an invitation?"

She looked down, with a slight smile emerging from the corner of her mouth, "No, superman. I'm just saying I have to get up early tomorrow to go to work.

He let his arms fall to his sides. "So when can we get together?"

"How about tennis Saturday afternoon? Then, later we can come back here, watch TV, and... whatever."

He knew he would have to press to do his regular assignment and do the interviews he wanted for this new story, but he didn't want to pass up being with Patty. "Okay, I'm in," he said. "Just don't beat me too bad. I'll get a dinner reservation at Hoffman's restaurant so you won't have to worry about cooking." He pulled himself up from the couch, grabbed his hat and jacket, and kissed her goodnight at the door. As he drove away, he wondered what he would find tomorrow in Elroy.

CHAPTER 4

Stan rolled down his car window and breathed in the brisk autumn air. The leaves were turning color, and the temperature was in the fifties—a perfect fall day. Elroy was an hour's drive from Sparta, but he figured he had plenty of time to accomplish what he needed to do and get back to the office by two, in time to cover the new factory opening. After locating Cashman's wife, he wanted to stop at the depot to see if he could find any of Cashman's old co-workers. As he headed out of town, he tuned the radio to WINT and started bobbing his head to Elvis Presley's latest hit, *Teddy Bear*.

Five miles out of Wilton he turned onto County Road H, which he knew ran close to the site of the train wreck. He wanted to refresh his memory of what happened. When he spotted the place he was looking for, he pulled off on the gravel shoulder. The train tracks were about a hundred yards away, on the other side of a recently mown hayfield, and the ground was soggy from last night's rain, similar to the morning of the wreck. He grabbed his camera from the passenger seat, got out of the car, and put the strap over his shoulder. There was a wide ditch between the road and the field—no problem. He bent his legs and leaped. His right foot slipped as he touched down, his arms flailed, and the camera went flying. He sprawled on all fours onto the muddy ground. Stan caught his breath, got up, straightened his cap that had gone sideways, and brushed himself off. The knees of his pants had mud ground in, and that wasn't going away. He looked for the camera and found the case sitting in a shallow puddle. He picked it up and opened the case. If the camera was damaged, Malloy would have his scalp. The camera looked okay. He put it back in the case and trudged across the field.

Nearing the tracks, he could see the edge of the river bank just a few feet beyond. The ground was overgrown with grass, shrubs, and weeds. The steel track glistened in the morning sun, resting on its raised rail bed and ties. At this point the ground was level, but the track curved to the left about thirty degrees, following the bend in the river. He stepped across the rails and looked down on the sluggish brown stream twenty-feet below. Large angular rip rap had been deposited along the bank to prevent erosion. From all appearances, it was hard to tell that anything had happened here four years before.

Stan closed his eyes and tried to recall what he saw when he'd arrived on the accident scene: It was ten o'clock in the morning—maybe an hour after the accident—when he arrived. It had rained the previous night. Firetrucks, police cars, ambulances, and private vehicles were parked haphazardly in the field with deep gouges in the ground where they had driven in. There were people shouting and running around. Some were helping extract people from the rail cars or tending to injured, while others were just standing around gawking. He felt like he was in a slow motion film. Steam was coming from the giant yellow and green locomotive that was entirely off the track canted to one side with its nose stuck in the ground like a rooting hog. There was a sizeable gap between the engine and three or four passenger cars, still upright but sitting at angles to one another. The tops of two passenger cars poked above the edge of the river bank. He tried to get closer but a sheriff's deputy told him to move back.

Passengers who'd managed to get out of the cars wandered about looking lost. A triage tent had been set up near the tracks where medical personnel were tending to the most seriously injured. A body, entirely covered by a sheet, laid beside the tent. He approached a doctor to ask him a question but was shooed away. He walked along the track until he came to the place where the engine derailed. The left inside rail was separated where a rail joint had broken off, but it was not badly distorted. However, the right rail, on the outer edge of the curve, was completely severed. Over thirty feet-long, it was twisted into a U-shape as if it was a piece of thin wire. Eight-foot long ties had been dislodged from the rail bed and strewn about like so much kindling wood.

He finally found Sheriff Bascom who agreed to give a brief interview. It wasn't much. He wouldn't confirm if there were any deaths and couldn't tell him how many were injured. Neither would he say if it was caused by human error or if there was a problem with the track itself. The main thing he got from the interview was the train engineer was found unconscious in the train cab, and he was being transported to the hospital in Sparta. After talking with the sheriff, he walked around the area, took several pictures, then returned to his car and drove to the hospital to see what he could learn about the condition of the engineer and passengers.

Stan opened his eyes and looked around once more. He was disappointed that he couldn't see anything new that might give credence to Cashman's innocence. As he stared across the field, Stan thought to himself, how could the train engineer not be at fault? During the trial, Cashman said he wasn't speeding, but what else could it be? What if somebody tampered with the tracks? How would one know? I'll ask the DA if he looked into that.

He aimed his camera across the field and took two wide-angled shots, just in case Irv wanted a comparative photo of the scene. Then he turned and walked back towards the car. When he got near the ditch, he cradled the camera in his arms, got a running start and leaped over with room to spare.

. . . . .

After reaching Elroy, Stan parked in front of Edna's Café on Main Street and went inside. He sat down at the counter, and the waitress, a plump-faced woman in her fifties, her hair pinned up with a comb, asked if he wanted a menu.

"Nope, just a cup of coffee, black, and one of those iced doughnuts in the case there."

"Coming right up."

When she returned with the coffee and doughnut, she asked, "Anything else?"

"Yes. I'm looking for 832 Grant Avenue. Don't know my way around here. Can you give me directions?"

"It's not too far. Grant is just two blocks over, and the address you're looking for is maybe five or six blocks up thataway." She pointed towards the rear wall.

"By the way," said Stan. "You wouldn't know anyone by the name of Lucille Cashman, would you?"

The woman raised her eyes to think. "I knew a George Cashman. He used to come in here once in a while. That was before he got sent to prison. Don't know any Lucille Cashman."

He thanked her, paid his bill, and left a quarter tip. Back in his car he turned onto Grant Avenue and found the address he was looking for. It was a compact two-story white frame house with a covered front porch. The bushes in front were overgrown and some of the paint was peeling around the windows. He parked at the curb and sat for a moment wondering how the woman would react since she seemed so afraid when she called. He shook his head, got out of the car, and went to the front door and knocked.

After a second knock on the door, a young woman, who hardly looked out of her teens, came to the door with a baby in one arm, and a toddler screaming behind her. "What is it?" she asked.

Even though he was pretty sure this wasn't his anonymous caller, Stan went through the drill of explaining who he was and that he was looking for a Mrs. Cashman. He told her this was her last known address.

"No, I don't know any Cashman," she said while bouncing the baby with one arm and turning to shush the toddler. "We moved here just a year ago, but maybe the lady next door can tell you something. She's been here a long time."

He thanked the frazzled young mother and walked over to the neighboring house, a neat white cottage with a flowerpot filled with geraniums hanging on the porch and a welcome mat at the front door. He rang the doorbell, and a tiny elderly woman, her white hair fixed in a bun, opened the door. "Can I help you?"

Once again Stan went through his spiel, hoping he could find some bit of information to give him a lead.

"Oh yes, I know Lucy. Felt so bad for the way things turned out for her with her husband going to jail and all."

"Do you know where I can find her?"

The old woman shook her head. "I'm not sure where she's living now. Haven't seen her around town for a long while. Could have moved away. She remarried you know."

Stan's eyes widened. "Oh really! She divorced George Cashman?"

"Yep. Less than a year after he went to prison. I thought it was kind of quick to drop her husband like that. But who am I to say?"

"Do you know the name of her new husband or where they might live?"

She shrugged her shoulders. "Nope. Lucy never told me, and it wasn't my place to ask."

"What about your husband? Would he possibly know?"

"There's no husband anymore. I'm widowed."

"Oh, I'm sorry Mrs...."

"No need to be sorry. He's been gone for more than ten years now. Sometimes I can't even remember his name. Still remember my name though. It's Grace Kinslaw."

He tried to suppress a smile. "Thank you Mrs. Kinslaw. You've been a big help."

As she turned to go back into her house, he stopped her. "One more thing, ma'am. Can you tell me how I can get to the railroad depot?"

She turned and pointed. "Yes, just go down Grant until you come to Railroad Street. It'll be on your left."

He tipped his cap. "Thanks again ma'am. Have a good day."

When he got in his car, Stan checked his watch—ten o'clock. Enough time to stop and see if anyone at the depot knew Cashman.

. . . . .

Elroy had less than two thousand people, and when he reached Railroad Street, he was surprised at the size of the depot. It was a two-story russet colored frame building with an open gable roof design. With its covered baggage loading area, the structure covered almost half a block. He pulled into the gravel parking lot and walked to the front of the building facing the four rows of tracks. A noisy diesel locomotive trailing a long line of boxcars idled on the outside track. He passed a door marked "Freight Office," and another one marked "Passenger Lobby," before reaching a last door simply marked "Office."

He tried the knob, and the door opened. He found himself in a large room where three rough-looking men in coveralls were huddled around a small table next to a pot belly stove playing cards. One appeared to be in his twenties, and the two others were older—one with a ducktail and long sideburns and the other heavy-set with shaggy gray hair and a full beard. They glanced up at him as he entered, but returned to their game. A rotund man with a ring of gray hair around his bald head and wearing a navy blue vest over his white shirt, was sitting at a built-in counter desk set against the windowed wall facing the tracks. He swiveled around in his chair and addressed Stan. "Yes, what is it?"

Stan introduced himself and explained that he was working on a story about the train wreck that happened four years ago and wanted to know if anyone knew George Cashman. The older man in the vest pointed to an empty chair. "Have a seat. I'm Harry Frost, the depot agent here. I knew George casually. But I don't know I can tell you anything you don't already know. These fellas here are section hands. They're waiting on a way freight coming through here soon. You can ask them."

Stan turned toward the three. "Any of you know George Cashman?"

The youngest one shook his head. One in the middle with the sideburns said, "I used to work as a brakeman on his train. Didn't have much contact with him, but from what I heard he was asking for trouble for a long time."

"Why do you say that?"

"When he got arrested and went on trial, we was all talking about it. One of my friends who knew him a lot better than me said Cashman would sneak booze on board his train. He seen him drunk before, but said he never told anybody cause he didn't want to get him into trouble. You know—didn't want to be a stool pigeon."

Stan took out his pen and notepad. "Who was this friend of yours? What's his name?"

"Ray Bickle. That's who told me."

"Do you know where I can find him? Where he lives?"

"No, No idea. It's been a while since I worked with him."

Stan made some notes and started to say something when the rapid click-clacking of a telegraph key interrupted. Heads turned, and Frost announced, "The 584 just passed LaValle. They'll be here in less than ten minutes. You fellas better end your game quick-like."

The oldest of the three, the one with the beard, looked at his cards and tossed down a coin. "I raise you two bits."

The youngest threw down his cards. "I'm out."

The one with the sideburns threw out a quarter. "I call."

The two bidders laid down their cards, and the bearded player shouted, "Two pair. I win," and gathered in his pot.

The one with the sideburns shook his head. "I guess you're buying the first round tonight."

After the section crew left, Stan turned to Frost. "Did you follow Cashman's trial at all?"

Frost leaned back in his chair. "Oh yes. Most of us were paying attention to what happened. He was one of our own. Though I didn't know him real well, I thought he was a good guy and hated to see what happened to him."

"You're not the only person who feels that way."

"What do you mean?"

"Somebody—a woman—called me to say she knew someone else caused the wreck. She didn't give me her name, but it made me curious and I decided to look into it. I want to see if I can find something the police might have overlooked. Bring it out in the open. Any idea what she might've been talking about?"

Frost shook his head. "I wish I could help you Mr. Ellis, but I'm afraid I can't. The investigators said he was going too fast for the curve."

"How can they tell that? Is there any kind of recording device in the engine that would tell how fast a train is going when an accident happens?"

"No. No recording device. Just a speedometer, something like in your car. When the engine stopped, the needle would probably just go to zero. The investigators have some mathematical formula they use to determine the speed based on the damage to the rail and other things."

"I see. What if the rail was already loose or broken through normal wear or tear, or what if someone damaged it on purpose?"

Frost rubbed one hand across the top of his head. "Section crews inspect the tracks at least once a month. That's part of their job, and the Northwestern puts a high priority on it. I won't say they couldn't miss something, but it's unlikely given the circumstances. As for somebody tampering with the tracks, I'm sure the police checked into that."

"But there'd be no way to be sure no one tampered with the tracks—would there?"

Frost shrugged. "I guess not. I'm not an engineer or investigator, but I'd think it'd be hard to say for sure."

Stan sighed. "Yes. I think so too. By the way, do you know anything about this Ray Bickle who claimed he knew Cashman was a drunk?"

Frost gave a soft chuckle. "I know who he is. Haven't seen him around lately. These train crews work on different routes all the time. But from what I've seen of him, he's quite a loudmouth. I never heard anything about Cashman drinking on the job, and I wouldn't put much stock in what Bickle said—but that's me."

Stan took a card from his wallet and handed it to Frost. "Thank you for your time. If you should think of anything about the train wreck that authorities might have missed, please call me."

When Stan got back in his car, he looked at his watch. A little past eleven, plenty of time to have lunch and get back to Sparta by two.

CHAPTER 5

Stan felt upbeat as he arrived at his office Monday morning. His date night with Patty was all he'd hoped it would be. After playing three sets of tennis in the afternoon—one of which he won—they went out to a nice dinner at Lakeside Inn. Then they went back to her apartment to watch TV and cuddle. She'd let him spend the night. After hanging up his jacket and cap and going to his desk, he shut his eyes and recalled the best night of his life—the caress of her hand on his chest, the tickle of her hair against his cheek, the touch of her lips against his. He was in love, and after Saturday night, he was sure she felt the same.

His reverie ended when Rose, in the next desk, barked out, "Stan! You must not have slept much last night. You all right?"

He shook himself awake, "Yes, yes," he said. "I was up late, but I'm fine now—very fine. Thanks for asking."

He had an appointment with the district attorney, John Hamilton, at nine. Despite being unable to locate his mystery woman, he considered his trip to Elroy worthwhile. His visit to the wreck site helped him reconstruct in his own mind just how things happened. As soon as he got to the office Friday morning Stan dropped off his article on the train derailment in Irv's in-box. He returned to his desk to get a start on part two of the story involving Cashman but didn't get very far. After thirty minutes he stopped what he was working on and went over to Irv's desk to let him know he was on his way to the DA's office. Without looking up from his typewriter, Irv nodded. "Good luck. Let me know how it goes when you get back."

•   •   •   •   •   •

Stan didn't like to dress up, but this morning he decided to wear a sports coat to try to make a good impression. He gathered some pertinent notes and stuffed them into his jacket pocket before leaving. Hamilton's office was in a red brick building directly across the street from the courthouse. On entering the office, Stan told the secretary he had an appointment, and she checked her calendar. "Please have a seat," she said. "I'll call you when Mr. Hamilton is available." Fifteen minutes later she told him he could go in.

Tall, lean, and broad-shouldered, the edges of Hamilton's slicked-back brown hair were touched with gray. Appearing to be in his early forties, he wore a vest and a maroon silk tie under his double-breasted pinstripe suit. Stan felt somewhat underdressed and was glad he'd thought to wear a jacket, even though he got it off the discount rack at Sears. After shaking hands, Hamilton invited Stan to have a seat in one of two cushioned chairs in front of his desk before taking his own seat behind the desk.

Leaning back in his chair, Hamilton said, "You're doing a story on the train wreck and wanted to talk about George Cashman. Is that right?"

"Yes, that's why I'm here." Stan started out by explaining that he had covered the train wreck for the Herald back in 1954, and he was doing a follow-up. Then he told the DA about the anonymous call from a woman who claimed Cashman was innocent of any wrongdoing. He said he hadn't been able to identify the woman yet, but he wanted to get Hamilton's perspective on the trial and see if he could shed additional light on what the woman might have been alluding to or who she was.

Hamilton stared at him from across his desk, twirling a pencil in one hand. "I think you're spinning your wheels on this, Mr. Ellis. But ask your questions."

Stan pulled his pad and pen from his jacket pocket. "Can you tell me some of the significant points in the trial and what you felt after the verdict was read?"

Hamilton cleared his throat. "I've looked over the case file, and I want to be clear. Mr. Cashman had excellent legal representation in Anson Puller, and he received a fair trial when he was convicted of negligent homicide. All the physical evidence available supported the allegation that the engineer was solely responsible for the derailment of that train, and the jury made its decision on that basis.

Stan sat up straighter. "I was at the accident shortly after it happened, and I saw how the track was bent and broken. But how can you tell it wasn't already damaged when the train crossed that section?"

"Mr. Ellis, you're not an expert, and neither am I."

"What about it being a problem with the track? They get rusted and worn out over time. There was rain the night before that could have washed out some of the roadbed."

"Did you attend the trial?"

"The first two days I did."

"Well, maybe you missed the important parts. I had a railway official on the stand—an expert in the field—who testified that the road had been checked two days before and that it was in good condition. Based on his analysis, he concluded that it was the force of the train traveling at an excessive speed that caused the train to derail. Simple as that. Furthermore, there was a freight train that traversed that route the previous afternoon with no problem."

"Okay, you've determined that Cashman was careless in going at an unsafe speed. Why did you feel it necessary to make the case that he was drunk and adding more years to his conviction?"

Hamilton laughed. "He made the case for himself. The whiskey bottle was found in the toolbox with his fingerprints on it."

"When was it discovered?"

"I think it was the next day.

"Were his the only fingerprints?"

Hamilton gave a slight smirk. "No. His wife's prints were on it too. You think she put it there?"

Stan shook his head. "No, of course not. But how do you know he actually drank the whiskey? Did anyone report smelling liquor on his breath right after the accident? Was any blood test done?"

Hamilton looked perturbed. "I don't know if anyone smelled liquor on his breath, and no there was no blood test. Regardless, it's a simple matter of logic. We made our case to the jury, and they agreed that there was no other explanation for his failure to lower the speed limit on a route that he had been over many times before."

"Okay, I understand the logic, and I don't mean to be presumptuous, but did you consider the possibility that somebody damaged the track on purpose, either for a prank or because they had something against Cashman?"

"Mr. Ellis. I think you've been watching too many Perry Mason shows. Of course, the police looked at that, and found nothing." Hamilton glared at him. "Anything else?"

Stan squirmed in his chair. "No sir. I think that's all I have. Thank you for your time."

"Any time," said Hamilton. "Glad to be of service. Have a pleasant day Mr. Ellis." He didn't get up from behind his desk and Stan turned and left.

.   .   .   .   .

The next morning at the office, just as Stan was getting his first cup of coffee, Irv came up to him before he even had a chance to hang up his jacket and cap. "That was a good story on the train wreck. I had a couple people yesterday tell me how it brought back memories—some not so good—but they liked the story."

Stan smiled. "That's encouraging. I'm working on the next part now."

"Did you listen to the Braves game yesterday?"

"Yeah, Burdette was really on. Allowed just one run. Looks like they'll be in the Series again."

"Looks that way," said Irv. "Oh, the boss said he wanted to see you as soon as you got in. Don't know what it's about."

Stan took a gulp from his coffee cup, laid the cup on his desk, and headed back to Ed Malloy's office. He knocked on the doorframe and when he saw Malloy wave at him through the window, he went in. "Irv said you wanted to see me."

"Yes, have a seat," said Malloy.

Stan sat down on a couch across from Malloy's desk and waited nervously for several seconds while he shuffled through some papers.

Finally, Stan said, "Did you read my article yesterday on the train wreck?"

Malloy looked up. "Yes, I read it. It was fine." He tapped his fingers on his desk. "I got a call from John Hamilton at home yesterday evening. He said you visited him earlier in the day to do an interview."

"Yes. That's right. I felt it went well."

"Hmmm. Hamilton came away with some concerns he wanted to share with me."

"What sort of concerns? I just asked him about the trial and how it was conducted so I could include a few of his comments in my next article."

"He was bothered by some of the questions you raised regarding the Cashman trial. He said you tossed out different ideas about how somebody other than Cashman might have been responsible. It seemed to him you were questioning his competence and the competence of the police."

Stan leaned back with a confused look on his face. "I wasn't questioning his competence. I was just asking questions. That's what reporters are supposed to do, isn't it?"

"Don't get yourself in a lather. You need to hear what he had to say. He told me we need to be cautious in how we deal with this kind of subject. I have to agree with him. I'm beginning to think you're on some kind of crusade to sensationalize this story you're working on, and that's not the approach I want to see. In fact, Hamilton thought what you were asking could cast a bad light on our public officials and make the city look bad. That's not in the public interest."

"I'm not trying to make anybody look bad. I'm trying to find out what happened. I had this anonymous caller who raised a question as to the man's guilt, and I feel a responsibility to follow up on that."

"We're not a tabloid like the New York Post, and we're not the Milwaukee Journal that has a staff and budget to take on investigations into corruption and whatnot. We're a small-town paper with a very narrow profit margin, and our purpose is to support our community and to report on things here that interest our reading public. You've written a decent feature about the train wreck, and perhaps we need to end it there."

"I still need to find the anonymous caller."

"You've been looking for more than a week with no results. I don't think you'll find her. Our fire department gets called out two or three times a year for false alarms. Just last spring some kid called in a false bomb threat at the school. They never identified him. This is the same thing. There's no point in going on."

"No, Mr. Malloy. I think this is real. We may be a small-town newspaper, but we're still part of the American press. When I was in school, professors talked about journalists as the fourth estate with responsibility as the guardians of the public interest. I think this story is in our public's interest. I have an appointment at Waupon Prison later this week to interview Cashman. Let me go and see him."

Malloy backed off. "Okay, you can get down from your soapbox. I won't stop you from interviewing Cashman, and you can write up a story on that. But I'm going to be looking it over very carefully, and if I find anything that I think will bring Hamilton down on my back, I'll kill it. Understand?"

"Yes sir. I'm sure Cashman will be able to tell me who this woman is and where I can find her. If I don't, then this will be the last I'll write on the subject."

After leaving Malloy's office, he stopped at Irv's desk. "I'm going over to the police station to check what they have on their crime blotter today. Anything else you have for me?"

Irv looked up at him from his desk. "Claire Westover, she heads up the Sparta Arts Council, called and said she wants to get something in the paper about the shows they're planning for the holidays. Can you stop and see what she has for us? Should be worth at least ten inches for the 'Local News' page."

"Okay, I should be back by two."

. . . . .

When he returned from his interview, Stan tossed his notes on his desk. Noticing Irv at the teletypes checking the wire service releases, he hollered across the room. "Anyone call for me?"

Irv turned his head around. "Yeah. Somebody called from the Waupon Prison. Said your interview request was approved. You've got an appointment with them at one o'clock tomorrow. Lucky you."

Stan started to raise his arms in a victory cheer but then remembered what he had scheduled. "Irv—I need some help."

"What kind of help?" Irv asked, as he ripped copy off the teletype.

"I've got an interview with Coach Parker tomorrow at one. I needed that for part of a pre-game story. Then I have a school board meeting tomorrow night at seven, but I think I can make that. Is there any way you could cover the interview for me?"

Irv nodded. "I can go see the coach, and I'll do the pre-game write-up for Friday's game, but I've got another thing going tomorrow evening. Give me a call if it looks like you won't be able to make the school board."

Stan relaxed. "You're the best."

CHAPTER 6

Stan scraped the early morning frost from the windshield before jumping into his car and checking his road map. Waupon was a three-hour drive, and he hoped his interview wouldn't be for nothing. As he backed out of the driveway, he tuned the radio to his favorite station. The smooth sound of the Platters began filling the air. The traffic was light as he left Sparta. He leaned back in his seat and unconsciously started tapping the steering wheel to the beat of the music, letting his eyes wander occasionally to the burst of autumn colors in the hills alongside the highway. As he neared the Dells, a busy tourist spot even in the fall, the traffic on the two-lane road became heavier. It was eleven thirty by the time he got to the state prison.

When he first caught sight of the monstrous prison structure, he thought it looked like something out of the Middle Ages. From the parking lot he could see two looming turrets poking high above the ageless limestone walls like a castle on the Rhine. At the corners were watch towers with gun ports. He walked through an arched entryway where he was met by a gate guard who checked him over for contraband before directing him to the reception lobby. There a desk sergeant asked for his ID before checking his name off a list and confirming his appointment for one o'clock. The sergeant told him he'd have to wait in the lobby. He checked his watch—a whole hour to waste.

The lobby was a large open space with a vaulted ceiling, constructed like a railway waiting room, with long benches, two in the center of the room and others along the outer walls. Most of the benches were occupied by several people, but he spotted one against the wall where an elderly woman sat by herself. He walked over to her and asked, "Mind if I sit here?"

She looked up. "Have a seat, mister. I don't mind having company."

He took a seat and started twiddling his thumbs. He hadn't realized he'd have to sit and wait so long and wished he'd brought along a book to read. He turned to the woman who had a ball of yarn in her lap and was busily knitting something. "What are you making?"

She looked over at him. "A cap. It's for my son. I like to bring him something when I come."

"I'm sure he appreciates it. Do you come here often?"

She kept her eyes on her knitting. "As often as I can. I try to come every two or three months. I can't afford to do more."

"Is he here for a long time?"

"He got twenty-five years—for somethin he didn't do."

"Really? Tell me about it."

She looked up and eyed him warily before deciding to tell him her story. "They put him in here for killing somebody in an armed robbery, but he wasn't involved at all."

"What exactly happened?"

"We from Milwaukee. There was a bank robbery downtown, and somebody got shot. They said it was three black guys who did it. My son was out with a girlfriend driving around near where it happened, and the police stopped them. They said they found some marijuana or somethin in the car and arrested him. Then they put him in a lineup and picked my boy out as one of them robbers. My boy had nothin to do with it. Didn't make sense to me. But I had no way to fight it."

"Doesn't sound like he got a fair shake. When did this all happen?"

"Five years ago."

"What's your son's name?"

"Jeremy. Jeremy Bridges."

Stan sighed. "You shouldn't give up. There's got to be someone who will listen to your case. Have you talked to a lawyer?"

She shook her head. "Costs a lot of money. Went to legal services though. They had me fill out some papers, but they so backed up with work and not enough people, they never did anything. Then, one time, a brother showed up at my house—dressed like he's goin to church. Said he was some kind of lawyer and he could help me file some papers to get my son out if I give him fifty dollars. Told me Rev'rend Thomas gave him my name. I trusted him. I give him the fifty and filled out some more papers. Never saw him again."

"Did you try to contact him?"

"I did. He gave me a fancy card, but when I tried to call the number, I got some car dealer. They didn't know him. I called Rev'rend Thomas, too. He didn't know him either. The guy was a crook, just trying to cheat an old woman."

"You should have reported it to the police."

She gave him a derisive grin. "Sure mister. You think the police are goin to do somethin?"

Stan shook his head. "I would hope so, but I think I understand your situation. Maybe you ought to go to the newspapers in your city. Tell someone there your story."

She frowned. "What good would that do?"

"You said you're from Milwaukee. The newspapers there have investigative reporters who may be willing to investigate things like what you described, and they won't charge you anything. I'm a newspaper reporter myself. Name's Stan Ellis." He pulled a business card from his pocket and handed it to her. "Actually, the reason I came here today is I'm working on a story about an inmate who may have been falsely convicted of causing a train accident near Sparta that resulted in multiple deaths. You know where Sparta is?"

She shook her head.

"I'm not surprised. It's just a small town about a hundred miles west of here. The guy I'm interviewing was the train engineer. I want to get his side of the story, and if it turns out he's innocent, I want to do what I can to get him released."

She pressed her lips together tightly and shook her head. "I think you wasting your time mister. Once they put someone in here, no chance they gonna let him go afore his times up. Nobody wants to admit they made a mistake. I know. My son's innocent, but nobody cares less you can afford a high class lawyer, which I can't. Nobody'll care about your man either."

"I hope that's not true, and I hope you'll think about talking to somebody at the paper there where you live."

"I'll think about it," she said and then returned to her knitting.

Stan leaned his back against the bench, pulled out his notebook, and began reviewing the questions he'd prepared and jotted down some new ones. A few minutes later the elderly woman put her knitting away in a bag by her side and stood up. "Gotta go see my boy now."

"Don't give up," said Stan. "Remember what I told you."

He saw a wry smile emerge at the corner of her mouth, but she didn't respond. He watched the woman slowly amble over to the receptionist desk to check in and then disappear through a rear door. He wondered how hard it must be for a woman to come to the prison month after month knowing there's no prospect of her son being free. He wondered, also, if that's how the woman who called him felt. He picked up the notepad he'd been reviewing and wrote down: *Jeremy Bridges, Milwaukee, 1953.* Maybe something to look into.

•   •   •   •   •   •

As the clock approached one o'clock, Stan went up to the reception desk, gave his name, and the sergeant directed him to the interview room where he was to meet Cashman. Entering the room, he saw a low counter with half-a-dozen chairs set in front. Four of the chairs were occupied by visitors who were talking with prisoners across a three-foot high counter. At the far end he noticed the woman he'd been talking to earlier in deep conversation with her son. A guard stood to the side with a clipboard. Stan approached the guard, gave his name, and told him who he was there to see. The guard checked his name off the list and told him to wait a moment. He made a call on a walkie-talkie and two minutes later, a guard brought out a prisoner wearing pajama-like prison stripes and set him down in one of the chairs behind the counter. It was Cashman, medium height, about five-foot-nine, and wearing wire-rim glasses. He had a round fleshy face, and in the baggy uniform, seemed rather obese. Forty-seven years old, with a receding hairline and thin graying hair, he looked a lot older. The guard on the visitors' side, motioned Stan to sit across from the prisoner, and told him he had a one hour time limit.

Stan thought that Cashman would be glad to have a visitor, but he sat without emotion on the other side of the counter, looking as if he'd just been rousted from bed. With heavy bags under his eyes, sagging jowls, and pale blotchy skin, Cashman didn't seem to be in the best of health. Stan sat down, smiled, and introduced himself.

Cashman nodded and responded listlessly, "What's a reporter want with me?"

"I'm writing a story about the 1954 train derailment that got you sent to prison. I wanted to meet with you because I got a call a week ago from a woman who said you didn't get a fair trial. She claimed that someone else was responsible for the train wreck—not you—and wanted my help."

Suddenly his face came to life. "Who was it called you?"

"I don't know. That's why I'm here. I was hoping you could tell me. I thought it might be your ex-wife, but I don't know how to find her."

"My wife? No, I don't think so. I haven't seen her for almost three years. In fact, nobody's been to see me since I don't remember when. I don't hear from anyone I used to know. Before she got the divorce, she came up here and saw me two or three times. Once she brought Billy. But after the divorce, she quit coming, and she never responded to any of my letters. I'd like to see Billy before I die, but I don't know if I'll make it through my sentence."

"Billy? Is that your son?"

He nodded. "He was just seven years old when I saw him last."

"Why did you say you might not see him before you die? You're probably eligible for probation in a few years."

"I've got advanced diabetes. Never took it serious until I got in here, and they diagnosed me. I'm taking shots now, but the docs tell me I'm going to need a kidney transplant before long. Can hardly feel the bottom of my feet."

"Did your wife know about the diabetes?"

"She knew. Doctors told me a long time ago I was becoming diabetic, and I needed to watch my diet, but I never paid enough attention. It was affecting my health, too. We argued about it some. It might have been part of the reason she divorced me."

Stan nodded. "Maybe she had a change of heart knowing how your condition has gotten worse. I'd really like to talk to her—find out if she was the one who called. I understand she remarried, but I don't know her married name. Do you?"

Cashman looked puzzled. "I didn't even know she got married again. But if anyone would know where she is, it would be her mother, Helen Grim."

Stan took his notebook from his shirt pocket. "Do you have her address?"

"She lives in Elroy, not too far from the elementary school. My parents had a place a couple doors down. I don't remember the exact address. It's on Elm Street. My parents are gone now, but you shouldn't have any trouble finding her by just asking around."

"That's a good start. Now what about the caller's statement that someone else caused the train accident? You pled not guilty during the trial, but I want to hear from you now. Were you drinking on the train that day and were you exceeding the train's speed limit?"

Cashman leaned forward breathing heavily and stared at Stan for a moment. "No, I was not drinking, and I was not speeding."

"Then do you have any other explanation for why the train derailed if you weren't speeding?"

He shrugged. "Maybe there were some loose ties at the curve, or the track was out of alignment somehow. That's the only thing I can think of."

"What about the liquor bottle with your fingerprints on it? Was it a brand you drink?"

He nodded. "Yeah, from what they told me it was Wild Turkey. That's what I kept at home. But all I know, is I didn't put the bottle in the engine tool box."

"How often do you open that drawer?"

"Not often, but I remembered opening it to get a flashlight on the day before the accident. I never saw any bottle, but I wasn't looking for one, and could have missed it."

"So for all you know it could have been in that toolbox for a long time."

"Yep. Could have been."

"You say you didn't put it there. Who else could have done it? What about the crew members on your train? Who was on board with you?"

Cashman rubbed his chin. "Let me think. Rudy Anderson was the conductor, and Ty Gibbon was the lone brakeman that day. Then there were the men in the dining car, the cook and one waiter. That's all."

"Any of them have any reason to get back at you for anything?"

"Only one I had any problem with was Ty."

"What kind of problem?"

"Oh, about two months before, we were switching out cars at the Wyeville switching yard, and somehow he didn't get a coupling right, and when we went over the hump, two cars separated, rolled back down, rammed into some box cars, and knocked them of the rails. I had to tell the train master what happened and give them Ty's name. Since he already had two other performance incidents on his record, he got a three-day suspension. He pissed and moaned to me after he came back off suspension, but then he let it go. I don't think he held it against me. He knew he messed up."

"Were there any crew members in the cab with you at any time during the trip?

"Nope, I was all alone."

"Isn't that unusual?"

"Not really. These diesels only need one operator in the engine. Oftentimes a brakeman will ride up front—mostly just to keep company. But I've made lots of trips without anyone in the cab with me, and this was a short passenger train. When you have a long freight train, it makes sense for one of the brakemen to sit in the engine so they can check the front-end cars at stops, while the other brakeman in the rear can check the back-end cars. But we had only seven passenger cars that day, so there was no need for an extra crewman."

"Were you in the engine the whole time from when you started that morning until the accident?"

"Yep. Except for a few minutes when we stopped for passengers at LaCrosse, and I went into the station to take a leak and get a candy bar from the snack shop."

"Couldn't somebody have snuck into the engine compartment then?"

"I don't think so. Crew was busy with the boarding."

"Were any of the crew called to testify at your trial?"

"Rudy and Ty were. They both denied any knowledge of how the liquor bottle got in the tool drawer and that was about it. Nothing they said helped me. The only thing that seemed to matter was that my fingerprints were on the bottle."

"I think I'd like to talk with this Ty Gibbon. Do you know where he lives?

"Elroy. Don't know the exact address, but you can find it in the phone book."

"Did you get together with him socially, like at your home, where he could have access to your liquor supply?"

Cashman shook his head. "Ty? No, he'd never been to my home. Other than work, we'd never had any social contact."

Stan scratched his head. "I can see why your lawyer had a hard time coming up with a good defense. When there's no other explanation, your left with the obvious. Can you think of anyone you had to your home who could have gotten into your liquor cabinet?"

"Other than my wife, the only other people who know where I keep my liquor are the guys I played cards with."

Stan's eyes lit up. "Who did you play cards with?"

"Some friends—we got together about once a month at one of our houses. Rollie Erickson was one. He's a retired conductor, lives in Elroy. We been friends for a long time. Then there's Fred Noonan. Works as a salesman at the feedlot in Elroy. Ray Bickle's the other one. He's a brakeman, lives in the area, but not sure exactly where. He's worked on a lot of the same runs as me, and we'd gotten to be friends."

"So you don't think one of them could have planted the bottle? Maybe as a prank?"

"No, that's not something a friend would do. It's something that could cost a man his job." He shook his head. "It cost me my job and more."

The name Bickle got Stan's attention, but he tried to not let on what he'd already heard. "What about this Ray Bickle? You said he's another brakeman who you worked with. Was he on the train the day of the wreck?

Cashman squinted his eyes while gathering his thoughts. "No. No, he wasn't there that day. Like I said before, there was just the one brakeman. I think Bickle was on vacation or took sick that week."

"You never had any run-ins with him?"

"No, nothing that I can think of."

Stan decided to not pursue the Bickle angle further. "I interviewed Harry Frost last week for the story I was writing. He had some good things to say about you. Didn't think you'd drink on the job."

"Yeah, Harry and I go a long way back."

After asking a few more questions without learning anything more that might point to Cashman's innocence, Stan laid down his pen. "My time is about up. Is there anything else you want to tell me before I leave?"

"No, but I just want to ask you, if you see my wife, tell her I understand why she felt she had to divorce me. If she's the one who called you, maybe something happened that made her feel sorry for me. If she seems to want to help me at all, ask her if she'd bring Billy up to see me sometime. That's all I'd ask."

Stan nodded. "Yes, if I'm able to talk to her, I'll do that. Either way, I'll call or write you to let you know what I find out."

"I appreciate you're trying to help me," Cashman got up from his chair, and a guard came up and escorted him out of the interview room. As Stan watched him disappear through a door he was gripped with a feeling of sadness over Cashman's condition, but also a heightened sense that he was doing the right thing in searching for the truth about the train wreck.

CHAPTER 7

The next morning, after checking in with Irv for any last-minute assignments, Stan headed out of town hoping he'd be able to locate his anonymous caller and finally get some answers. When he arrived in Elroy, he stopped at the library and asked the lady at the front desk for a local telephone book. He quickly found the name of Lucy's mother, Helen Grim, and the address of 478 Elm Street. The other person he wanted to talk to was Ty Gibbon who Cashman said lived in Elroy. He found Gibbon's name listed on the same page living at 230 Railroad Street. After writing both addresses and phone numbers down on his notepad, he went up to the librarian and asked her for directions to 230 Railroad Street. She thought for a moment before pointing to her right. "I think that's the rooming house directly across the street from the railroad station. It's just a couple blocks from here."

Stan stopped at the rooming house first. It was a three-story white-framed building with front balconies on the two upper floors and a full length porch on the first floor where three wooden rocking chairs sat empty. Stepping onto the front porch, he immediately went to the black mailboxes attached to the wall next to the doorway and located Gibbon's name on the box labeled #7. He went inside and found himself in a narrow vestibule with a stairway to his left and a darkened hallway straight ahead. He took the stairs to the second floor and followed the hallway to the end before reaching apartment #7. When he knocked, there was no answer. He went to a neighbor's door, knocked again, and a blurry-eyed, gray-haired man in a tank-top undershirt, looking like he'd just got up from a long nap, answered the door. "Yah, what is it?"

Stan tried to smile and said, "I'm looking for Ty Gibbon. He didn't answer his door, but I was wondering if you know when he'd be home."

The man yawned and stretched his arms. "Don't know. He works different hours, different days. Just like me. If he didn't answer, he ain't home. You'd best leave him a note in his mailbox, and he'll contact you if he wants to see you."

Stan let out a sigh. "I'll do that. Thanks for your help."

Standing in the dimly lit entryway, Stan pulled out his pen and wrote out a note asking Gibbon to contact him at the Sparta Herald. He folded up the paper, put one of his business cards inside, and dropped it in Gibbons' mailbox.

• • • • •

Helen Grim's house was on a shady street across from the town's elementary school, just as Cashman had said. It was a well-maintained one-and-a half-story cottage with a railed-in front porch. A flower box overflowing with colorful pansies decorated the front windowsill. He knocked on the door, and after a few seconds a diminutive white-haired woman in a rumpled blue dress answered the door. Her hair was tightly curled, and she had deep lines in her weather-worn face, but her blue eyes sparkled. "If you're selling anything I don't need any," she said.

Stan smiled. "No, I'm not selling anything. I was looking for Helen Grim."

She frowned and looked up at him. "That's me. What is it you want?"

After he explained who he was and that he was trying to locate her daughter, she let him in and invited him to take a seat on the living room sofa. A formal 8x10 portrait of an attractive middle-aged woman with a bright smile and a somber-faced man with a receding hairline and wire-rimmed glasses sat on top of a chest of drawers along with several smaller framed family photos. Helen took a seat in a big overstuffed chair that made her look even smaller than she was He pointed to the larger picture. "Is that you and your husband?"

"Yes. That was taken more than thirty years ago, six or seven years before my husband Joe died. He was only forty-six when he passed. Had a heart attack."

"He reminds me a little of Jimmy Stewart—the eyes and the slant of the mouth."

She touched her lips with one hand. "I don't know about Jimmy Stewart, but I thought he was handsome. We had a wonderful marriage." She sighed. "That's a long time ago now. It was very hard at first. The kids were still in school, but we made it." She pointed to the chest. "That picture there—that's Lucy with George and their baby son taken a couple years after they were married."

Taking a notepad and pen from his pocket, he cleared his throat. "Let me tell you why I want to talk with your daughter. I got interested in writing a story about George Cashman's trial when I received a call from a woman about a week ago. She said she had information that someone other than Cashman caused the train wreck that sent him to jail. She said she wanted my help, but she hung up without giving me her name. I think it was his wife—your daughter."

"She isn't his wife anymore."

Stan nodded. "I'm sorry. I meant former wife. Yesterday I went to Waupon Prison and talked to George. He didn't know where Lucy was living, but he told me to come see you. He said you would know."

"How's George doing?"

Stan shook his head. "He's having trouble with his diabetes. Looks kind of overweight. A little depressed and lonely, I'd say. He said your daughter hadn't been to see him since the divorce and he missed seeing their son."

She nodded her head slowly. "I liked George. I didn't know she hadn't been to see him. Don't know why she hasn't gone up there."

"Have you seen her lately? Can you tell me where she's living now?"

"She's living in Kendall. The house is on Hardy Road, but I can't tell you the exact address without looking it up. Haven't been to see her in several months. I don't drive, and it's hard to get over there unless I can get a ride with someone. She was over here a month or so ago."

"I see. Did she seem upset about anything then, or did she talk about Cashman?"

"Didn't talk about George. She was upset though about the way her husband's been treating her and, especially how he handles Billy—that's my grandson. I don't want to go into details, but I suspect he's gotten physical with both her and Billy. I don't want that in the paper. Married couples have spats, after all, but she did seem worried about the way things were going. Since she divorced once, she doesn't want to think about going through that again."

"So, what's her married name now?"

"The name's Bickle. He's a railroad man too."

Stan's mouth dropped open. "You mean Ray Bickle?"

Helen bent her head to the side. "Yes, Ray Bickle. Do you know him?"

"N-no. But I've heard his name before. George told me he was a friend who used to come to their house quite often to play cards. How well do you know Mr. Bickle?"

"I can't say I know him well. I never knew him before they got married, and I've only seen him a couple times I can remember—once, shortly after they married, when they brought Billy over for me to watch while they went on a three-day honeymoon, and once when I went over to their house to visit Lucy. I been over there a couple other times, but he wasn't there."

"What did you think of him?"

"I can see why Lucy might've been attracted to him. A nice full head of hair, closer to Lucy's age than George was, and strong as an ox. Got forearms like Popeye—you know, the sailor in the Sunday comics. I'll say this for him, he works hard around the house. Lucy said he repainted the outside of the house himself a couple years ago. They got a big yard with lots of bushes and a garden, and Lucy said he takes care of it all. Last May, when I was there, the flowers were all out, and it looked really nice. The place used to be his grandparents. According to what Lucy told me, Ray went to live with them when he was around ten after his parents divorced. So he grew up in that house. When his grandparents died, he got the property to himself."

Stan smiled. "So you like him?"

Her face turned to a frown. "No, I don't like him. He has shifty eyes, and I don't like the look of his face. He's controlling. Lucy has to get his permission to do anything or go anywhere. She said he's especially jealous of her talking with other men, which sometimes makes it hard for her since she works in a grocery store and tries to be friendly to everyone. There's a kind of meanness to him. I wasn't really surprised when she told me about what's been happening. I can tell from a man's face what kind of person he is."

"You can?" said Stan. "What kind of face do I have?"

She cocked her head and looked directly at him. "It's not a pretty face— but I think it's an honest face. Yes, it's an honest face."

Stan chuckled and then became serious. "Were George and your daughter having problems before the train accident?"

"Getting kinda personal aren't you?"

Stan stammered. "I'm sorry. I was just trying to understand Lucy's motivation for calling me and get a better feel for what questions to ask her when we meet—assuming she'll talk to me."

Helen crossed her arms. "Yes, there were some problems she told me about. There was a big age difference you know."

"Yes, I gathered that."

"If I tell you something confidential, you won't put it in the paper will you?"

Stan shook his head. "Anything you want off-the-record is off-the-record."

Helen leaned forward and, with one hand cupped against the side of her mouth, said in a hushed tone, "Off-the-record, he couldn't do it. They were okay at first, but then the diabetes..."Stan's lips formed a perfect "O." He dropped his head to look at his notes and then continued. "I... I guess that happens sometimes, particularly with diabetes. I figured there was a big age difference. Can you tell me how they met?"

Helen looked up at the ceiling for a moment. "George lived with his parents a couple doors down from us. We'd known them for years. When my Joe died, Lucy was a teenager and our son Calvin was away with the army. George would come over and help take care of the lawn and fix things around the house that needed to be done. He got very close to Lucy. He taught her how to drive a car and he helped her with some of her studies."

"Didn't she date guys her own age?"

"She did some in high school. But she was a shy girl—still is. After high school she got to seeing George more whenever he was home, and when he asked her to marry him, I guess she just felt comfortable with him and said yes. They moved in with me at first, but after Billy was born they bought a place over on the other side of town. Things weren't perfect, but they seemed to be doing okay until that train wreck."

Stan looked at his notes again. "You mentioned your grandson. How old is the boy now?"

The old lady leaned back and put her elbows on the chair arms. "He's eleven, and a beautiful young man. I have hopes for him. That's one reason I'm talking to you, probably more than I should. I worry about what kind of situation he's in. Maybe Lucy'll open up to you the way she hasn't to me. We talk on the phone once in a while, and she tries to defend that husband of hers, but I get the feeling she doesn't totally believe what she's telling me. Something's not right."

Stan nodded. "Well, I'm just a reporter, but if I'm able to talk to her, I'll tell her how you feel, and if she needs any help, I'll do what I can to point her in the right direction. As for what I might write, don't worry. I won't divulge any off-the-record stuff we've talked about."

"Thank you Mr. Ellis."

Putting his pad and pen in his jacket pocket, he said, "Before I leave, could you look up the street address where your daughter's living?"

"Sure."

Helen got up from her chair and went to the next room. Stan heard her dialing a phone, but apparently there was no answer. When she returned, she handed him a piece of paper. "Now here's the address and her telephone number. You should try to see her at work, at Hogan's grocery, rather than going to the house. I called to see if she was home, but she didn't answer. She must be at work. I don't think it would be helpful if you try to talk to her when her husband's around."

Stan rose from the couch and took the paper. "Yes, I understand. I'll stop by the store and if she isn't there, I'll give her a call later. He leaned forward, enfolding her tiny outstretched hand in his two large hands. Thank you so much for your help Mrs. Grim." He put on his jacket and cap and left.

CHAPTER 8

Kendall, a bustling little farming community eight miles north of Elroy, was a place Stan had driven through many times, but he'd never stopped there. Its businesses were all on a three block stretch along Route 71 that cut through the village. Watching both sides of the road, he passed a gas station, a car repair shop, a bank, a hotel, a tavern, and a post office before spotting Hogan's grocery on the second block. When he walked in the door, he immediately recognized the girl at the cash register as the one in the picture he'd seen in Helen Grim's house—a cute girl, about five feet tall, rather thin, with blonde hair. The only difference was she now wore her hair in a ponytail. He waited until she finished with a customer, grabbed a packet of gum and went up to the register. "Are you Lucy Bickle?" he asked.

She turned and looked at him with a smile. "Yes. Why?"

"I'm Stan Ellis. Reporter for the Sparta Herald. I think you called me about a week ago about George Cashman."

Her smile gave way to a frown. "How did you find me?"

He was so busy congratulating himself on finally locating her, it took a moment to think what to say. "I... uh... I went to see George at the prison. He gave me your mother's address in Elroy. She told me."

Her eyes narrowed. "She shouldn't have. I... I made a mistake in calling you. It was nothing. Five cents for the gum."

He laid a nickel on the counter. "If it was nothing I don't think you would have called. Your mother seems worried about you too. Can we meet somewhere and talk? I'd like to tell you about my meeting with George."

She looked around. A customer pushing a basket was coming towards her register. "I have a lunch break at twelve thirty. Meet me at Libby's."

He looked out the window and saw a hand-painted sign atop a storefront directly across the street with the words 'Libby's Eats' in big red letters. He gave a nod. "I'll meet you there."

As he walked out of the grocery store, he checked his watch—quarter to twelve. Libby's was a small restaurant with five or six counter stools, three booths along the wall, and four small tables in between the counter and the booths. There were two men in work clothes at the counter. The tables were empty, but the first booth was occupied. He went to the last booth, sitting where he could see the door. When the waitress came by with a menu, he told her he was waiting for someone else, but he'd order now. He opened the menu and asked for a hot beef sandwich and a cup of coffee. After ordering, he grabbed a local newspaper from the counter and returned to his booth. He was on his second cup of coffee when Lucy walked in the door. She scanned the room, saw Stan, and came and sat down across from him. "Okay, I'm here. What do you want?"

"I think you know what I want. I'm the reporter you called a week ago. I'd like to get your story."

Before she could say anything, the waitress came over and dropped a menu on the table. "Hi Lucy. What can I get you?"

Pushing the menu aside Lucy said. "Hi Betty. Nothing for me."

Stan spoke up. "Go ahead and order something. I'm paying."

Looking flustered Lucy pointed toward Stan. "This... this is Mr. Brown. He's one of our suppliers. I needed to talk to him about some change orders." She picked up the menu and glanced at it quickly. "I'll have an egg salad sandwich and a Coke."

The waitress smiled and picked up her menu. "Okay, I'll be back."

Stan took a sip of his coffee. "So why the deception?

She shook her head. "My husband comes in here sometimes. The only reason I came here to meet you is because you said you met with George. Is he okay?"

"I wouldn't say he's okay. He worries that he won't live long enough to get out of prison. Said the doctors told him he needs a new kidney."

Lucy lifted her eyebrows. "Oh no! That's awful."

"So why didn't you go visit him? The one thing he asked me to tell you was how much he missed seeing his son. He couldn't understand why you stopped coming, but then, he didn't know you'd gotten remarried. Certainly didn't know about you marrying his old buddy Ray Bickle."

She glared at him. "What do you know about Ray and me?"

"Just that you divorced George and married Bickle less than a year after your husband went to jail.

She put her two hands to her cheeks and lowered her head. "I know, I know. It was wrong, the way I acted. I would have gone to see George, but Ray wouldn't—."

Betty came over with her sandwich and Coke. "Anything else?"

"No," said Lucy.

When Betty went back behind the counter, Lucy peeked around the corner of the booth to see if anyone was close. Just one customer on a stool at the far end of the counter talking with the waitress. The booth in front seemed to be empty. "Ray wouldn't let me go," she said.

"I guess that explains it. But you have to admit it looks pretty odd you marrying your ex-husband's good friend so soon after George was sent away."

"I know it does."

"Aside from that, you said you felt wrong about the way you acted. Why did you say that? Did it have something to do with the train derailment?"

She looked down at the tabletop. "I guess I felt guilty." She continued to avoid looking at Stan, saying in a subdued voice, "I gave Ray that bottle of liquor that they found in the train after the wreck."

"What?" Stan leaned half-way across the table. "Did Ray tell you he put it in the engine cab?"

"No, not directly, but they said at the trial the bottle had both George's fingerprints and mine on it. It had to be the same one. Who else could have done it?"

"So you think he did something with the liquor bottle. Could he, also, have done something to the tracks to cause the train to derail?"

She twisted her head around to see if anyone was looking their way. "I can't say. I've said too much already. I was desperate when I called you, and I'm not sure how much I should trust you."

Stan straightened his back and raised his chin. "Your mother said I have an honest face."

Lucy gave a slight smile. "She's a sucker for tall men."

Changing his mood to serious, Stan asked. "Are you still in love with Ray?"

"No. Not anymore," she said. "Taking up with him was the biggest mistake of my life."

"You ought to tell the police you suspect him of being involved in the train wreck. Tell them what you know, and if he's not treating you right, tell them that too."

"I told you before I can't. I'm afraid of him. The police aren't going to do anything to protect me."

Stan leaned back in the booth and thought for a moment how to respond. "You don't actually need to go to the police. I can go and tell them what I've learned. You're an anonymous source for me, and I don't have to tell them where I got the information. But if you tell me, based on what you know, just what happened leading up to the train wreck and afterward, it may be enough for them to start a new investigation. I don't need to give your name."

"I don't know. I need time to think. I need to get back to work."

"Can we meet again? Just talk?"

She looked at him cautiously, then shook her head. "I... I don't think so."

He pulled out a card from his pocket. "Here's my work and home phone. If you change your mind, call me."

She took the card, put it in her purse, and left.

CHAPTER 9

Dispirited after his meeting with Lucy, Stan walked into his office Friday morning, hung up his cap and coat, and went directly to the coffee urn. Irv came up and patted him on the shoulder. "Did you find the woman you were looking for?"

Stan nodded. "I did, but it didn't go exactly as I'd hoped."

"Was it the guy's wife like you thought?"

"Yeah, but she divorced him and remarried. That made it harder to find her. She works in a grocery store in Kendall. We talked over her lunch hour, but she didn't give me much. I think she just felt sorry for him and maybe she's having some problems in her new marriage, but I didn't get anything I can use as far as the Cashman conviction goes. I'll get my story to you by the end of the day."

"That'll be fine," said Irv. "Were you able to reach any of the train passengers?"

"I did. I interviewed two people up in La Crosse who were on the train that day, and I talked on the phone to the daughter of one of the passengers who died. I was hoping when I found that woman caller, it would lead to some breakthrough that could prove Cashman innocent. But I'm afraid it's just a tragic story with no happy ending."

Irv drew a cup of coffee for himself. "Sometimes you don't know how a story will come out until you follow through on it. I really thought you might be on to something, but if that's the end, then accept it, and go on to the next one."

Stan nodded. "You're right. Got something else for me today?"

"As a matter-of-fact, I do. There's a retirement ceremony in City Hall at one o'clock for Jack Davis."

Stan looked at him, unsure of the name.

"The fire chief. Retiring after thirty-five years. Should be a happy story for the front page. They'll have food."

Stan managed a smile. "Okay. Sounds good. After that I'll head over to Tomah to cover tonight's high school game. Appreciate you doing the pre-game workup."

.　　.　　.　　.　　.

Although he told Irv he'd try to forget the Cashman story, Stan couldn't stop it from whirling around in his mind like a blinding sandstorm. Saturday evening he and Patty met up with Glen and Carol at Clutter's Bar to relax and get their minds off work. They feasted on burgers, fries, and beer and talked about sports while a jukebox played rock n' roll in the background. Two pool tables were set up in the rear of the bar area, and when Patty and Carol began talking about plans for a baby shower, Glen and Stan excused themselves to go shoot a game or two.

Around eight o'clock they all left the bar and went their separate ways. Stan and Patty returned to her apartment to watch television. After sitting together on the couch for a half-hour, Patty looked at Stan. "You seem distracted. What's wrong?"

"I guess it's that Cashman case. The girl I talked to yesterday—his ex-wife. She could be in some danger, but I don't know what to do."

"What do you mean in some danger?"

"I think her new husband had something to do with causing the train wreck, but she wouldn't say it in so many words. She said she won't go to the police because she's scared of the guy."

Patty stroked his arm. "There's not a lot you can do. If she'll go to the police, they can put a restraining order on him, but she has to make a move to report him. I know how you feel about wanting to help people in need, but there's a limit to what you can do. Try to get it out of your mind."

He put one arm around her shoulder, turned her head, and kissed her lips softy. "Easier said than done, but I'll try." She wrapped her arms around his neck, pulled him close, and returned a lingering kiss that made him forget for a time what he'd been worried about.

Sunday morning, Stan woke up feeling he'd done all he could, and it was okay to move on. He went for a five-mile jog through the park, then down to City Hall, and back. After returning home, he was fixing himself some bacon, eggs, and hash browns when his phone rang.

"Hello?"

There was a silence on the phone. Then a woman said. "Is this Mr. Ellis?"

"Yes. Who's this?"

"It's Lucy Bickle. We talked on Thursday."

"Oh—Mrs. Bickle. I've been thinking about you."

"I've been thinking about our meeting too. Mom said I should trust you. So if you're still interested, I'll meet with you to tell you what I know about the train wreck."

"I'm interested. Where do you want to meet and when?"

"My husband left this morning for work. He'll be gone until Tuesday. You can come to my house tomorrow morning around ten. It's a ways out of town. So there's no neighbor close that might see you. Do you know my address?"

"Your mother gave me your address, and I think I put it in my desk drawer at work. But to be safe, can you give it to me again?"

"It's 250 Hardy Road. The number's on the postbox."

After hanging up the phone, he pounded the counter with his fists. "I knew it!"

• • • • •

Stan pulled his car into a parking space along Kendall's Main Street to look over the county map he'd brought along. He looked at his watch—quarter to ten. He checked his map and then drove two more blocks, turning onto White Street. The car rattled over railroad tracks and then passed several well-kept Victorian style houses with gigantic elm trees gracing the yards. After crossing a bridge over a small stream, he turned right onto Hardy Road. From there the houses began to thin out. He drove slowly for a mile-and-a-half until he spotted the post box he was looking for. A white bungalow with a broad covered porch sat about thirty yards off the road. A blue and white Chevy sedan sat in the gravel driveway. *What do I say if he answers the door?*

Stan stopped just behind the Chevy, got out, and went up to the door. He knocked and after a few seconds Lucy opened it. She was wearing a frilly blouse and blue slacks. He noticed a slight bruise on the side of her mouth.

"The car? Is your husband here?"

"No, she said. I took him to the station in Elroy. He'll get his train there. Billy's at school. So we can talk."

Stan breathed out a heavy sigh. "I was a little worried he might be here when I saw the car."

"I wouldn't have let you come if he was here."

He followed her into a neat, but somewhat cramped kitchen where a Formica-topped dinette table with three chairs occupied one wall opposite a tiled kitchen counter with a window that looked out on the backyard. A black and white cat sat in a corner looking up at him and then scampered out of sight when he went to pet it.

"Do you want coffee or anything? The coffee's from this morning, but it'll just take a minute to heat."

"Yes, coffee's good. Thank you."

While she turned on the stove to reheat the coffee pot, Stan laid his hands on the edge of the sink and looked out the window. The backyard was big, extending probably forty yards to a line of aspen trees, beyond which there seemed to be an open field. A towering oak dominated the yard, bordered on both sides by a variety of deciduous and evergreen shrubs, none of which he could identify except for the hydrangeas that still held some blooms. There was a good-sized garden off to the right where two rows of yellowed corn stalks and several bright orange pumpkins were all that remained from summer's harvest.

"You've got quite a spread back here. Must take a lot of work just to keep up with it."

"It does, but that's Ray's job. I guess you could say gardening is his hobby. When he's home, he's always doing something outside. When we got married, he said he'd take care of the outside, and my job was taking care of everything inside."

Taking a coffee cup out of the cupboard, she filled it to the brim, and set it on the table. She took a Coke from the refrigerator for herself, popped the top off, and sat down at one end of the table. Stan slid out the chair at the other end and sat down across from her. "What changed your mind about talking to me?"

"Ray and I had an argument last night."

Stan touched the edge of his mouth, the same spot where Lucy showed some bruising. "Looks like it was more than just an argument."

She nodded. "Yes. He got real mad at me. He talked to someone who saw us at Libby's, and he wanted to know who you were. I told him you were a salesman—like I told Betty at the restaurant. He started getting rough with me. Said he didn't believe me. When Billy tried to intervene he threw him clear across the room."

Stan winced. "Was he hurt?"

"No. Luckily he wasn't—no bones broken or anything—but he could have been. When that happened, I jumped on Ray. He slapped me across the face hard, and I went down. After that he just stormed out of the room swearing. I can't take much more of him, but I'm afraid to go to the police and turn him in. I talked to my mother this morning after I took Ray to the station. I told her about our talk in the restaurant. She said I should contact you."

Stan took a gulp of coffee. "What can I possibly do to help? You should go to the police."

"No! I won't do that on my own. But I got to thinking about what you said."

"Which was...?"

"You said you could tell the police my story without giving my name, and then they would investigate."

"I did say that, but you've got to realize that at some point, if Bickle is arrested and goes to trial, you'll have to step forward publicly."

She nodded. "I understand, but I don't want him to know what I'm doing before he's arrested."

"Okay, let's say I go to the police with your story. You told me you weren't certain he caused the wreck—only that you gave him a liquor bottle. The police would need more than that."

She shuffled her hands nervously on the tabletop. "I know. I wasn't telling you the total truth. After the trial was over and George was sentenced to prison, Ray was pestering me about putting in for a divorce and I wanted to wait. One night we were together, and he'd been drinking quite a bit. He got angry and started yelling about all he did to get George out of the way. When I asked him what he did, he said he caused the train derailment. When I told him he must be crazy to do something like that, I thought he might hit me, but he didn't. Instead, he bragged about how he'd done it."

"Did he have help?"

"He never mentioned anyone else. Ray's a strong guy, and you have to understand he'd been over that route a hundred times and knew every twist and turn in the track. He told me he went out there after midnight and removed the bolts and clamps that held the rails in place. Then he used a crowbar to bend the rails just far enough apart to make sure the front wheels would go off the track. After that he said he just went home and waited to see what would happen."

"There are several trains a day that pass over that route. How could he be sure that George's would derail, and not an earlier train?"

"I asked him that, and he said he checked the route schedule before he went out to make sure there wouldn't be any other trains before George's."

"Did he tell you he put the liquor bottle in the train cab?"

"No, but I'm sure he did. When I asked him about that he just laughed at me and said it wasn't his fingerprints on the bottle."

Stan ran his hands through his hair and sighed. "After he told you all this, you were okay with it?"

She bit her lower lip. "I knew it was wrong, but I thought I was in love with Ray. When he finished telling me what happened, he teared up and told me he how sorry he was, and that he loved me and did it for us. He said he didn't mean for anybody to get killed, but just wanted to get George out of the way. I felt I had to keep his secret. If I had to do it over again—"

Stan gave a reproachful shake of his head. "I know, everyone wants a second chance when they make a mistake. Sometimes there are no second chances. It took a lot of planning to get everything to mesh. You swear you didn't know about it beforehand?

"I swear. I didn't know that's what he was planning."

"Okay, I believe you. But from what you've said, you were... umm... it looks like you were having an affair with Ray? That's why he did it?"

She bent her head down. "Yes, it had been going on for almost a year. George and I were having some problems. Ray started coming on strong... I wasn't thinking straight." She made both her hands into fists and shook them.

"I was such a fool! I should have turned him in then. George shouldn't be in prison. Ray should be."

"Unless you get the police involved, that's not going to happen. You don't think Ray will suspect you if the police start asking questions?"

"He might suspect me, but there are other ways the police could find out. I'm sure he must have bragged to some of his buddies about what he'd done, and they could have told the police."

Stan scratched his chin. "But if the police do begin an investigation, it could involve you too. You could be considered an accessory for withholding evidence."

"Do you really think they'd arrest me? I didn't know what he was going to use the whiskey for. And he didn't tell me until after the trial what he did." She shrugged. "Even if they do, it'll be worth it to get Billy and me out of this situation."

"Okay. I have a friend in the sheriff's department who I can talk to. I'll get with him and see how we should proceed. I'll do everything I can to keep your name out of it."

"Please. That's important."

"I may need to get in touch with you again, depending on what happens. How can I do that and be sure your husband doesn't find out?"

She thought a moment. "You can call my mother, and she can get in touch with me." She got a scrap of paper from a counter drawer, wrote down the number, and handed it to him. Her hand remained touching his for a couple seconds as she looked up at him. "Thanks for helping me Mr. Ellis."

When he returned to his car and started the motor, he sat for a moment thinking about how she looked at him. There was genuine fear in her eyes. He hoped he hadn't promised more than he could deliver.

CHAPTER 10

By the time Stan got back from Elroy, it was nearly noon. Rose was the only one in the newsroom when he walked in. "Where's Irv?"

"There was a robbery over at the Cities Service gas station. He went over there a half-hour ago. He said he left some things on your desk for you to work on."

On his desk was a pile of wire service stories to go through. A note beside the pile read: *May be out all day. Interview set up with Mrs. Sheridan 2 p.m. at library about new children's annex opening Saturday. Need write-up for tomorrow paper. Thanks. Irv.*

When Stan returned from the interview, he sorted through the AP and UPI copy, picked out the five he thought Irv would want to include and added them to the mock-up next to Irv's desk. It was already five o'clock by the time he finished his library story. His mind kept going back to his meeting with Lucy and what he was going to do about it. Rather than return to his apartment, he decided to stop by Patty's. He'd promised he wouldn't release Lucy's name to the public, but the seriousness of the situation was weighing on him. He needed to tell somebody, and he knew Patty would keep whatever he said to herself.

When he got to Patty's, she answered the door wearing her uniform. Jessie was yipping away behind her but quieted down when she saw it was Stan and retreated to her place in the kitchen. "I wasn't expecting you," she said. "You know I'm on the evening shift this week. I was just heating up a frozen dinner before going to work."

"I won't stay long. I just needed to talk to you about something that came up today."

"Come and sit at the table while I eat. You want a beer or anything?"

"Yeah, a beer would be good."

She opened a bottle of Schlitz and set it in front of him, then took her dinner out of the oven and sat down across from him. "What happened?"

Stan took a swig of his beer. "Sunday I got a call from Cashman's ex-wife. I went to see her this morning."

Patty's eyes popped wide. "Is she going to the police?"

"No. She's still afraid to do that. She wants me to go to the cops and tell them what I know from an anonymous source, hoping they'll investigate and find out the truth."

"What is the truth?"

"She told me her current husband, Ray Bickle, admitted to her that he sabotaged the train tracks the night before the wreck."

She stopped eating and looked up. "Oh my God!"

"I plan on talking to Glen about who to turn this information over to. My question to you is, am I doing the right thing? Lucy may not be telling me the truth. She may just be using this to get back at her husband. I'll look like a fool if I'm being played. And if she is telling the truth, she could be charged herself with participating in a crime."

"You told me before that you felt the case against Cashman had some holes in it. Now you have information that supports that, and it might exonerate him. If you don't use the information, you'll always question yourself. I think Lucy knows what she's doing. She sounds like a brave girl, but you have to trust your gut instincts. What do you feel?"

He stared down at the table for a moment and then looked up. "I think she's telling the truth. I think I'll stop by Glen's place to get his thoughts. I won't give him Lucy's name though."

"You won't need to. He'll probably figure your anonymous source pretty quickly."

As he left Patty's apartment he checked his watch and saw it was a little after six. He didn't want to interrupt Glen and his wife if they were having supper, so he decided to stop first at the A&W to get something to eat before heading over. Glen and Carol married just six months ago. At the time, Stan worried that it might change their relationship—him being single and all—

but they'd stayed the same close friends, and he and Patty continued to get together with them fairly often. In a way, he envied Glen for being settled with a wife and his own house now, but he wasn't quite ready to make that big leap.

By the time he arrived in front of the house it was almost seven, and Glen answered the door with a dish towel over his arm. "Hey, buddy. What brings you here? We just finished supper. But come on in and take a load off." He pointed toward the living room.

Carol emerged from the kitchen, her baby bump evident under her pink apron. "Hi, Stan. Would you like some coffee and pie? It'd be no trouble."

"No thanks. I'm sorry to interrupt your evening, but I just needed to talk to Glen about something, and I didn't think it could wait until tomorrow."

"That's fine. You guys go talk. I've got things under control in the kitchen."

Stan took a seat on the couch, and Glen sat down in his easy chair. "What's happened? Something come up on your Cashman investigation? Did you find your anonymous caller?"

"Yes, I did."

Glen fluttered his hands for more information. "Who is it?"

"I promised I wouldn't give the name. What the person told me, on condition of keeping his name secret, is that a man named Ray Bickle sabotaged the train track causing the wreck. My source wants to remain anonymous but wanted me to make the information available to the authorities, hoping they would start a new investigation. I know I need to go to Sheriff Bascom, but I wanted to talk it over with you first."

Leaning forward Glen said, "Do you know who this Ray Bickle is?"

"He's a train brakeman who's worked a lot with Cashman, and they were apparent friends, since Cashman said he had him over to his house regularly to play cards."

"What's the motive?"

"He was having an affair with Cashman's wife. After Cashman went to jail, his wife got a divorce and married Bickle. When I talked to Cashman last week, he was completely in the dark about the affair or that his ex-wife married him."

Glen settled back in his chair. "It sounds like a neatly wrapped package, but it's one thing to have someone make an allegation and another to prove it. I think I know what you're aiming for, but Bickle isn't likely to confess and a wife can't be forced to testify against her husband. If they deny everything then we're nowhere."

"I understand, but the information about the affair wasn't brought up during the trial, and I would think it creates a lot of suspicion and puts an entirely new light on how the wreck happened."

"Yes, but unless we have first-hand witnesses or admissions of guilt, that's all it is—a suspicion."

Stan's shoulders slumped, "I really believe my source is telling the truth. I don't think there needs to be a lengthy investigation to tell if it's the truth or not. She's depending on me. Can't you go to bat for me with the sheriff?"

Glen smiled. "You slipped there, good buddy, by saying 'she.' I think I can guess who your anonymous person is, but I'll keep your secret." He sighed. "I need to fill Lieutenant Welk in on what you've found out and see if he'll agree to set up a meeting with Sheriff Bascom. He's the man we need to convince."

．　．　．　．　．　．

The next morning at ten Glen met Stan in the lobby of the sheriff's office. "I gave the Lieutenant a rundown on what you told me, and he agreed to set up the meeting with the sheriff. Anything new come up?"

"No," said Stan. "How did he react when you told him?"

"He was a little skeptical of an anonymous witness, but he agreed it was worth pursuing. He's in with the sheriff now. Let's go see if they're ready for us. When you talk to the sheriff, just look him straight in the eye. He puts a lot of stock in that."

They checked in with the secretary, and she said the sheriff was waiting for them. When they entered the inner office, Sheriff Bascom was sitting behind a large wooden desk and Lieutenant Welk was in a cushioned straight-back chair off to the side. There was a three-person sofa facing the desk, and without getting up, Bascom waved a hand to indicate to them 'have a seat,' while he continued to concentrate on an open folder on his desk.

At sixty years old, the sheriff was a long-time fixture in his job having been elected five straight times on the Republican ticket. Standing six-foot-three, with a mane of wavy white hair, and an arrow-straight posture that belied his age, the sheriff was still a commanding presence in any circle.

Highly respected—not just within the county but within the state's law enforcement community—he was known as gruff, but fair, and a no-nonsense type of man.

Stan knew that his whole plan to have an investigation depended on the sheriff's support. Sitting stiffly on the couch, he interlaced his fingers in his lap to keep from showing how nervous he was. After thirty long seconds the sheriff raised his head, put the folder to the side, and addressed Stan. "I've been looking over the file on George Cashman. Lieutenant Welk tells me you think you've uncovered information that points to someone else's involvement in the train wreck and that it could have a bearing on his conviction."

"Yes sir. That's right," said Stan.

"I understand you've got a witness, but you didn't want to give a name. It would make our job a lot easier if you gave us a name."

Stan didn't want to have the sheriff end the meeting right there, but he promised Lucy he wouldn't give out her name. He forced himself to maintain eye contact. "I understand sir, but I can't do that. It's a matter of journalistic integrity."

Bascom squinted his eyes and bore into Stan for a moment. Then he said, "Okay, young man, I can respect that. Tell me what you've heard."

Stan went over the story Lucy had told him about Ray Bickle's friendship with Cashman, how he had access to the whiskey bottle that was found in the train engine's cab, and how he admitted to his anonymous source that he sabotaged the train tracks. When he told of the affair between Lucy and Bickle, the sheriff interrupted. "I didn't see any mention about an affair in the arrest file. If that was happening, I'm certain Cashman would have brought it up in his defense."

"That's the thing," said Stan. "He didn't know about the affair. I went to Waupon last week and talked to Cashman. He was completely surprised about his wife marrying Bickle. When I look back to that trial, I have to think the jury might have looked at things differently if they'd been made aware of the affair, and the verdict might have turned out different."

Bascom stroked his mustache. "I admit an affair does draw suspicion, but it doesn't tie directly to what you're saying about sabotaging the tracks. Reopening an investigation costs money, and I'm not about to do it on just some hearsay. Why should we trust this informer of yours?"

"Bickle admitted his guilt to my source, and I believe this person revealed the information to me out of a sense of guilt for not coming forward earlier. I saw the fear in the person's eyes and I believe what the person told me."

"Okay. If you were doing the investigating, who would you want to talk to?"

"First, Ray Bickle. Second, his wife. After that, maybe the friends who he played cards with once a month. Their names are Rollie Erickson and Fred Noonan. They both live in Elroy. One of them might be able to confirm the affair."

Bascom looked at Lieutenant Welk. "Do you think this warrants a new investigation?"

"Sheriff, that's got to be your decision, but I think there's enough to initiate some interviews."

Bascom nodded. "I think there's some basis for that. I'll need to run it by the DA to get his opinion first. It's not easy to overturn a conviction. Who do you want to put on the case?"

Welk said, "Since Glen here has taken such a direct interest in this, I'd go with assigning him to the case along with Sergeant Palmer, assuming the DA goes along with it. What do you say, Glen?"

"I'd welcome the chance to do it, sir."

"All right," said Bascom. "I think we're finished here. Mr. Ellis, thank you for bringing this to our attention. I would appreciate it, for now, that this matter not to be brought up in the press. We need to see how this thing falls out."

"I understand sheriff. I won't write anything until it's cleared for the public."

When they walked out of the office, Glen clapped Stan on the back. "You did it buddy. The DA won't stop it. I can't wait to get an interview with Bickle."

Stan nodded, but with reservations. "I just hope I'm not being played."

CHAPTER 11

There was a knock on the front door. Lucy turned down the burner on the stove so as not to burn the stew she was preparing and went to see who it was. Opening the door, she met two men in khaki shirts and brown pants, wearing standard police 8-point duty caps. One seemed to be well over six feet tall. She had to crane her neck to look up at him. The other one was shorter and stockier, like her husband.

The tall one said, "Good morning ma'am. I'm Sergeant Palmer with the Monroe County Sheriff's Office and this is Deputy Horner. We're here to see if we can talk to Mr. Ray Bickle. Is he here?"

Lucy knew why they were here. She'd set the wheel in motion. Now she wasn't sure she was ready to go through with it. But did she have a choice? "Yes," she said. "He's out back mowing the lawn. What's this about?"

"It's about an investigation were doing about a Chicago & Northwestern train wreck that happened a few years ago near here. We understand Mr. Bickle worked for the railroad at the time of the accident, and he may be able to shed some light regarding what happened."

"Oh, sure. Come in, then." She stepped back and pointed to the living room. "You can wait there while I go and get him."

Three or four minutes later, Bickle, in dirty blue jeans and a checkered flannel shirt with his sleeves rolled up, appeared in the doorway of the living room. Lucy stayed in the kitchen. "My wife says you wanted to see me. Something about a train wreck?"

Both officers rose from their seats and offered to shake hands. Bickle, with his own hands covered with grit and grass stains, shook each of their hands confidently. Then Palmer said, "Yes, we're reopening an investigation into the 1954 train accident where three people died. I'm sure you're familiar with it. We received a tip regarding the cause of the accident that, if true, could have an effect on the train engineer's conviction."

Bickle took a seat in a straight-back chair and the officers returned to the couch. Without showing any emotion Bickle asked, "What does that have to do with me?"

Palmer said, "Your name came up as someone who worked on the same train with George Cashman, the engineer who was convicted, and you were also friends with him. We're interviewing others who were friends of his or who worked with him to try to verify if the tip we received is valid or not. We're not here to accuse you of anything. We're just looking for information."

"Okay, so what do you want to know?"

"Since this is a formal investigation we'd like to ask you to come to the sheriff's office for an interview so we can properly document responses. It's voluntary on your part, and you don't have to come this afternoon. We don't want to interrupt what you're doing. We know you have a job to go to, so it's up to you how you want to handle it."

Bickle looked down and scuffed the rug with one shoe. "I'm off again tomorrow. I guess I can go up there and talk to you. What time do you want me there?"

Palmer said, "How about one o'clock?"

"Okay, I can make it then. You guys gonna pay me anything for my trouble?"

Palmer looked at Glen and then turned back to Bickle. "I think we can come up with a voucher to cover your meal expense and gas. Are you familiar with Sparta and where the sheriff's office is?

"I been to Sparta, but never to your place."

"We're right next to the courthouse. You shouldn't have any trouble finding us. When you enter the lobby, just tell the deputy at the desk that you're there to see Sergeant Palmer."

The two deputies got up from the couch, Bickle got up from his chair, and they shook hands again. This time Bickle seemed less confident as he showed them to the door.

When they left, Lucy came to the living room, and they watched from the front window as the two officers got in their cruiser and drove off. Then Ray turned to Lucy and with narrowed eyes said, "Did you know anything about them coming here?"

Lucy gave a rapid shake of her head. "No, I don't know why they came."

She turned away and headed into the kitchen. Ray followed her, grabbed both her upper arms, and pinned her against the wall. "I think you do know something. How would they know to link me to the train wreck?" His hands easily wrapped around her upper arm and he began to squeeze.

"Maybe one of your friends told them something."

"I didn't tell any of my friends anything about it. I only told you." His hands dug deeper into her arm muscle.

She struggled helplessly to pull away. "Ow! Ow! It must have been George then. He must have suspected something between us."

"You're a lying bitch!" He kept holding her with one hand, and with the other reached into a pants pocket and drew out a card. "I found this in your purse. It says 'Stanley Ellis Sparta Herald Reporter.' Did you talk to him?"

Cowering under his grip, she gave a quick nod.

Just as he raised his right hand to slap her, the front door opened, and Billy called out, "Mom. I'm home. I stopped at Gary's house first."

Bickle let go of her arm and lowered his voice. "We can settle this later. I may have to have a talk with Stanley sometime."

Lucy hollered back to Billy who was in the living room. "Go and wash your hands and get ready for supper."

Ray kept her pinned against the wall, looking down at her with a smug grin. "I'm going up there tomorrow and tell those cops I know nothing about how the wreck happened. If they ask about our relationship, I'll tell them we started seeing each other when my wife got sick and after they arrested your husband. If they call wanting to talk to you, you're going to tell the same thing, aren't you sweetie?"

"Yes, yes, I will," she said pushing him aside. "I need to go check on Billy. Then I'll finish fixing supper."

After they finished eating, Lucy cleaned off the table and told Billy to go upstairs to do his studies. A few minutes later, while she was washing the dishes, Billy came into the kitchen. "Mom, can you help me with this arithmetic problem? I can't figure it out."

"Did you ask Ray? He should be able to help you."

"I did, but he said to ask you. He wanted to watch his TV program."

She tossed the dishrag into the sink and stomped into the living room. "Ray, what's wrong with you? Why can't you help Billy? You're not doing anything."

He slammed the beer bottle he was holding onto the side table and glared at her. "Hell I'm not. I'm watching my program. He's your responsibility—not mine. Now leave me alone."

"No, I won't leave you alone. When you married me, my son came with the deal. I thought you accepted that. You used to do things with him—took him fishing sometimes and played ball with him. Now you treat him like he doesn't belong. Why?"

He turned toward her with a scowl. "I don't have the patience for kids. Found that out when I was babysittin him, always whining or arguing about something. If I would have wanted to have kids, I would have had them with Alice. I work my ass off and bring home decent money to support you both. That oughta be enough. Now leave me alone. He picked up the beer bottle, took a swig, and went back to watching TV.

She took Billy by the arm and led him into the kitchen. "Come on. I'll help you."

At ten o'clock, after getting Billy settled, Lucy went to bed, but Ray stayed up drinking and watching a late movie. As she laid in bed, she thought how things could have been different if she hadn't betrayed George and allowed herself to be swept up by Ray. She regretted what she'd done. She wanted out, and she hoped with all her might that her opening up to the newspaper reporter wouldn't backfire on her. When he entered the bedroom around midnight, Ray came over to the bed and shook Lucy awake. When she opened her eyes, she saw him looming over her like a hungry jackal about to pounce on its prey. The strong smell of alcohol on his breath was overpowering. "Take off your clothes," he ordered.

She didn't say no, even though having sex was the last thing she wanted to do. She knew if she did, he would get rough and force himself on her. It was useless to fight. Back before they were married and for the first year afterward, his aggressive sexiness excited her. It was so different from what she had with George. It was fun then. But it wasn't fun anymore—not after he started hitting her. Now when he touched her, she felt repelled, but she didn't dare resist. She slowly got up from the bed, robotically removed her nightgown and panties, and laid back down on the bed, waiting for what was to come. She let out a gasp as he flopped down on top of her, and her mind flowed elsewhere. *He wants to control me. He may control my body, but he won't control my mind. I have to do something, and I will.*

CHAPTER 12

Glen checked his watch. It was one o'clock and Bickle hadn't shown yet. He looked at Vic who was waiting with him in the lobby of the sheriff's office. "Maybe we'll have to drive over to Kendall to get him. You think?" Just then Bickle walked in the front door. He'd spruced up since the last time they saw him. He had on patterned cowboy boots and wore a brown leather jacket over a blue denim shirt and tan slacks. Vic went up to him, shook hands, and took him to the front desk to sign him in.

They walked Bickle back to a windowless interview room and had him sit in a straight-back chair beside a small table. Vic pulled a chair to the table and sat opposite Bickle, while Glen sat at a distance, letting Vic initiate the questioning. After explaining again why they were reopening the investigation into the 1954 train wreck, Vic asked, "How well did you know George Cashman?

Bickle appeared relaxed, leaning casually against the back of the chair. He explained that he had worked off and on with Cashman for five or six years before the accident, but their work assignments didn't always coincide. "There were times I'd ride with him in the cab, so we got to know each other pretty well," Bickle added.

"Were you on the train that crashed?" Glen asked.

"No, I wasn't at work that day. I was out sick."

"When was the last time you rode on the same train with Cashman?"

Bickle raised his eyes to think. "Maybe two, three days before. I forget when I took off sick that week, but I know I wasn't there when the train derailed."

"Were you friends with Cashman outside of work?"

Bickle nodded. "For two or three years before the accident, I was part of a group that played cards once a month, usually at George's house or at Rollie Erickson's. Other than that we didn't get together at all. George didn't care to go out drinking in the bars with the guys. He liked to do his drinking at home."

Vic broke in. "Do you know if he drank a lot?"

"I can't say how much, but I know he liked his whiskey. When we played, that bottle of Wild Turkey was always out."

"That leads me to a serious question I have to ask," said Vic. "Do you know if he ever drank on the job."

Bickle rubbed the side of his face with one hand. "Now you're putting me on the spot. George is a friend. But I have to tell you the truth I guess. There was a couple times when we were riding together that he pulled a pint out of his coat and asked if I wanted some."

"Did you take him up on his offer?"

"Sure—just a friendly pick-me-up to get through a long day. Nothing that would affect my work. Same goes for George. As far as I know, he never got to where he couldn't operate the train."

"Appreciate your honesty." Vic turned to Glen. "Any questions?"

"I do." He looked squarely at Bickle. "The report we received alleges that before the train accident happened Cashman's wife was having an affair with someone. Were you having an affair with his wife?"

Bickle's eye's widened. "Whoa! I know where you're coming from. You think because I married Cashman's wife, we had something going on behind his back."

"Did you?" asked Glen.

"Hell No! We started seeing each other after he was arrested and after my wife got sick. Lucy was depressed, and I was too. We kind of supported one another. Then when he went to prison and my wife died, it just seemed that it was meant to be, and we decided to get married."

Glen nodded thoughtfully. "I'm not going to play games with you. The word going around is that you were having an affair with Bickle's wife. You still say it's not true?"

"Not true."

"If it's just a rumor, where do you think it could have come from?"

"Oh, I think George probably came up with that idea after he found out we were married, and he's looking for a way to get himself out. Investigators looked at the accident after it happened and said he was going too fast and that caused the accident. I can't say if he was drinking or not cause I wasn't there, but the jury decided he was. I feel sorry for what happened to the old boy, but he ain't pinning anything on me."

"You said you were out sick on the day the accident occurred. You were at home all that time?"

Bickle shrugged. "Sure. Where else?"

"Can anyone vouch as to where you were? Did you see a doctor?"

"No. I just had the flu and stayed home until I got better. I didn't need a doctor. My wife's the only one who could vouch for me." He bowed his head. "But she's not around anymore to back me up. It's just my word."

Glen said he had nothing more to ask and looked over at the sergeant. "We're finished here today," said Palmer. "We have a few other people we'll be interviewing before we wrap up our investigation. If we need to talk to you again, do you have any problem with coming back?"

Bickle nodded. "I guess I can. I got nothing to hide—just as long as it doesn't cause me to lose work-time. Tomorrow I'll be on a run out to Iowa. Be gone for a couple days."

After he left, Glen looked at Vic. "We'll find out how much we can believe once we interview his wife, and those two other card-playing pals of his."

• • • •

The next morning, the two officers interviewed Rollie Erickson, the retired train conductor, who was one of Bickle's card-playing friends. They met him in the lobby when he came in and escorted him back to an interview room. Portly with a round jowly face, he wore a navy blue suit and striped tie with wide suspenders stretched over his expansive belly. After going quickly over their reasons for asking him to come in, Palmer asked how well he knew George Cashman.

"I've known him for maybe twenty years. I worked the same trains with him for about ten years before I retired six years ago. A couple years before I retired, we started getting together for cards once a month or so," said Erickson.

"Did you know him to drink to excess?"

"Not really. We'd drink beer, and sometimes whiskey at our get-togethers. Nothing wild or crazy. I'm not exactly a wild and crazy kind of guy, I think you can tell."

"When you knew him did you ever know him to drink on the job?"

He shook his head. "Nope. Never saw anything like that."

"We're doing this new investigation because of an allegation that somebody other than Cashman was responsible for the train derailment. In other words, somebody sabotaged the train. Do you know anyone who might have something against Cashman, who might have reason or opportunity to do something like that?"

Again he shook his head slowly. "No, I can't think of anyone."

Palmer turned to Glen to raise a question. "Ray Bickle was one of your card-playing partners. How well did you know him?"

"As best I remember, he started working with me a year or two before I retired," said Erickson. "Kind of a brash young fellow, a jokester, but a good worker. Strong as a bull. George invited him into our group when Ollie Carson moved to Madison to live with his daughter. Ray could be a little crude sometimes with his jokes, but he added a little spice to the group, I guess you'd say."

"The inspectors said the train accident was the result of excessive speed. You've been around trains your whole life. Do you think it's possible that the inspectors might have overlooked something, and someone could have sabotaged the track?"

Erikson thought for a moment. "Sure it's possible. I remember a situation back in '42 when we had a train derailment on a milk run down near the Montfort turnout. Inspectors at first said the engineer was speeding, then later it came out that a section hand hadn't completely closed the turnout switch. But in most cases inspectors are going to be hard to fool."

"Maybe they accepted the speed theory and didn't look any further. If you wanted to derail a train at that spot in a way that would fool inspectors, what would you do?

Erickson rubbed his chin. "Well, each rail is about forty feet in length connected by what's called a joint bar. I guess if it was me I'd look at removing the bolts from the joint bar, and that might be enough to cause a derailment. But to make sure, I'd also remove the bolts from the tie plates connecting the rails to the ties. Once the train derailed and tore up the rail underneath, I think it'd be hard for an inspector to tell if someone had tampered with it. But a person would have to want to do that awful bad. It'd take some knowledge of what was needed and it'd take time."

Glen looked at him. "Yes, someone *would* have to want to do it awful bad. That's the only questions I have." He turned to Vic. "Anything else?"

"No. I think we're finished. Thank you Mr. Erickson."

Fred Noonan, the feedlot salesman, was waiting in the lobby when Glen escorted Erickson out at ten o'clock. He was a short wiry guy with greasy slicked-down hair and a small weasel-like face, dressed to impress in his blue checkered blazer and narrow black tie. Glen greeted him and took him back to the interview room where Vic had remained.

Again they explained why they were reopening the investigation. Palmer asked him to explain his relationship with George Cashman.

"I've known him for quite a few years. When I went to work for the feed store we did a lot of business with the Northwestern, I would run into George sometimes when his train was loading grain and we would talk. But I didn't get to really know him until they invited me to be part of their card group. I guess that went on for about three years until the train wreck happened and then George was sent away."

"Did Cashman invite you to join the group?"

"No. It was Ray Bickle. Me and him were old army buddies."

Palmer noted the connection and then asked. "One of the things that Cashman was accused of was operating the train while drinking. From what you know, was he a heavy drinker?" asked Palmer.

Noonan grinned. "Really, all I know is when we got together for cards. He enjoyed his liquor, and we all did. We had a good time, but none of us would get falling down drunk. I told them that at the trial, but that prosecuting attorney, he tried to make a big thing out of it. I told them I didn't think George was an alcoholic."

Glen asked, "You've known Cashman for a lot of years. You spent time in his house. Do you know of any problems he was having with his marriage?"

Noonan gave a vacuous grin, "Don't everybody have some problems with their marriage? Whatever problems he might have had he never told me. The way he talked about Lucy, he felt lucky to have her."

Palmer said, "Do you know of anyone who might have something against Cashman and wanted to get him in trouble?"

He shook his head. "Most everybody liked George. I don't know anyone who would want to get him in that kind of trouble."

They asked several more questions without any new revelations before ending the interview and escorting him back to the lobby. After he left, Glen and Vic went back to Glen's desk to go over the morning's results.

"Doesn't look like we got anything today that would change the sheriff's or the DA's opinion about Cashman's guilt," said Vic. "Even though these guys were supportive of Cashman, nothing they said would convince a jury Cashman wasn't responsible for what happened. No enemies who'd want to do him harm. Nothing about marital problems. Some question whether he's an alcoholic. I checked. It was more than ten years ago, but he did have a couple DUI's on his record. This investigation is going nowhere fast."

"I agree," said Glen. "So tomorrow we go talk to the wife, right? According to Bickle, he should be still out of town."

"Yes, she's the key to this. I'll give her a call now to see if she'll come up here, or if we need to go down there."

Palmer checked through the file for Bickle's home phone. He made the call, and Lucy answered. When he finished, he said to Glen. "She wants us to come down there at nine tomorrow. Her husband has the car so she can't come here. She said she has to be at work at one, and I told her we'd be finished in plenty of time."

"Did she say when her husband's supposed to be back?"

"Tomorrow night late."

CHAPTER 13

Sergeant Palmer was already at his desk looking over some paperwork when Glen walked in at seven thirty. "When do you want to leave?"

Palmer looked up. "You'll have to take the Bickle woman's interview yourself. The sheriff wants me to go over to Tomah this morning. They had a break-in at a pharmacy last night and a bunch of drugs taken. He said the police chief in Tomah is asking for our help because there may be a link to some recent break-ins around the county."

Glen got to the Bickle house just a few minutes before nine. No car in the driveway which was good. If they did the interview at the office back in Sparta, they could tape record it. Now he'd have to depend on his note taking. He wished Vic was with him so at least they'd have each other to verify what she said. He grabbed his notebook from the passenger seat, went up to the porch, and knocked on the door. Lucy answered it right away and invited him into the living room. She offered him coffee, and he took a seat on the couch while Lucy went to the kitchen to get it. When she returned with the coffee, she took a seat opposite him in an upholstered chair. Not wanting to dive directly into hard questioning, he took a sip from his cup and noted the fresh floral arrangement she had sitting on the coffee table between them.

"Nice flowers. From your garden?"

"Yes. Ray's the gardener in our house. They're hydrangeas. That'll probably be the last of them for this year. Ray cut them for me before he left—probably to make up for an argument we had."

"Well, they look very nice here." He opened up the notebook on his lap. "I don't want to take too much of your time, so let's get right to the matter at hand. As Officer Palmer and I told you before, we're starting this investigation into the 1954 train wreck because of new information that came to light from an informant. That informant claimed that someone other than George Cashman was responsible for the train derailment." He leaned forward. "I'm not going to beat around the bush, Mrs Bickle. We believe that informant was you. Are you the one who gave that information to Stan Ellis?"

At first she looked away. Then she turned and said, "Yes, it was me. But I told him not to give out my name because I'm afraid of my husband."

Glen took a deep breath. "All right Mrs. Bickle. We can handle that if you'll let us. But you need to tell me everything you know so we can take the appropriate action."

"If I do, what happens to Ray?"

"If we find what you tell us directly connects him to the train wreck, and is credible, and the district attorney thinks it will support a conviction, then we can arrest him. He'll eventually go to trial."

She lowered her head and thought a moment before responding. "Okay. What do you want to know?"

"First of all, how did the whiskey bottle get into the cab of the train engine?"

"I'm not positive, but I think Ray put it there. One night when we were together he asked me to give him the half-empty bottle of whiskey in George's liquor cabinet. He had me put it in a paper bag, and he took it with him. That was just a few nights before that train wreck. I thought he just wanted it for himself to drink."

Glen began transcribing her words onto his pad as she spoke. "What makes you believe he put that bottle in the train?"

"Because he wanted to hurt George. To get him fired. Maybe put in jail."

"Why would he want to do that?"

She looked down. "Ray and I were having an affair. Ray thought if George was fired or went to jail, it would be easy for me to get a divorce and we could get married. I wasn't happy in my marriage, and Ray wasn't happy in his."

"How long had this affair been going on?"

"Probably about a year. I got to know Ray when he'd come over to play cards. He started coming on to me, and I didn't discourage him. George was gone a lot on trips, and when Billy was in school, it was easy for us to get together without anyone knowing. He talked about getting married, and he wanted me to file for divorce from George, and then he'd do the same with his wife. I told him I didn't want to because of Billy. But he kept pressuring me."

Glen looked down at his notes for his next question. "You said you thought Ray was taking the liquor for his personal use. When did you realize Ray may have put the liquor bottle in the train?"

"During the trial. One of the investigators said it had my fingerprints on it along with George's. I knew George didn't put that bottle in the train then, because I gave it to Ray. I didn't say anything to anyone, though. I was still hoping they wouldn't find him guilty, or at least not send him to prison. And I guess I was afraid I'd be accused of something too."

"So at some point you asked Ray about it?"

"Yes, but not until after the trial was over, and George was sentenced. We were together at my house one night and we were both drinking. Ray was pushing me to start divorce proceedings, and I wanted to hold off. Then Ray got angry and started spouting off about all he'd done to get Ray out of the way so we could get married. When I asked him what he'd done, he said he unbolted the train tracks the night before the wreck to cause the train derailment."

"And you just went along with it?"

"No...well, I guess I did. He said he did it to prove to me how much he loved me, and he made me promise not to say anything, or we could both be in trouble. I let him talk me into keeping quiet and agreed to file for a divorce so we could get married."

Glen shook his head. "Did Ray admit that he also put the liquor bottle in the train to make it look like George had been drinking?"

"No. He wouldn't say yes or no when I asked him. He just laughed at me and said it wasn't him. I suppose he could have given it to someone else, but he never mentioned anyone."

"Were you with him the night he went out to sabotage the track?"

She shook her head. "No. He would have been with his wife. She was still alive."

Glen narrowed his eyes. "Yes. That's right he *was* married then. Do you know how she died? She must have been pretty young."

"She was three or four years older than me—early thirties, maybe. Ray said it was a heart problem—something congenital, and she smoked too."

Glen nodded. "Yes, I suppose smoking can aggravate it. Earlier, you said that you were afraid of saying anything about the whiskey bottle when it came up at the trial because you might get accused of something yourself. Why are you telling me this now?"

"Because then I thought Ray was the answer to all my problems, and I didn't want to lose him. Now I know Ray *is* my problem, and I want out. He's always looking over my shoulder, we argue, he beats me, he's mean to Billy, and I want out."

"Do you want to file a complaint for abuse?

"No! I don't think anything will come of it, and it'll just make him madder. I can't do that."

Glen paused to write down what she said. "All right then, if what you say is true, I think we may have enough to take action against Ray and maybe get George released from prison. Of course, I'll need to discuss this with my bosses. Will you be willing to testify in court to what you've told me?"

She glanced at the wall and bit her lower lip. "If you can assure that my son and I can be protected from Ray."

"We can do that," said Glen. "But you shouldn't say anything to Ray about what you've told me this morning. He doesn't even have to know that I came here."

·　·　·　·　·

When Glen got back to the sheriff's office, he typed up his report and took it over to Sergeant Palmer who had returned from his assignment in Tomah. He told Glen to wait while he read it over. When he finished, Vic said, "What she says is pretty damning, but at this point, it's just his word against hers. Her statement contradicts everything Bickle told us. But who's telling the truth— it's just a 'he said-she said' situation." He shook his head. "I can take this to the sheriff and talk to him, but I don't know that he'll buy this as sufficient."

"You might be right. Why don't we wait until Monday before going to talk to the sheriff? Maybe I can come up with some other angle to look at."

Glen went home to an empty house after work since Carol was working a late shift at the hospital. He looked through the refrigerator, grabbed a beer, opened the bottle, and took a long swallow. While staring into the open refrigerator considering what to have for supper, he decided to call Stan and invite him over. He knew Stan would want to know where they were in the investigation. Maybe he had an idea or had come up with something new. He took four hamburger patties from the freezer compartment and set them out to thaw before calling.

After a not so healthy meal of fried burgers, chips, and slaw, while bantering over non-work subjects, Glen pulled two more beers from the refrigerator and suggested they go to the living room and talk about the investigation. Without giving specific details about the interviews, Glen told Stan that Lucy had reaffirmed what she'd told Stan.

"Our problem," said Glen, "is Bickle is saying something totally opposite, and we've got no corroboration on what Lucy says. Which means there's no case."

Stan grimaced. "That's bad."

"We talked to Cashman's two other card-playing buddies and neither of them had anything bad to say about Bickle. He seemed to be the life of the party."

"I think people tend to see what they want to see. People ignore things that don't seem to fit into the reality they expect. That was part of Cashman's problem. He was just too naïve. But that girl Lucy—she's genuinely scared. I'd like to do something to help her."

"I'd like to, too. But she doesn't want to make any formal complaint against the guy. And we can't prove what she says happened—even that there was an affair."

Stan bent over and put his hands on his temples. Then his head popped up. "There's a woman I talked to who might be able to confirm the affair."

"Who are you talking about?"

"I talked to an old woman in Elroy who lives next to the place where Cashman used to live." He lowered his head. "What was her name? Ah, Grace—Grace Kinslaw."

"Why? Did she say anything about it when you talked to her?"

"No, but I think she might be able to identify Bickle, if he was spending time at Lucy's house while Cashman was away. Wouldn't that be confirming?"

"It could be. We don't have any picture of Bickle. I didn't find any arrest record on file for him when I checked."

"I know what kind of car he drives. It's a blue and white Chevy Bel Air. I could get a picture of it and show it to her."

"What year was the car?"

Stan thought a moment. "Oh crap! I think it was a '55. That wouldn't help us for something that happened a year before."

Glen responded, "Maybe I can find out what he drove through the county motor vehicle files. I'm not sure if I can get a photo of him, though."

"What about a picture from a high school yearbook? I know he went to school in Kendall, so there should be a picture of him in the yearbook. There's a little library I saw in Kendall. They should have copies."

Glen rubbed his chin and smiled. "Okay, you've sold me. If we can get this stuff together over the weekend, I'll bring it up with Sergeant Palmer Monday and see if he'll agree to go talk to this woman. I'll take care of looking into the motor vehicle files. You see if you can find a yearbook with Bickle's picture."

"I'll drive over to Kendall tomorrow morning," said Stan. "I'll come by here tomorrow evening to let you see what I'm able to come up with."

CHAPTER 14

Glen came into the office earlier than usual Monday carrying a 1941 high school yearbook and an envelope with a photo of a maroon 1951 Chevy sedan. He looked over at Palmer's desk. He was talking to another deputy, and Glen went to get a cup of coffee and waited until he was free. When the deputy left after five minutes, he went over to Palmer who had his head down writing. "Excuse me sergeant."

Palmer looked up. "Morning Glen. What is it?"

"Last Friday you said that without any corroborating witness to prove Bickle was having an affair with Cashman's wife, the sheriff probably wasn't going to okay an investigation."

Palmer nodded. "That's right. Did you come up with something?"

Glen smiled. "I think I found someone who might be able to confirm it."

Palmer raised his eyebrows. "Really? Who?"

"It's a woman named Grace Kinslaw. Stan Ellis put me on to her. She's a former neighbor of Cashman's and might be able to identify Bickle as being at Cashman's house when he was away." He opened the book to the page with Bickle's senior picture and laid it on Palmer's desk. I'll go see her today and show her the picture. If she can ID him as being a frequent visitor to Cashman's house before the train wreck happened, we'll have our corroboration. Won't that give us what we need to make a case?"

Palmer nodded. "It's still a bit circumstantial, but yes, I think it might be enough to convince the sheriff to take the next step. I'll go with you."

That afternoon the two officers drove to Elroy and parked at the curb in front of Grace Kinslaw's house. Before getting out of the car, Palmer said, "If this doesn't pan out, we're going to put the investigation back in the can."

Glen frowned. "I understand, but we should at least let Mrs. Bickle know that we're closing down the investigation. She's afraid of that guy and we should try to convince her to make a complaint."

"We do need to let her know, but we don't need to be soliciting complaints. That's not our job."

They got out of the car, went to the door, and knocked. A little gray-haired woman, slightly bent over, but with a lively face, opened the door. She looked up at them and raised her hands. "Whatever I did, I surrender."

Without breaking a smile, Palmer said, "We're not here for anything you did ma'am. I'm Sergeant Palmer and this is Deputy Horner. We're here to ask you some questions about your former neighbors, the Cashman's. Would it be all right if we came in?"

She stepped back. "Yes, come in. I talked to a nice reporter several days ago. Is it about the same thing?"

"Yes," said Palmer. "We've reopened an investigation into Cashman's conviction, and your name came up as someone who could provide some useful information."

She ushered them into the living room and asked them to sit down on the sofa while she went to the kitchen to heat up a pot of tea. She came back a few minutes later with a tray of cookies, cups, and a full teapot. After pouring them each a cup, she settled into her overstuffed easy chair and asked, "Now what do you want to know?"

Palmer said, "Have you lived here in this house a long time?"

"Oh yes. My husband and I moved into this house shortly after we married, more than fifty years ago. It was a new house then."

"I understand the Cashmans lived next door. How long did you know them?

"Let me see," she said. "They had a child that was a mere baby when they moved in. That must be about ten years ago, I guess. Of course, after that thing happened with George and then she married that other man, I haven't seen them since. That was what? Four years ago?"

"Yes, it was about four years ago Cashman was sent to prison. And it's around that time, four or five years ago, that we thought you might be able to help us identify a certain person of interest. We have some reason to believe that Mrs. Bickle might have been having an affair with someone before the train accident while she was living next door to you. We know that George Cashman was absent a lot because of his work. Did you ever notice any male visitors to the Cashman house on a more or less regular basis when Cashman wasn't home?"

"Oh my! Now you're going to make me look like a nosy person—but I couldn't help but be curious when I saw a strange man come to the Cashman's house quite often. I knew it couldn't be a repairman or anything because it was the same car all the time. I don't know who the man was or why he came. Maybe he was a brother or something. But if she was having an affair..." She cupped her hands to her mouth in faux surprise and said, "Oh my!"

Palmer turned to Glen, "Show her the pictures we have."

Glen pulled the photo of the car from the envelope. "Does this look like the car you saw in the next door driveway when George wasn't home?"

She picked up her reading glasses from the side table, put them on, and leaned her head close to the picture. "Yes, it was a maroon-colored car with a sloping back just like that."

Glen put the photo back in the envelope and placed it to the side. "Now we need to ask how well you saw the person who was driving that car. Do you think you could identify him from a photo?"

"Probably. After they got married, they were packing up things to move, and I went over to take some cookies to them and ask if I could help. They didn't need my help, but they took the cookies. Her new husband, he didn't really say anything to me, and she didn't tell me his name, but he was the same person I saw earlier visiting."

Glen said, "Very good. We'd like you to look over some pictures in this old high school yearbook to see if anyone resembles that man." The names on the page he opened to were covered over with tape.

She leaned forward and squinted her eyes. "These are all boys. The person I saw was older."

"Yes," said Glen. "These are high school pictures from 1941. He would have been thirty-one in 1954. Do you see anyone who resembles the person you saw?"

She looked harder and after a few moments pointed with a thin index finger. "Yes, I think so. I think it might be this one. He had a particularly strong jaw like this boy, but the hair was different." Then she pointed to another photo. "Or maybe it could be this one. The eyes look like his." It's one of these two."

Both Glen and Palmer looked at each other and nodded.

"Did I do okay?" she asked. "I can't make up my mind between these two."

"Yes, you did fine," said Palmer. "If we decide to continue with our investigation, we should have a more current picture of the man for you to look at. Would that be okay?"

"Yes, I'll help any way I can."

"One more thing I have to ask. Are you willing to testify in court as to the man you saw visiting the Cashman house? You would need to identify in court the actual person you saw back in 1953 and 54."

She nodded firmly. "Yes, of course."

"Good," said Palmer. "If we get to that point, we'll have a current picture of our person of interest. We want to thank you for your time and willingness to be of assistance. We'll contact you if we need anything further."

As they got up from the sofa to leave, she said, "You haven't drunk your tea! You must try the tea and take the cookies with you."

The two men picked up the dainty teacups and downed the contents while she went to the kitchen and quickly returned with a bag in which she put the cookies. They thanked her for the cookies, and she watched from the front door as they backed out of her driveway.

As they drove out of town, Palmer said, "We got the car nailed, but we didn't get a positive ID on the guy."

Glen responded, "No, but Bickle was one of the two she picked out, and if we have a current picture of him, I'm sure she can pick him out of a lineup. We should call him in. Get him to react. We know he lied about having the affair. We can hold him overnight and put a scare in him."

"Yeah, maybe he'll make another mistake. When we get back to the office, you can call him and see if we can get him to come in sometime this week—the sooner the better."

When they got to the office, Glen went straight to his desk, put in a call to Bickle's home, and he answered. After explaining who he was, Glen said, "Since you were up here we've come up with some additional information that we're trying to verify, and we think you may be able to help us with that."

"What do you want to know? I can tell you over the phone."

"In these kinds of investigation, we like to conduct our interviews on site here in our office. Would you be able to come up here tomorrow around ten o'clock?"

There was a pause before Bickle responded. "I'd like to help you, but I was just getting ready to head out the door to go to work. I'm going to be on the road for a couple days. I think I could come up Friday if you need me."

Glen pressed his lips together in frustration. "Friday? Yes, that'll be all right. What time can you be here?"

"I should be able to make it there by ten o'clock."

Glen looked at his calendar. "Okay, that'll be fine. I'll be expecting you then."

CHAPTER 15

Lucy watched from the kitchen doorway as Bickle hung up the phone. "What was that about? You don't have to go to work until Wednesday."

Bickle looked at her and smiled. "That was Deputy Horner from the sheriff's office. You met him. He was here just last week."

She nodded nervously. "Yes, I remember. What did he want?"

He walked toward her. "They wanted me to go up there and talk to them again. I think it's a trap. Somebody gave them information about me. You wouldn't know anything about that, would you?"

"Uh, no."

He came up to her and put his hands on her shoulders. "You know a man and his woman need to take care of one another no matter what. Isn't that what we said when we married, 'through thick and through thin?' They need to be true to each other. Are you true to me sweetie?"

She stiffened at his touch. "Sure I am Ray."

He rubbed her shoulders gently. "I know you are, babe. So tell me, when did you talk to those sheriff deputies?"

Her head went down, and she stuttered, "I... I didn't go and talk to them. I didn't have the car. I just stayed home."

His grip tightened on her shoulder blades. "I didn't say you went there, I asked you *when* you talked to them. I don't think you're being truthful darling."

She swallowed hard. "Yes... yes, they came here when you were gone. I couldn't stop them from coming. But I didn't tell them anything they didn't already know. I don't know what all George might have told them"

"Honey, your face tells me you're not being totally truthful with me like you said you'd be." His hands slid down the t-shirt she was wearing to cover her small breasts. She wasn't wearing a bra, and he massaged the tips of her breasts gently with his fingers.

She tried to move away, but he held her firmly, pinned her against the wall, and put his hands back on her breasts. "Don't do that," she said.

"Why? You usually like it. Just tell me the truth. Did you tell them anything about our affair?" He pinched her nipples gently.

"Please don't, Ray."

He squeezed hard. "Ooww... Let go!"

"Tell me what you told them."

"All right. I told them about the affair. They probably already knew from George anyway."

"Maybe he did. But he didn't know about you giving me the whiskey bottle or that I messed with the track. You didn't tell them about that, did you?"

"No."

He squeezed both her nipples hard between his thumbs and forefingers. She screamed, twisted her body, and cried out. "Yes I did. I did it because I felt guilty about what's happened to George. I'm sorry I ever got involved with you!"

He released her and slapped her across the face. She fell back against the kitchen counter and looked at him with both fear and anger. Bickle stared back at her and growled, "Too late for regrets babe. You did get involved with me. You were just as anxious as me to dump that blubbery husband of yours and get married. Now you want to betray me? Those guys want me to go up there so they can arrest me based on what you told them. Well, you're stuck with me, and whatever comes, you and me are in it together whether you like it or not."

"What are you going to do?"

He sneered at her. "It's not what I'm going to do. It's what you're going to do.

"What do you mean?"

"I mean you're going to go back up to that sheriff's office tomorrow and tell them everything you told them before was a lie, because you were trying to get back at me for some fight we had."

"I can't do that!"

He smiled and put his hands on her shoulder again. "Oh, sure you can babe. You know how I get angry sometimes and take it out on Billy. You don't want that."

She hung her head. "No. I don't want that."

•   •   •   •   •

The next morning Bickle drove with Lucy to Sparta. He stopped in front of the sheriff's office and turned to Lucy before she got out of the car. "You know what to say now, don't you?"

She nodded her head. "I know."

"That's a good girl. I'll be waiting at Birdie's Cafe up the street. Come there when you finish, and we can go home." She got out of the car, and he watched her as she mounted the steps and went in the front door of the building.

Lucy walked up to the reception desk and gave her name and told the deputy on duty she wanted to talk to Sergeant Palmer. After buzzing his desk with no answer, he said, "Sorry he's not in now. You want to tell me what you wanted to talk to him about."

"No, I'd rather not say right here. What about Deputy Horner? Is he here? He'll know who I am if you give him my name."

The deputy buzzed to the back again, and this time he was able to reach Glen. "There's a woman out here, name of Lucy Bickle, who wants to talk to you. You got time to come out and talk to her?"

A minute later Glen came out to the lobby, his face a mask of concern. "Hi Lucy. I didn't expect to see you today. Is everything all right."

She nodded. "Yes, but I need to talk to you alone about something."

"Sure, we can go back to one of the interview rooms and talk."

Once in the interview room, she took a seat beside a small table, and he asked her if she wanted anything to drink. "A glass of water, please."

After bringing back the water, Glen sat down in a chair opposite Lucy. "What's going on?"

She took a deep breath. "When I talked to you last time I told you a lot of stuff about my husband Ray—about how he did all those things to get George in trouble and to cause the train wreck."

"Yes, your testimony is going to help free George I think."

"Well, what I said wasn't true."

Glen grabbed the arms of his chair. "What? You don't mean that? Has he threatened you?"

"No. No. It's not like that. What I told you about Ray and me having problems was true. I was so angry with him, I wanted to get back at him, and so I told you a lie. I don't want Ray to get into trouble. Ray isn't always that way, and when Ray came home later that night after I'd talked to you he was all apologetic for getting mad at me, and we had a good talk."

Glen felt a sinking feeling in his stomach. "What'd he say?"

She took a deep breath and lowered her head. "Ray started talking about how he was going to change the way he behaved and said he'd be a better husband to me and father to Billy. He seemed so ashamed of how he'd acted, and I told him what I'd done and said I was sorry. He felt I betrayed him—and I did because of my anger. He's afraid now he'll get arrested when he didn't actually do anything. I don't want to let that happen. It's awful embarrassing for me to come and admit I lied, but I have to be honest."

"Look at me now, Lucy, and tell me you're telling the truth."

She raised her head and looked at him, but her eyes connected with his only briefly. "I'm telling the truth."

Glen stood up. "I want to see if Sergeant Palmer is around. He needs to hear this too. Wait here while I go look for him."

Five minutes later he was back in the room with Palmer. The sergeant asked her to go over again what she'd told Glen, and she did. After she finished, he said, "Your recantation of your earlier statements amounts to a false accusation of a crime. That in itself can warrant criminal prosecution. Are you aware of that?"

She looked up at him with doe-like eyes. "I wasn't aware of it. But it doesn't change anything. Ray didn't do anything."

Palmer nodded. "We're not going to charge you with anything right now. But we may be in contact with you later, after we review the entire case and let the sheriff take a look at it. You're free to go now Mrs. Bickle."

She left the room, quickly exited the building, and walked hurriedly to Birdie's where she found Bickle sitting in a rear booth sipping on a cup of coffee. "I did it. I said what you wanted me to say."

He smiled, "And did they buy what you said? Are they going to close their investigation?"

"I think so. But they might charge me with making a false accusation."

He shook his head. "Nah. They wouldn't bother with that. We're in the clear babe. Let's go home and celebrate."

CHAPTER 16

Glen stared at the telephone on his desk. Lucy's recanting of her story yesterday was like a punch to the gut. The call he'd just made, telling Bickle there was no need for him to come in for the interview because they were shutting down the investigation, compounded the sick feeling he already had in his stomach. When Bickle asked why, Glen had to tell him they just didn't have enough to pursue the case any further. He could almost hear him laughing his head off. He was sure Bickle was guilty of causing that train wreck and had threatened Lucy, but now there wasn't a thing he could do about it.

After Lucy had left the interview room, Glen suggested to Sergeant Palmer that there might be other acquaintances of Bickle who could back up Lucy's allegations. Palmer said he'd go and talk to the sheriff and see what he wanted to do. When he came back to his desk later that afternoon, Palmer told Glen the sheriff was livid that we'd wasted a week's time on an investigation that he felt was doomed from the start. "You should be happy," said Palmer. "You're back on your regular patrol duty and don't have to worry about Bickle or his wife anymore."

That afternoon he made his rounds through the rural communities of Norwalk and Cashton, checking in with his business contacts and local officials as to their goings-on. He enjoyed his work on the road, but it didn't mean he'd be able to forget what Lucy had told them, or stop being concerned about what would happen to her now.

Glen kept his feelings to himself at work, but at home he couldn't hide them from his wife. That evening, sitting at home watching TV, Carol said, "You've been terribly moody the last couple days. You've hardly talked. What's wrong?"

"It's that Cashman case we had to shut down. It bothers me to think what'll happen to that girl who we interviewed. I'm uncomfortable with just dropping the case. The husband's an abuser, and we should be doing something, but Vic told me we have to stay out of it. He says it's not our job to interfere in any family business unless we're asked. It bothers me a whole lot."

"You need to get your mind on something else. Tomorrow I'm off. I don't think Patty is scheduled either. I'll give her a call. Maybe we can go out somewhere and have a little fun. What about bowling? We haven't done that for a while."

"Okay, maybe it'll change my mood.

*   *   *   *   *

Friday evening Glen and his wife met up with Stan and Patty at Barclay Lanes. After bowling two frames in which the girls won one, and the guys won the other, they decided to call it quits and go into the bar to get something to eat and to talk.

Stan and Glen each ordered a hamburger and fries along with a pitcher of Old Style, while Patty and Carol ordered Cokes and grilled cheese sandwiches with chips. The television in the bar area was tuned to a sports show. The announcer was talking about the Braves beating the Yankees in the second game of the World Series the day before, and the place was abuzz with sports talk. Glen, though, remained mostly quiet, munching morosely on his burger while Patty and Carol talked shop and Stan eyed the television.

Refilling Glen's glass, Stan said, "I know what's bugging you. It's that girl Lucy and the Cashman case, isn't it?"

Glen nodded. "Yeah, that's it. In my head, I know that the sheriff didn't have any other choice but to close the investigation when she recanted her story, but it doesn't mean I got to like it."

"I felt terrible when I heard about the investigation being shut down," said Stan. "I mailed a letter today to Cashman to let him know what happened. The guy's going to be devastated."

"Any reaction from your boss?"

"Yeah, when I told Mr. Malloy, he just shook his head and said I told you so. End of story. It makes me angry as hell, because I know Bickle was lying and had everything to do with that train wreck. So do you."

Glen nodded. "I do, but my hands are tied from doing anything more."

"I understand why you, being in law enforcement, can't get involved. But I don't have that constraint. I may not be writing any more stories about the train wreck, but that doesn't mean I can't try to help her on my own."

Patty stopped what she was going to say to Carol and turned to Stan. "What does that mean? What are you thinking of doing?"

"I'm thinking of contacting Lucy again to try to get her to file a complaint with the county welfare office. I've already talked to Judy Wickham. She's the head social worker there. She said they would start an investigation if they had a formal complaint. It doesn't necessarily have to be the woman herself— someone like a relative or neighbor who witnessed something going on could file the complaint."

Patty's face turned to a scowl. "Stan why? Why do you think you have to do this? You've tried to get the sheriff's office to investigate. You did your best. It's time to stop."

"I didn't really plan on doing anything," he said. "But I got a call from Lucy's mother yesterday. She said when she found out that the Cashman investigation was closed, she got a ride with a friend and went to see her daughter during the day when her husband wasn't home. She said Lucy broke down crying and told her that Bickle had roughed her up and made her take back what she'd told the police. She tried to convince Lucy to go back to the authorities and tell the real truth, but she wouldn't, and she made her mother promise she wouldn't go to them either because she was afraid Bickle might hurt her too if he found out. She said she called me because Lucy had listened to me before and asked that I meet her one more time. I couldn't refuse."

Patty breathed a heavy sigh. "You could have refused, and you should have. This is something that could be dangerous for you. I'm sorry for this Lucy, but I don't want to see you hurt."

Stan bobbed his head back and forth. "I already told her mother that I'd do it. I'm not going to back out. Mrs. Grim said she'd call me back after she checks with Lucy again to set up a meeting time and place."

Glen said, "I think Patty's right. You've done enough to try to help this girl. You're taking a big risk in getting involved like that. Domestic abuse problems can get really nasty, and you could exacerbate it without intending to."

"I'll be careful. I won't get too involved. I just want to try to persuade her to go get help. I'll give her the social worker's number, and then it'll be up to her. Her husband will never know."

"Just be careful, and let me know if things seem to be getting out of hand."

CHAPTER 17

Bruton is racing back, back to the wall. He's looking up, and it's out of here! A two-run homer for Hank Bauer! Down 4-0 in the seventh, things weren't going so well for the Braves, but it was only game three and the Braves had won the first two. Stan turned off the radio and picked up the paper when the phone rang. It was Helen Grim.

"I was wondering when you might call. Were you able to talk to Lucy?"

"Yes, I talked to her on the phone. Did you get a name of someone she can call that can help her?

"Yes, I reached a social worker at the county welfare office. She said Lucy could contact her directly."

"That's good. Now Lucy still says she doesn't want to talk to anyone else about her situation. She says she wants to be left alone, but I know she doesn't really mean it. She's just a scared little kitten."

"Well, if she doesn't want to meet, I guess that's it."

"No, I still think if she talked with you face to face she'll come to her senses. I came up with an idea for you to meet her without Ray knowing about it. Please do this for me."

Stan sighed. "What do you want me to do?"

"Lucy takes Billy to Sunday school most every Sunday. It's the Congregational Church on Spring Street. She usually doesn't go herself but waits for it to get over. You could catch her there at the church tomorrow morning. While Billy attends his class, you'll have time to talk with her. The

Sunday school starts at nine so you should get there a few minutes before then."

"All right. I'll try to talk to her. But if this fails, I don't think there's any more I can do."

"I understand Mr. Ellis. I really appreciate what you're doing, and Lucy will too in the end."

"I'll call you later Sunday to let you know how it goes."

•   •   •   •   •

The next morning, at quarter to nine, he sat waiting in his car outside the Congregational Church in Kendall. At five to nine he spotted Lucy walking up the sidewalk toward the church with a boy trailing close behind. He got out of the car and walked toward her. She didn't notice him until he was almost upon her. "Oh! Mr. Ellis. What are you doing here?"

"Hi Lucy. Your mother called me and asked if I'd meet with you and let you know that the investigation had been closed down."

She looked at him warily. "I knew that already. You didn't come all this way to just tell me that."

Other people were passing by on the sidewalk on their way into the church. "Can we talk somewhere more private?" said Stan. "I just need a few minutes."

She turned to her son. "Billy, go ahead to your class. I'll be waiting outside your room when you finish."

Billy ran off to go to his class, and Stan said, "We can talk in my car if you want." He pointed. "I'm parked right over here."

They walked over to the car and got in. "Now," she said, "What's the reason you came here? Was it really my mother who called you?"

"Yes, she did call me. I wouldn't have come unless she asked me. She's terribly worried about your safety. She thinks your husband coerced you into recanting your story to the sheriff's office. I think so too."

Lucy gave a peevish look. "You can think what you want. It doesn't matter. I said what I wanted to say, and that's the end of it. I was just mad at Ray, and I shouldn't have tried to get him in trouble. Nobody can prove otherwise. It's really none of your business anyway."

"You may be right. But certainly your welfare is your mother's business. She's worried that your husband will hurt you and Billy. I agreed to come see you because I'm sort of responsible for pushing you into going to the police in the first place."

"You don't need to worry about it. I'll be fine now. That's all done with."

"You're not concerned any more about George?"

"I feel bad for him, but I can't help him."

He noticed a mark on her neck area. "You know there's a red welt near your collar bone. How'd that get there if everything is fine now?"

She put her right hand on her neck. "I don't know."

He put his hands on the steering wheel and stared ahead. "Maybe you don't want to take my advice, but you need to know there are places you can go to get help if you want to. I talked to this social worker at the county welfare office. Her name's Judy Wickham. She said all you need to do is call her and she can see that you can get to a safe place. She can initiate action to get a protective order against your husband." He pulled out a card from his shirt pocket and held it out for her.

Lucy took the card from him and looked at it. She put it in her pocket and started to open the car door. Before getting out, she turned toward him. "I am grateful for what you've tried to do, but you need to stay out of my life from now on. It only makes it more difficult." She opened the door and, without looking back, walked back toward the church entrance.

Stan started up the car's engine and sat for a moment looking into space. This was probably a wasted trip, he thought, but at least he'd tried to help. It was frustrating for him, feeling he'd come so close to getting Bickle arrested for sabotaging the train only to have everything blow up in his face. He'd exhausted every lead he had. Nothing else to do. Then he remembered one lead he hadn't followed up on. He'd left a note for that railway brakeman—the one who lived in the rooming house in Elroy. It'd been two weeks, and the guy had never called him back. Something to hide, maybe? He searched his memory, finally recalling the name—Ty Gibbon. Mr. Malloy would jump on him with both feet if he knew he was doing anything more with the Cashman case. But it's Sunday. *I'm on my own time. Since I'm down this way, I might as well drive over to Elroy and see if I can catch Gibbon at home.*

After getting stuck at a railroad crossing by a freight train that seemed to have no end, Stan arrived at the rooming house on Railroad Street and went directly up to the second floor. As he approached the #7 apartment he heard sounds coming from inside. He pressed his ear to the door and heard what sounded like a television playing. He knocked on the door and after a second knock, a short squat fiftyish man in his undershorts and a white t-shirt opened the door. "Yeah, what d'ya want?"

Stan offered a smile and introduced himself, adding, "I left a note in your mailbox a couple weeks ago. Did you get it?"

The man looked up at him cautiously. "Yeah, I got it."

The man didn't invite him in, but left Stan standing in the open doorway waiting for the man to continue with an explanation. After a moment of silence, Stan said, "Well, the reason I wanted to talk with you is that I'm writing a look-back series on the train wreck—the one in 1954."

The man stood with his arms crossed over an ample belly, "Yeah, I worked that train. The cops questioned me after the accident, and I had to testify at the trial. I just want to forget it now."

"I understand it's not a happy memory. But I thought, since you were a part of the train crew that day, you could provide some interesting commentary on what you experienced. It would be a nice addition to the story I'm working on."

"I don't want to be part of any story. Just leave me out of it. You can find whatever you want from the trial record."

"Well, there may be some things that were missed in the trial. Cashman was accused of bringing liquor into his cab and becoming drunk. I've been looking at the possibility that someone other than Cashman could have put the liquor bottle in the engine cab. You must have known Cashman pretty well. Would it be all right if I came in and asked you some questions?"

"Nah, I don't want to get involved with any of that. I like my privacy. Don't want my name in any newspaper. Just leave me alone."

He closed the door in Stan's face. At first he thought of knocking again and giving him a piece of his mind. Then he decided it wasn't worth the trouble. He went back to his car and drove back to Sparta, wondering whether this guy really had something to hide. After all, he did have a motive to get back at Cashman.

CHAPTER 18

When Lucy returned home from church, there was a car in the driveway. It looked like Fred Noonan's Plymouth. She could tell it was his, because the trunk lid had a big dent in the back. She parked to the side of his car and went inside with Billy. She looked out the kitchen window into the backyard and saw Ray and Fred talking beside the garden. He was one of the gang of four who played cards regularly at her house when she was married to George. After she married Ray, she learned that Ray and Fred had served together in Germany during the war, and they'd remained close friends ever since. Now, instead of playing card games at her house, Ray would go out on weekends to some local bar with his male friends, and usually came back smelling of beer and cigarette smoke. She didn't like it, but she learned quickly after they were married to keep her mouth shut about it if she didn't want a fight she couldn't win.

Lucy opened the back door and hollered out. "I'm home from church. I'm going to fix some pancakes and sausage for brunch. If Fred would like to stay he's welcome."

Fred hollered back, "Thanks Lucy. But I got things I have to do. I gotta be going."

She closed the door, and soon Ray came into the house by himself. "What was Fred doing over this way on a Sunday?"

"He came over to see some farmer near here about a new contract for grain deliveries. How was church? Did you get all your sins forgiven?"

She shrugged. "Church was fine." She looked up at him somberly. "And no, I'm still living with my sins."

He shook his head. "You take things too seriously. You gotta forget things in the past. Live for the future. I'll go wash up and let you finish making breakfast."

After eating, Ray left to go into town to get some fall fertilizer for the garden and flower plots. When he returned, he carried several bags to the backyard and put them in the shed. Lucy was in the living room watching a television show when he came back in the house and sat down beside her on the couch. "I saw Jenny Cutler when I went to Cooper's for the fertilizer. She said she was at church this morning. Did you see her?"

Without taking her eyes off the television screen, Lucy said, "No. I don't remember seeing her. I didn't actually go into the service. I stayed in the library until Billy's class was over."

"Well, Jenny said she saw you. When she was going into the church, she said she saw you talking with some guy. Billy came into the church, and then you went and got in a car with a guy."

Her head jerked around. "I didn't..."

He grabbed both her arms. "Don't tell me you didn't do anything, she saw you with him. You cheating on me now? Who was it?"

"I wasn't cheating on you honest!"

He began shaking her. "Who was it?"

"A deacon at church. I wanted to talk out some things."

"I don't believe you. What's his name? I'll call him."

"No, I don't want to get anyone else involved."

He released her arms and hollered, "Billy, come down here. I want to talk to you."

A moment later Billy came down the stairs and into the living room. "What is it?"

Ray put his hands on the eleven-year-old's shoulders. "Your mother and I were discussing the man she met at the church this morning. She said it was one of the church deacons. Do you know who it was?"

"No, I don't."

"Did you ever see him before?"

"No, never did."

"Boy, I don't believe you. I think you're lying to protect your mother. Didn't they tell you in church today it's a sin to tell a lie?"

"I don't know who he was."

"You need some punishment for lying, young man. Unbuckle your pants and lean over that chair."

Billy moved in front of his mother, and when he did, Bickle grabbed him by one arm, twisted the arm behind his back, and pulled up. "Ow!" Billy yelled.

Bickle forced him face down over the arm of an easy chair, removed the wide leather belt from around his waist, and gave it a crack in the air. "After a few whacks of this maybe you'll tell me the truth."

Bickle raised his arms and swung hard—once, twice, three times. Finally, Lucy jumped up and grabbed his arm. "Stop it! I'll tell you. I'll tell you."

He lowered his arm and turned to Lucy. "Is it that reporter?"

She nodded and motioned for Billy to go back to his room. "Yes, Stan Ellis. But it's not what you think. I wasn't cheating on you."

"You expect me to believe that?"

"It's true. I didn't know he would be there. He said he wanted to try to convince me to go to the authorities and file a formal complaint against you for the way you treat me."

"What? How do I treat you? I provide an income. I put food on the table. I give you all the loving you want. What else do you want?"

"You also beat me sometimes."

"Aah! So I'm a little rough sometimes. That's just to keep you in line. You didn't mind before we were married. What's the real reason? He's got the hots for you. Right?"

"No! My mother asked him to meet me. That's why he came to the church."

"Your mother! That fucking bitch. Why is she getting involved?"

"She got involved *because* she's my mother."

"Well, she needs to stay out of our business. What about this Ellis, what exactly did he say?"

"He said I should file a complaint against you with the county. He said if I called them, they'd help me get away from you."

"And what did you say?"

"I told him I didn't need any help, and I wasn't going to file any complaint—that we'd made up, and everything was okay between us. I told him to leave me alone, and that's how it ended."

He squinted his eyes. "You telling me the truth?"

She nodded.

"I'll take your word for now. But this Ellis guy, I don't know. I think he has the hots for you, and I may need to do something about that."

"Just leave him alone. He's not going to bother us anymore."

CHAPTER 19

Stan parked in front of Patty's apartment building, and as he got out of the car, he noticed a green car pass by and stop at the next block. He thought it curious because it looked like the same car that was parked across the street from his house when he left. He trudged up the stairs to Patty's apartment, a bag of groceries in his arms. He'd called her earlier and asked if it would be okay if he could come over. He was upset with the way things had gone with Lucy that morning, and he hoped being with Patty would help calm him down. She said she was on the midnight shift for the next week, and she didn't have anything much in the refrigerator, but to come over if he'd be okay with left-overs. He offered to bring some fixings for supper and prepare the meal for her, and she'd accepted.

He knocked on the door, and she opened it right away. Jessie, sitting on her haunches beside Patty didn't bark this time, just sat there expecting a treat. Patty took the bag from Stan, and he dug into his pants pocket for a doggie biscuit to oblige Jessie who took it eagerly and went to her corner.

Stan followed Patty into the kitchen where she was rummaging through the grocery bag. "So, shining prince, what wondrous delicacies did you bring for your princess?"

Stan smiled. "I'm afraid it's not pheasant under glass, but I think I can make something you'll like. The butcher at Culver's cut me some nice thick pork chops that I think I can do a respectable job on. Then mashed potatoes, gravy, some green beans with bacon, and a salad with Italian dressing. Oh, and I got some dinner rolls we can put in the oven too. Does that sound okay?"

"Sounds scrumptious. I'll get you an apron and you can get started. Since you say you want to cook, I'll let you take care of everything except the salad. I'll do that."

When they sat down to eat, Stan was concerned how Patty would react to his cooking. This was the first time he'd prepared a meal for her that wasn't limited to hamburgers or sandwiches and chips. He opened a bottle of wine, and they both toasted to one another. He had to wait a few minutes, before she had a few bites of her food and gave him a thumbs up. Then he was able to enjoy the meal himself.

Towards the end of the meal, Patty went to the kitchen and brought back a coffeepot and poured a cup for Stan and herself. Up to then, neither had mentioned anything about his visit to Lucy, but it was never off his mind. "I went to see Lucy Bickle this morning. Met her in front of her church."

"I was wondering when you were going to bring it up. How'd it go? Is she going to take your advice?"

He shook his head. "Didn't go so well. She told me to get my nose out of her business. She said she'd made up with her husband, and she can handle everything herself."

"You believe her?"

"No. Not a bit. I gave her the card from the social worker, and she took it. I don't know if she'll do anything with it, but she at least thought about it."

"Are you done with that little adventure now? You've done everything you could and more."

"I guess so. I did call back her mother and told her about my conversation with Lucy. She asked me for the number for the social worker, and I gave it to her. She said she might file a complaint if Lucy doesn't. I hope she does—Oh, I also stopped in Elroy and talked to a railway worker that was part of Cashman's train crew."

"Why did you do that?"

"It was just a loose end that I was curious about. Cashman had turned him into the railroad authorities for something he did. So he had a likely motive for getting back at Cashman. I thought he could have been involved in putting that liquor bottle in the train engine, and I wanted to see what he had to say for himself, but he didn't want to talk. I'm done with it now."

She reached across the table and took his hand. "I'm glad to hear that. I've been so worried about your being involved—of what could happen to you."

He smiled and patted her hand. "No need to worry anymore."

Stan left Patty's around nine o'clock and drove straight back to his place. He lived in a three-room upstairs apartment in a large two-story brick house that had once been owned by a prominent local family that had sold the house and converted it into four separate apartments. On the drive home he noticed the headlights of a car that seemed to be following him. When he reached home, he pulled into one of the parking spaces at the side of his house. As he went to the front door to go into his apartment, he noticed a car parked a half-block away near a street light and wondered if it was the one that had been following him. It looked like a Plymouth Belvedere, the kind his uncle drove, but a different color. This one was dark green, or blue, and had a dent in the trunk lid. He couldn't recall ever seeing it around the area before but finally shrugged it off, figuring it must be someone visiting.

It was after eleven o'clock when he went outside to drop some garbage into one of the cans near where the cars were parked. As he lifted the garbage can lid, he heard the squeal of tires. He looked toward the street and saw a car peel past the end of the driveway. Stupid teenagers, he thought, as he put the garbage lid back on and went back to his apartment.

On his way into work the next morning, Stan stopped at the police station to check on what bookings were made over the weekend. There were the usual—four DUI's, one burglary, two drug arrests, a domestic brawl broken up, and two arrests for battery involving a bar fight. He collected the information and headed off to the office to write it up. He felt good when he walked into the newsroom. Spending the evening with Patty had allowed him to release a lot of the frustration he'd been feeling over the Cashman case. Now he could put it behind him.

He dropped the booking report on his desk, and after filling his coffee cup, he stopped at Irv's desk feeling like he'd emerged from a dark cave and into the light. "I'm ready for something new. I'm done with Cashman. You got anything hot for me to take on—a typhoid epidemic threatening the county, Soviet spies discovered in the courthouse, discovery of gold along the Kickapoo River?"

Irv popped his head up from the copy he was reading. "Oh, I didn't see you come in. Glad you got the Cashman thing behind you. Ed will be glad too." He looked through some papers. "No, I don't see anything too earthshaking here." He picked up one sheet. "Here's something you could check out though. The Norwalk Village Council is putting out bids for construction on a new water tower. It may not be as exciting as what you're looking for, but why don't you go over there and see what you can dig up for a story. Bert Knutson—he's on the village council—is the man to see if he's available."

"That sounds like it'll keep me busy for a day or so. I'll try and call him and set something up for this afternoon."

Stan was able to reach the village office and made an appointment with Knutson for two o'clock. After lunch he took off for Norwalk, a fifteen mile drive from Sparta. He noticed when he stopped at the first stop sign that the brake pedal seemed to go down farther than normal and he thought he'd need to have that checked out when he had time. He took Route 71 out of town and thought no more about it. The blacktop road was straight, and he maintained a leisurely speed of fifty-five, but as he approached an intersection with County U, a tractor pulling a trailer piled high with a load of hay turned into his lane, not fifty yards ahead. There was a car coming in the opposite lane, and he couldn't pass. He slammed on the brakes to avoid running into the rear of the trailer. The pedal went to the floor. Within ten feet of the trailer he swung the steering wheel hard to the right, and the car veered off the road, bounced down a small embankment, through a wire fence, and into in a cornfield where it came to a stop, a hundred feet off the road.

Stan checked himself over and decided he wasn't hurt except for some bruises. He wasn't so sure about the condition of the car. Even if he could drive it out of the field, he didn't dare drive it without any brakes. He got out of the car and looked toward the road. The tractor driver was long gone. Norwalk was another five miles. He went back to the road and started hiking. It wasn't long before a pickup came along. He stuck out his thumb, and the driver, a ruddy-faced man in his fifties with 'FARMALL' printed on his billed-cap, stopped and rolled down the passenger window. "I'm just going as far as Norwalk. I'll take you that far if you want."

"That's where I was headed. Thanks," said Stan as he got in the car. "I appreciate your stopping for me. My brakes failed, and I ran off the road back there to avoid hitting a tractor. I don't think he ever saw me."

The driver looked back before pulling onto the pavement. "I'll be damned. You got a problem mister."

"I know it. You wouldn't know a place in town that I could get someone to give me a tow to a garage, would you?"

"Bergen's Garage. Dolph's a friend of mine. He'll take care of you. I'll drop you off there when we get to town. You have business in Norwalk?"

"I was going to meet someone there—Bert Knutson. I'm afraid I'll be late and screw up my meeting."

The driver looked at him. "Ahh, don't worry. I know him, and I'm sure he'll wait for you."

When they got to the garage, the driver got out with Stan and introduced him to the owner, Dolph Bergen. Stan explained his situation, and they settled on a price for the tow. The man who gave Stan the ride turned to go back to his pickup, but Stan stopped him and held out his hand to shake. "Wait sir. I didn't get your name. I really want to thank you for stopping and giving me the ride. I'm Stan Ellis."

The man cocked his head to one side and smiled. "I know who you are. I'm Bert Knutson. When you finish up here, come on over to the village office and we can talk."

. . . . .

Stan rode in the tow truck with Dolph to show him exactly where his car was located. It took an hour before they had the car back at the garage. While Dolph worked on the car, Stan walked over to the village office, just two blocks away, and met with Knutson. When he returned to the garage, it was five thirty, and Dolph was standing at the counter filling out a form.

"What's the verdict on my car?" asked Stan.

Dolph put down his pen and looked up. "You had a leak in the brake line. I guess that you could figure that out yourself. I replaced the hose, but your front suspension is shot and should be replaced. And the front end is going to need realignment. If you want me to do it, I'll need to keep it here for a couple days."

Stan pawed at his cheeks. "I really need to get back to Sparta to file my story. Any place I can rent a car?"

"I can give you a loaner if you leave the car with me to do the repairs. It should be ready tomorrow afternoon."

"Okay, how much will it be?"

"I'll write up an estimate, but first I need to show you something." He pulled an oily piece of hose from under the counter. "This is your old hose. It didn't leak from normal deterioration. It was sliced open with a knife. I think someone did this on purpose."

"Let me see that," said Stan. He took the hose and saw that it was indeed a clean cut. Somebody meant to send him a message.

CHAPTER 20

Stan wanted to make out a police report as soon as possible, hoping they would investigate his accident. Norwalk had a small three-person department with an office on Main Street, and after finishing up with Bert Knutson and getting what he needed for his story, he stopped there to file a report, but they wouldn't take it. The patrolman on duty said that because his accident happened outside the village limits, he needed to talk to the county sheriff. Disappointed at being rebuffed, he drove home determined to do just that.

After checking in at the newsroom the next morning, Stan went directly to the sheriff's office. He didn't recognize the deputy on the front desk, but when he told him what he was there for, he gave him an accident form to fill out. After completing the form, the deputy looked at it and said, "One-car accident. No one else involved. You really didn't need to file this, but we'll put it on file. You just need to get with your insurance company."

Stand raised both his hands. "No, actually there was another person involved. That's why I wanted to register this report. I need to talk to an investigator. Someone tampered with my brake line and caused me to have the accident."

"Oh, really? I'll get somebody you can to talk to about it. That wasn't clear from what you wrote down. Have a seat and I'll check who's available."

Stan waited ten minutes, and finally Vic Palmer came through the rear door into the lobby. He saw Stan and held out his hand to shake. "Hi Stan. I hear you had something you need to talk to me about. I thought you were finished with the Cashman case."

"I am. Or I thought I was until this thing happened."

He told Palmer about his belief that he was being followed by a dark-colored sedan on Sunday evening, and how he heard a car speed off from the front of his apartment late at night. He described how he noticed a problem with the brakes when he left home, and how the brakes were completely gone when he tried to avoid hitting the tractor and ran off the road. Then he pulled the hose piece encased in a plastic bag from his jacket pocket and held it up for Palmer to see.

"The mechanic who worked on my car showed me this. You can see it's been cut cleanly. Do you think you could get fingerprints?"

Palmer eyed it carefully and shook his head. "It does look like it's been cut, but since you had the car in a garage and the hose replaced, there's no chance we can get any useful fingerprints. You said you thought a car was following you. Did you get make of the car? The license plate number?"

"I think it might have been a 53 or 54 Plymouth. I didn't get a license number, but I did notice the trunk lid had a dent in it just above the license plate."

"Well, without the license plate number that's not going to help us. I don't think there's anything we can do at this point, unless you can spot that car and get a license plate number for us. I don't suppose you have anybody in mind who might have it in for you."

Stan waited a moment before replying. "There are a couple I can think of. I went to talk to a railway worker in Elroy named Ty Gibbon. He was on the train with Cashman when it crashed, and Cashman told me he had it in for him because he turned him in for a mistake he made and got him suspended—."

Palmer frowned while writing down the name in a notebook. "I thought you were done with that."

"I was, but I had tried to talk to him earlier. He never called me back, and I was still curious whether he had any involvement. Since I was in that area I stopped by his place Sunday, but he didn't want to talk to me. Then Monday this thing happened with my car."

Palmer shook his head. "That's not much of a reason for somebody to go to the trouble of cutting the brake line on your car. Without any direct observation or fingerprints to link anyone to a crime, there's not much we can do about it. If you can come up with a license plate, then we could check that out, but just leave the criminal investigation stuff to us from now on. You said there was another person."

"Yeah, Ray Bickle is the other possibility," said Stan. "I went and saw his wife on Sunday to see how she was doing. Her mother asked me to..."

"You did what? You're just asking for trouble, aren't you? Does Bickle own a Plymouth?

"No."

Palmer shrugged his shoulders. "I don't know what you expect us to do. Bickle may have a beef with you. He may have one with us. But based on what you've told me, there's nothing to link him to the accident. I don't like Bickle any more than you do. I think there's probably domestic abuse going on. But his wife already told us she lied about the entire thing. If something happens between her and her husband she can report it to us or she can go to the local police there in Kendall. Les Chapman is the chief there, and he can handle whatever needs handling."

"I understand. The only reason I went was because her mother asked me to. After I talked to Lucy, her mother said she might call the county social services department about it."

"That's okay if she does. If they think there's justification, then they'll look into it. That's part of their job. It's not yours. I suggest, for your own good, you stay as far away from them as you can."

Stan let his shoulders sag. "Okay, sergeant. I will. Thanks for taking time to see me."

"I'll make up a report. You can leave the hose with me, and we'll keep it in our evidence room in case you have another incident."

•　　•　　•　　•　　•　　•

When Stan left the sheriff's office, he went back to the Herald office and got back to working on the Norwalk water tower story. He didn't say anything to Irv or anyone else in the office about his near catastrophic accident. Palmer had made him feel like a fool for going to see Lucy and getting in the middle of a family argument. Palmer was probably right, he thought, but he couldn't help it. He thought she needed help, and the police weren't going to do anything unless something really bad happened first. So he tried. She didn't want his help. That should be the end of it. But it didn't stop him from thinking about it.

After finishing work, he stopped off at Patty's apartment before going home. When she opened the door, she was in her nurse's uniform. "Why didn't you call?" she said. "You know I'm working nights. I have to leave in a half-hour."

"I won't stay long. I just had to talk to you. A lot happened in the last two days, and I need to unburden myself."

She stepped back from the doorway. "Okay, c'mon in. If you'd like a beer, there's some in the refrigerator."

He went to the refrigerator and grabbed a bottle. "You want one?"

She hollered back from the living room. "No, silly. I'm going to work. The hospital management doesn't appreciate beer breath on its employees."

"Oh, yeah, Sorry." Stan came into the living room, sat down on the couch, and took a long swallow of his beer. Patty, sitting across from him in an armchair said, "So tell me what happened."

"Yesterday I had a car accident while driving to Norwalk. My brakes failed, and I ran off the road trying to avoid crashing into a tractor. Ended up in a field and had to get towed into town."

Patty got up from the chair, sat next to him, and put a hand on his leg. "Were you hurt? You look all right?"

"I wasn't hurt, but I sure could have been. I had to leave the car at a garage in Norwalk to get repaired. I need to go back down there tomorrow to pick it up. I'm using a loaner now."

"Did the brakes go out all at once? Shouldn't you have noticed something earlier that the brakes were going bad?"

"Normally I would have, but I don't think this was just an accident. I'm pretty sure somebody cut my brake line to cause the brakes to fail."

"No! What makes you say that?"

"I think I was being followed home when I left here Sunday evening, and whoever was following me came back later that night and cut the brake line."

"Who would do something like that?"

"I think it could have been the guy I talked to Sunday in Elroy. His name's Ty Gibbon."

"Did you recognize the car?"

"No, I don't know what kind of car he has, or even if he owns one. I just thought he had acted strange and maybe thought he had something to hide. The only other person I can think of would be Bickle. If he actually did what Lucy said he did, he wouldn't think twice about trying to stop me if he thought I was still trying to investigate the train wreck."

"Did you go to the sheriff's office?"

"Yes. I talked to Sergeant Palmer, and he made a report, but he said they couldn't do anything unless I could come up with a license plate on whoever was following me, which I don't have."

"I don't think Bickle would be that foolish, but if it was him, if you don't have anything more to do with him or his wife, then I don't think he'll try anything again."

"I hope so. I don't like to just run away when somebody threatens me, though. At first, I was energized just by the idea of getting a big story. I don't have that anymore, but when her mother called and asked me to help, I felt like I had to. Was I wrong?"

"No, Stan. But you let your heart rule your head. You need to be sensible. If you get that kind of feeling again, promise to call me first before you do anything."

He hung his head and nodded. "I will."

CHAPTER 21

Lucy had just gotten home from work and was sorting through some laundry, when she heard a knock at the front door. She went to the living room and peeked out a side window to see a stout gray-haired woman in a gray business suit, carrying a brown briefcase. She opened the door. "Can I help you?"

The woman smiled. "Yes, my name's Judy Wickham. I'm a social worker with the Monroe County Welfare Office. Are you Lucille Bickle?"

"Yes, I am. What's this about?"

"We received a report of domestic abuse involving your husband. When we receive such a request, my office is responsible for investigating and providing assistance."

"I didn't report it."

"Yes, I know, and I understand. May I come in and discuss it with you?"

Lucy backed away from the door. "Yes, I... I guess it's okay, but my husband is here. He's in the basement doing something now. He's not going to be too happy about this."

The social worker followed Lucy into the living room. "You should call him so I can explain why I'm here."

Lucy went to the basement door. "Ray. We have a visitor. You need to come up here."

When Ray got to the living room he seemed surprised to see an unfamiliar well-dressed woman sitting on his couch. He looked at Lucy. "We don't need any insurance Lucy if that's what she's here for."

The woman stood up without offering to shake hands. "I'm not an insurance salesperson, Mr. Bickle. I'm with the Monroe County Welfare

Office, and I'm here to investigate a complaint. I need to talk to your wife alone."

He looked at Lucy with a dark frown. "You called her?"

She shook her head. "No, I don't know who did."

He turned to the social worker. "Who called you? I want to know."

"I'm not at liberty to divulge that information Mr. Bickle since the complaint is against you. I will say it was not your wife. We are, however, responsible for investigating any credible complaint that we receive. You should know, also, before coming here I met with your chief of police, Chief Chapman, and told him I was coming here. If you should interfere with our investigation, I would need to notify him to take appropriate action."

Bickle stood glaring at her but didn't respond.

"Now I would like to meet with your wife alone if you don't mind." She looked at Lucy. "Is there somewhere we can talk in private?"

"We can go in the bedroom."

"I got things to do in the basement," Bickle grumbled. He turned and stomped out of the room and down the stairs.

The social worker followed Lucy into the bedroom and closed the door behind her. Lucy sat on the bed and the older woman took a seat on a straight-back chair to the side.

"Can you tell me now who made the complaint? Was it that reporter Stan Ellis?"

"No. It was your mother. She said that you had told her that your husband had beaten you and your child, and she was fearful for your safety."

"How much do you know about my situation?"

"I know that your first husband was sent to prison four years ago for negligent homicide, and that you married Ray Bickle less than a year later. I know that you went to the county sheriff's office less than two weeks ago and claimed your current husband was responsible for the train wreck, and then you recanted your statement a few days later. I know you have a son who you seem to care very much about."

"Well, I didn't ask my mother to call you. What if I don't want to cooperate with you? You can't make me, can you?"

"No, if you won't admit to the abuse or seek help I can't force you. However, if I determine that the abusive environment is affecting your son, then I may make a recommendation regarding his welfare without your consent."

"What? You can't just take my son away?"

"No, it would have to be done by a court. I'm not saying that would happen, but when a child is involved, that's something I have to take into consideration. Is he in school now?"

"Yes, he'll be home in about two hours." She lowered her head, put her hands to her forehead, and rocked back and forth. "I don't know what to do. You come here out of the blue and expect me to make a decision like this. I want to do what's right, but it's hard."

"I understand that it's hard. I've talked with many women in similar circumstances. Fear is the common denominator, and it takes a lot of strength to fight against it. The abused often feel that any attempt to escape is hopeless. I can only say from my experience that those who choose to stay in an abusive relationship rarely come out well. I'm here today to offer you some hope for yours and your son's future. There are certain points in that kind of relationship where you have a chance to escape, and this is one of your chances. Do you want to take it or throw it away?"

Lucy began to cry. "Yes, he has hurt me. I hate him. I don't care so much for myself, but for my boy. I'm afraid for him. I'll tell you what you need to know!"

"Good. You won't regret your decision. In order to get a protection order, you're going to have to file a petition and appear before a judge. Once he approves it, your husband will be restricted from having contact with you. That means either he will have to move out or you will have to move out, but you won't be alone in this fight." Wickham took out a pad from her briefcase. "You said he hurt you. Do you have visible marks that you can show me?"

Lucy removed her blouse and showed the social worker bruises and scratches on her arms, neck, and chest, which Wickham noted on her pad. She then asked Lucy to go into specifics about the physical abuse her husband inflicted upon her and her son. Lucy even told her that Ray had forced her to recant her statement to the sheriff's office. After writing everything down, Wickham said, "From what you've told me your husband does pose an immediate threat to you and your son. I think you should leave—the sooner the better.

"But where would I go? I have a job. Billy is in school."

"Those things can be worked out. I can take you to a safe house today where you can stay for a period of time until legal issues get sorted out. Or, if you have someone you can go to and feel safe, you could do that. What do you say?"

Lucy took a deep breath. "Oh God. That's a big step. If I tell Ray, he'll blow his top."

"You don't need to tell your husband you're leaving. Just leave a note and go. I'm sure I can get an interim protection order to prevent your husband from doing anything, and he'll be given notification to leave you alone."

Lucy shook her head. "The only place I know to go is to my mother's house in Elroy. I know she'd take me in. I don't really want to go anywhere else. But I have my job at the grocery store. And Billy's in school."

"We'll pick Billy up at his school. I'm sure you can work something out with the grocery store to take some time off. If you want to do it, do it now Start packing your things and pack up some things for Billy, and we can leave."

Lucy got up from the bed. "All right. I'll do it."

"Okay," said Judy as she pulled a sheet of paper from her briefcase. "This is a form I'd like you to sign asking for an interim protection order." She handed the form and a pen to Lucy and she signed it. "Do you have a photo of your husband?"

Lucy nodded and pulled a photo of her husband from her wallet and handed it to the social worker.

Judy got up from the chair, gave Lucy a hug and said, "I'll go wait in the car while you pack. Don't make a lot of noise. It'll be best if we leave without him knowing."

Lucy got out a suitcase from the closet and started throwing things in from her dresser and closet. She went to the bathroom to get what she needed there and then went upstairs to Billy's room and began tossing things he would need unto a sheet and tied it all up in a bundle. When she came down the stairs, Ray was at the bottom waiting for her.

"Where in the hell do you think you're going?"

She jutted out her chin. "I'm leaving you Ray. Where I'm going is none of your concern."

He looked around. "Where's that damn woman? What did you tell her?"

"She's outside waiting for me, and I told her everything that you've done to me and to Billy. I don't have to take it anymore, and I won't. Miss Wickham said that the police would protect me."

He grabbed her by the shoulders and pushed her into the bedroom. "You'll take whatever I give you. You don't have a choice."

"What do you mean I don't have a choice?"

"You were just as much a part of the plan to wreck that train as I was. If I get caught up in that and go to jail, you'll go to."

"I don't care about that. I don't care if I end up in jail. At least Billy will be free of you. I'm going to divorce you."

He pushed her prone onto the bed, opened the drawer to the side table, took out a snub-nosed revolver, and held it, with the barrel pointed upward, in front of her face. She looked up, wide-eyed. "Let me tell you how it's going to be," he said. "I'm not going to stop you from walking out of here now. I wouldn't want to upset the lady waiting outside. But if you do, I will find you; I'll kill you; I'll kill Billy; I'll kill your mother; and then I'll kill myself. If that's what you want, then you can go."

Lucy's chest heaved as she began hyperventilating. "You would do that?"

Bickle gave a venomous grin, and Lucy rolled over and started crying.

"What are you going to do? Make up your mind before that bitch comes back in here."

Lucy got up from the bed and wiped tears from her face. "I'll go out and tell her I'm not leaving."

His face transformed into a cheery smile. "That's what I wanted to hear. That's my girl. I'll wait here while you tell her."

She pushed past him and went outside where the social worker was sitting in her car with the motor running. Lucy came up to the open window and Judy said, "Where's your suitcase?"

"I changed my mind. I'm not going."

"Did he threaten you?"

"No. We just talked. He said he's sorry for what happened and promised everything's going to be different from now on. He wants me to stay, and I...I don't want to leave him.

Judy started to respond, but Lucy interrupted. "Can I have that paper I signed? I don't want you to turn it in."

"I'll hang on to it in case you change your mind."

"I won't change my mind."

"This may be your one chance, Lucy. Don't let him control you like this. He's not going to change. I'll go back in with you to get your suitcase." She started to open the door.

Lucy held the car door shut. "No, I don't want you to. You don't understand."

"Oh, my dear, I do understand. All too well. You're making such a big mistake."

"It's my life. I have to do what I have to do." Lucy turned away and went back into the house. Judy waited to see if she would come back outside. After two or three minutes when she didn't come out, Judy backed out of the driveway and drove off.

Ray was waiting in the hallway when Lucy came back inside. Her body stiffened as he came up to her, wrapped his arms around her, and tried to kiss her. She turned her head to the side. "Baby what am I going to do with you? I guess I'll have to turn over a new leaf to get us back to where we were when we first married. To show you how I'm going to change, tonight I'm going to make supper for us. I already started some chili, and I can have it ready by six o'clock. You go put your feet up and relax, and I'll take care of supper."

She looked at him warily. "Okay. You can fix supper. I'm not much in the mood for doing anything right now. I'm going to lie down until Billy comes home. Please don't make him upset."

"Sweetie, that's the last thing I want to do. I'm going to be a changed man. You just wait and see."

CHAPTER 22

The next morning, on the way to the Elroy depot, Ray asked Lucy what her plans were for the day. "I have to go to work at ten, but I don't feel much like it," she said. "I woke up with a terrible headache this morning, and it still bothers me. Maybe it was that chili you made last night. Too spicy."

"I thought you liked spicy. You probably got the headache because of all the aggravation yesterday. Just need to put that behind you."

"I'll try, but you got to keep your promise to change."

He grinned. "I always keep my promises. By the way, who was it that put that damn woman from the welfare office on my ass? Did she tell you?"

She shook her head. "No, she wouldn't tell me."

"I'll bet it was that reporter up in Sparta. What's his name—Ellis. I think he's got the hots for you. You need to stay away from him, you hear?"

"Yes Ray, I hear."

When they got to the depot, Ray got out and Lucy switched around to the driver's seat. Ray leaned in the driver's window. "Now I'll be back seven o'clock Sunday evening. You be here to pick me up. Don't get into any trouble while I'm away."

She shook her head. "No, I won't. I may stop over at my mother's before I go to work though."

"That's okay. Give my regards to the old lady," he said with a toss of his head before walking away.

It was only a five-minute drive from the depot to her mother's house on the other side of town. When her mother opened the door, she saw a pained expression on Lucy's face.

"What's wrong? Did anything happen?"

"Oh, mother... my life is so complicated. Nothing happened yet, but I'm worried about what might happen. Why did you have to call the welfare office? It's only made things worse."

Helen took her daughter's arm. "Come. Let's go in the living room and talk. I have some tea on the stove, and that will settle you down."

She brought a tray with tea out to the living room and set it down in front of Lucy. "Now tell me what happened. I did call and talk to a woman last Wednesday about your situation, but I didn't think she would act so quickly."

"A lady named Judy Wickham came by yesterday around one. She tried to talk me into leaving Ray right then and go with her. She told me she could find me a place where I'd be safe. At first I said no. But after she said she could get a protection order against Ray, I finally agreed to go with her—but told her I wanted to come stay with you."

"Was Ray home when this was happening?"

"Yes, but he went to the basement to work on something while I met with the social worker. She had me sign some paper and then went to her car while I packed some things. But just before I was leaving, Ray came up and stopped me." She took in a breath. "He threatened me."

"How did he threaten you?"

"He said if I left, he'd kill me, Billy, and you, and then commit suicide."

Helen closed her eyes tightly and grimaced. "Oh Lord! Did you tell the social worker?"

"No, I knew that would only make it worse. Ray meant what he said. I went outside and told her I changed my mind and I was staying with Ray. After that, she left."

Helen got up from her chair and sat beside Lucy on the couch and put an arm around her. "I didn't realize he could be that crazy. Somehow you have to leave him."

"I can't mother. He meant what he said."

"Something needs to be done. Maybe I should call the social worker directly. Does Ray know I called them?"

"No, I didn't tell him, but he thinks Stan Ellis did it."

"Well, I guess that's good for me, but I'm not so sure it's good for Mr. Ellis."

"I don't think Ray will do anything now that I've told him I'll stay with him. Ray promised that he'd change. He doesn't want me to leave him, and maybe things will be better."

"I wouldn't count on it. I just might call Mr. Ellis to let him know what you said. He needs to be aware just in case he runs into Ray somewhere."

"No. You don't need to do that. I'll let you know if Ray starts acting up again, but I think it's going to be all right. I just needed to talk to you and get everything off my chest. Thank you mother for being there for me." She leaned over and kissed her on the cheek.

•   •   •   •   •

Later that day, after returning home from work, Lucy busied herself doing some laundry in the basement and then hanging it outside. Billy came home from school just as she came back inside. "What's for supper?"

She was feeling better after taking Alka Seltzer in the morning, and hollered back to her son, "Leftover chili. Is that okay?"

"No, it's too spicy for me. Make me a sandwich."

She ate a bowl of chili by herself and made Billy a tuna sandwich. After doing the dishes, she played a board game with him for an hour, and then watched television until it was time to go to bed. She woke up with a stomachache during the night and threw up some of what she ate. She took some more Alka Seltzer and went back to bed. The next morning, she woke tired and had a throbbing headache, but the stomach pain had subsided. It was Saturday, the busiest day at the store, and Blanche wouldn't appreciate her calling in sick. Besides, she only had to work four hours on Saturday. She called the parents of Billy's friend Bobby and got their okay to leave him with them and left home a few minutes before nine.

Lucy made it through the workday, but her headache didn't go away. When she got home, she took some aspirin and went to the bedroom to lie down. While lying in bed, she remembered she hadn't put away Billy's clothes she'd taken out Thursday when she was preparing to leave. She dragged herself out of the bed and went into his room. The underwear, socks, pants, shirts, and a heavy jacket were scattered on the floor beside the unmade bed. She made up the bed and then picked up the clothes, putting the underwear and socks in the dresser drawer, and then opened up the closet to hang the other things. She tried to hang the heavy jacket at the far end of the closet since he wouldn't be needing it for a while. But when she stretched to hang it, the jacket dropped from the hanger to the floor. She wedged herself into the closet and bent down to get the coat and felt a wooden box underneath. She knew she hadn't put it there, and knelt down to get a closer look, but it was dark, and she pulled it out of the closet. It was a small wooden chest with a metal hasp but no lock on it. As far as Lucy knew this had been an extra bedroom before she moved in, but there was a sewing machine on a table and Ray's wife may have used this as a sewing room.

Lucy opened the top and saw there were clothes inside—a woman's sweater was on top. Beneath it were two cotton blouses, and then a wool skirt. *Ray must not have checked here when he got rid of the rest of her things after she died. I guess I can give these to the church.* Lucy removed the clothes revealing some letters, a few pieces of inexpensive jewelry, and a small blue book with no title on the outside. She picked it up, went and sat on the edge of the bed, and opened it up. It was a diary. The first entry was in 1952. *Could this be Alice's?* She began reading.

January 2, 1952

For my New Year's resolution this year I promised myself I'd start keeping a diary, so when I'm an old grandma I can look back at what I was doing and thinking in the past. I want to have kids more than anything, but so far Ray and I haven't had any luck. I've been to the doctor, and he says there's nothing wrong with me, and I'm only twenty-nine so there's still time. Ray is very strong and we try a lot. So eventually I'm hoping it works. I don't care much for my job at the creamery, but I'm hoping to get a promotion to shift supervisor....

Lucy began flipping pages. She wanted to see if Alice ever suspected anything about her affair with Ray.

May 4, 1954

I had supper alone tonight. Ray is on the road again. He's been gone a lot lately. He says he does it for the extra pay he gets on the long-hauls. I guess it's worth it to him, but we could get by without so much overtime. The doctor said we have to have sex at certain times in order to improve my chance to get pregnant. But he doesn't seem to care anymore. I don't know why. I hope he's not playing around. That worries me because...

Lucy was engrossed now and turned more pages.

June 1, 1954

Yesterday wasn't a good day for me. Mr. Henderson called me into his office and I thought I was going to get the promotion, but he told me he selected Grace Weiler instead. Ray didn't get home until ten and had been drinking, so I should have known how he'd react. I expected sympathy, but what I got was blame for not getting the promotion so he could afford to get a new car. Today wasn't any better. This morning I was gathering his clothes for the wash, and I smelled something on his shirts— something like perfume. There was a bit of lipstick on the collar too. Maybe he was at a bar and dancing with someone. I don't know, but I'm not happy.

June 12, 1954

Ray is out tonight playing poker with friends. I'm alone again as usual. He did take me out last Saturday, but he won't give up his time with friends, at least that's where he says he's going. I've about given up on having a baby. Now he says he doesn't want one. That wasn't what he said when we got married. I think he may be seeing someone else, but I'm afraid to bring it up to him. He gets so angry and when he does he gets mean...

Lucy started to turn to another page when she heard Billy come in downstairs. "I'm up here," she shouted. She closed the lid on the chest, shoved it back in the closet, and dropped the book on the nightstand next to her bed. When she went downstairs, she prepared spaghetti and meatballs for Billy, but she didn't feel like eating a lot, and fixed a can of chicken noodle soup for herself. After cleaning up the supper dishes, she watched television with Billy until ten when she ordered him up to bed. Once he had closed the door to his room, she went to her bedroom, undressed for bed, and picked up the little blue book to see what else Alice had said.

June 19, 1954

Tonight is Saturday, and Ray went out with his friends again. I don't like being left alone so much, but he does work hard and earns a good living for us. I know I'm not that pretty, and I should be grateful for him marrying me. I just worry that he's finding someone else. I don't know who, but I'm worried about that. I'll do anything to keep him, if he'll just...

That was the night before the train accident, thought Lucy. She wondered if Alice wrote anything about that. She turned the page.

June 20, 1954

I was asleep when Ray came home last night, but he was kind of noisy and I woke up. It was about two o'clock. I thought he'd be drunk, but he didn't seem to be. He said he was just playing pool at one of the bars in town, and he just had a couple beers. I noticed that his pants and shoes were kind of muddy and asked him about it. He said he had to change a flat tire on his way home and lost his footing and slipped down into the mud. Sounds a little suspicious, but I'll have to take his word for it. Later today, I heard on the news that there was a train wreck over by Wilton and some people died. When I told Ray, he was surprised and said that's the train he sometimes works. He was awful glad he had the day off. I'm glad too. No telling what would have happened to him.

Lucy reread the June 20 entry. Ray evidently never said anything to Alice about calling in sick. That didn't exactly track with her saying he was out with the boys at a bar. Did he keep everything else secret from her too? She kept skimming through pages to see if there was any other mention of his involvement in the train wreck. It was mostly mundane stuff. Alice seemed to be growing more suspicious of Ray's fooling around, but there was no indication she knew of Lucy. They lived in different towns, and the two had never met face to face. Lucy came to the entry of November 5. George's trial had ended two days before.

November 5, 1954

I didn't write anything yesterday. It was a horrible day, and I couldn't. Tonight Ray is out of town again, and I'll write what happened just for my record. Ray's friend George Cashman was convicted of causing the train wreck back in June of this year. When Ray came home, I asked him if he heard about it, and he said he had. I thought Ray would have been upset, but he wasn't. He just said he had it coming. I thought it was strange the way he reacted. He mentioned that he felt sorrier for George's wife. I didn't understand why? I asked him point-blank if he was seeing somebody else. He said no. I told him about the lipstick on his shirt and he shrugged it off as some floozy in the bar who came up to him. I don't really believe him. I'm starting to wonder if it's Cashman's wife he's playing around with.

The next entry in the diary was three days later.

November 8, 1954

Yesterday I had it out with Ray. I wanted to see what Cashman's wife looked like. I knew her name was Lucy, and that she worked over at Hogan's grocery. I went there shopping yesterday and saw her at the cash register. I hoped she would be old and ugly. But she wasn't. Very pretty. I didn't say anything to her, but just let her check me out. I thought I could smell that same kind of perfume I smelled on Ray's shirt. After supper I told Ray what I suspected, that he was having an affair with her. At first he denied it, but then he admitted it and said he wanted a divorce. I told him I wouldn't give him a divorce. I told him I knew he was lying about having a flat tire the other night, and that if he tried to divorce me I'd go to the police and tell them about his affair with Cashman's wife. He got really mad then and slapped me and pushed me to the floor.

I think I hit my head on the bedstead and must have been knocked out. I woke up a while later in bed with a bandage wrapped around my head. Ray was sitting on the bed and offered me a glass of water. I didn't expect to see him there after the fit he had thrown. But he was a different man than the one who I'd just seen, and I was glad for that. He said it scared him when he saw me unconscious with a cut on the back of my head. He said it made him realize how much he cared for me. He said he knew he was wrong to have the affair and asked me to forgive him. I told him I would if he would tell Cashman's wife that it was over. He promised he would, and that he would make it up to me. I wasn't sure if he really meant what he said, but this morning he made breakfast and seems to be sincere. I can only hope it continues.

Lucy was stunned with what she'd read. He'd told Alice he would break up with Lucy, but he never did. He never told her Alice had refused to agree to a divorce. He said he couldn't ask her for a divorce because she was sick. He lied about that. What else was he keeping from her?

January 20, 1955

All this week I've been feeling miserable. Ray says it's probably just the flu that's been hanging on. I missed three days of work. I've had some nausea, and I just feel tired all the time. Day before yesterday I called the doctor because I was having diarrhea and dizziness. Also felt some heart fluttering. I mentioned it to the doctor, and he couldn't find anything wrong with my heart. He said I might be getting a touch of pneumonia and should drink a lot of fluids. Ray's been good when he's been home. Tonight when he came home he gave me a package. Said he wanted to cheer me up. It was a beautiful music box. Sometimes he can be so sweet. Lately he's been fixing supper since I've been feeling so low. Tonight he fixed a hamburger casserole. My appetite's been poor. I only ate half of what he put on my plate.

The intervals between the diary entries were getting longer. Lucy flipped to the last entry.

February 21, 1955

I had to quit my job at the creamery last week. The boss told me they needed somebody full-time, but said he'd hire me back when I get well. Ray said not to worry about it, but I do. I'm not sure I will get well. So tired. Spending most of day in bed. When I try to get up, I get dizzy. I've lost a lot of weight in the last two months. I weighed myself yesterday and was just 98 pounds. I used to be 135. Last night I threw up again after supper. My headache was constant all night long, and I had a hard time breathing. This morning I had those heart palpitations like before. Ray said he'll call the doctor again if it gets worse. I'm supposed to have lots of fluids, and Ray fixed a nice beef broth with some vegetables. I wasn't hungry, but I got it down. I'm getting drowsy. Write more later.

Lucy closed the book, laid it on the nightstand, turned off the light, and laid her head on her pillow. *What does all this mean, and what should I do with it? Oh God, how do I get myself out of this situation?*

CHAPTER 23

Lucy woke up Sunday morning, still unsure of what to do about the diary. She didn't want Ray to see it, and she didn't think the police would give it a second look after what she'd been through with them. She got up from bed and went to the bathroom to shower. Her stomach felt better this morning, and the headache was almost gone. I guess I'll take Billy to church today, she thought, while letting the water cascade over her. After finishing the shower, she went to Billy's room to get him up.

"Hurry up," she said. "It's getting late. I don't want you to miss Sunday school." He resisted at first, but her promise to make him pancakes and bacon for breakfast eventually drew him out of bed. After breakfast Lucy drove Billy to the church. Normally she waited in her car until his Sunday school class was over. After walking with Billy to his classroom, she paused to glance over a bulletin board announcing various church activities.

A woman came up beside Lucy. "Good morning. I saw you drop your son off at class, are you staying for church?"

She turned to see a tall elderly woman wearing a colorful broad-brimmed hat. She'd noticed the woman before, but they'd never spoken. "Oh, no. I wasn't planning on staying."

"Oh, why don't you? If you feel shy about not knowing anybody or sitting alone, you can sit with me. There's no need for you to sit outside waiting for your son's class to get over. We have a nice choir. I think you'll enjoy it."

Lucy thought about it a moment and then said, "Okay, I guess I can do that. I need to let my son know where I'll be."

When Lucy returned from the classroom, they started walking toward the sanctuary and the older woman said, "I'm Wilma Crossley. I've noticed you coming quite regularly to bring your son to Sunday school. I know most people in town, but we've never met before. Are you from this area?"

"I'm from Elroy. I just moved to Kendall about three years ago."

As they reached the door of the sanctuary, an usher gave them each a service bulletin, and they took a seat in a rear pew.

Wilma said, "You didn't tell me your name."

"It's Lucy. Lucy Bickle."

Wilma raised her eyebrows. "That name sounds familiar. I knew a Gladys Bickle. She and her husband have been gone a long time. Any relation?"

"It was probably my husband's grandmother. He lived with his grandparents and kept the house when they died."

The church organ began, and Lucy turned her eyes to the bulletin in her lap. On the cover was a quotation from 2 Corinthians 7:9, the subject of the day's sermon: *Now I rejoice, not that you were made sorry, but that your sorrow led to repentance. For you were made sorry in a godly manner, that you might suffer loss from us in nothing.*

The pastor stepped up to the pulpit and began the service. The sermon focused on repentance and the need of believers in Christ to change their sinful ways to achieve salvation. As he talked, she reflected on the direction she was heading. When the service was over, she thanked Wilma for inviting her into the service. When they parted she found Billy waiting in the hallway. "Let's go home," she said.

As she started the car engine she recalled the words of the preacher who stressed the need of Christians to become truly repentant for their sins. Until then, she wasn't sure what to do with the diary she'd discovered. She'd thought about just putting it back where she found it, but the preacher's sermon nagged at her. I've committed a terrible sin, she thought. I have to make it right. I can't keep the diary a secret. When she got home she went straight to her bedroom and retrieved the diary from the bedstand. She told Billy, "I'm going to go over to grandma's for a while. Do you want to come, or stay here?"

"I'll stay here," said Billy.

•   •   •   •   •

Lucy arrived at her mother's house shortly after noon. She grabbed the diary from the front seat and hurried up the front steps. She tried the front door but found it was locked. She regretted not having called ahead and then remembered her mother was probably still at church. She started to leave the porch when she saw her mother coming up the sidewalk. As she drew near, her mother waved and called out, "You should have called ahead. Don't you know most people go to church Sunday mornings?"

"Sorry mom," she said as Helen came up the porch steps. "I forgot what time your church was. Actually I went to church this morning myself. But it was over earlier. First time in a while."

"Well, that's a change for the good. I was wondering when I'd hear from you again. I thought you might be still mad at me for calling that social worker."

"No, I'm not mad at you mom. I know you did what you thought was best. Right now, though, I just can't leave him. He said he would change."

"Well, I can't make you. But I wish you'd rethink it. You know you can always stay with me."

"I know."

"Let's go inside and talk. What's that you got in your hand?"

"It's a diary. I found it in the house." She raised it to show her. "Ray's first wife wrote it."

Lucy sat at the kitchen table while her mother got out a coffeecake and began boiling water for tea. "Is Ray home now with Billy?"

"No, Ray's on the road."

"When do you expect him back?"

"Tonight. I have to pick him up at the depot at seven. I left Billy home alone, but he'll be okay for a couple hours."

Her mother brought the tea and coffee cake to the table and sat down across from Lucy. "Does Ray know about the diary?"

"No, and I don't want him to know about it either. I wanted you to read it and tell me what you think."

Lucy pushed the diary over to her mother who took her reading glasses out of a pocket and began reading. "Oh my... Oh my," she said repeatedly as she read.

After sitting silent for a half-hour, Lucy asked, "Did you see Alice's entry in October 1954 after George's trial where Ray told her he wanted a divorce, and she accused him of having an affair with me."

"Yes, I read that, and how he beat her up. A person like that doesn't change. That's why I think you have to get away from him. He doesn't deserve any more chances."

"I know how you feel, mom. Read some more. Go to the entries in late January where she starts getting sick. That's about the same time I filed for divorce."

Helen began reading again, shaking her head as she progressed through each entry. When she finished, she closed the diary. She tsk-tsked and looked up at Lucy. "That poor woman. How long after that did she die? Such a young girl."

"She died about a month after that last entry, sometime in March."

"Did the doctors come up with any explanation for why she died?"

"I don't know. I wasn't involved, and the only thing Ray told me was that she was a heavy smoker, and there were complications from a congenital heart problem. That's all I know."

"Oh Lucy, something doesn't seem right. It's too much coincidence. Her dying like that just after you put in for a divorce. Didn't you suspect anything?"

"Ray never told me about his fight with his wife and her refusal to give him a divorce. He just said she was getting sick and he couldn't divorce her in that condition. I wanted to believe him. But now, with this diary... It looks like he might have done something to cause her death. The problem is, there's no proof. I don't think the police would do anything with the diary since Alice never accused him directly of doing anything. Instead, she praised him."

"Well, we need to do something. Maybe the police wouldn't be interested, but I think our reporter friend, Mr. Ellis, might help us."

"Mother! I told him I didn't want his help anymore. After all that's happened, he'll think we're crazy if you call him again."

"No, he won't be able to resist at least taking a look at the diary. Leave the diary with me, and I'll call him tomorrow. I have his work phone."

Lucy threw up her hands. "Okay Mom, I don't want to argue. Do what you think's best. I'll be working tomorrow, but I'll call you later in the week when Ray's not around."

· · · · ·

Waiting in her car in the depot parking lot, Lucy checked her watch when she heard a train whistle blow—five minutes to seven. *That must be Ray's train.* Fifteen minutes later Ray tossed his duffel bag in the back seat. He hopped into the passenger seat, reached over putting both hands on her cheeks, and kissed her on the mouth. "Miss me babe? I missed you. I got you a little present in Chicago. I'll show it to you when we get home."

When they arrived home, he brought out a wrapped package from his bag and gave it to her. It was a jewelry box and inside was a pearl necklace. "Do you like it?" he asked.

He hadn't given her any gift like this since they were married. She wasn't sure how to react. Maybe he was truly changing, she thought. She put the necklace around her neck, looked at herself in a mirror, and turned around and gave him a kiss. "Thank you Ray."

CHAPTER 24

Stan dropped the police blotter report on his desk, picked up his stained coffee cup and walked over to the coffee urn where Irv, with a somber look on his face, was filling his own cup. "Why so glum? I know it's Monday, but the sun is shining, the economy's up, and most of the world's at peace."

"Hmph. Maybe so," said Irv. "But I'm just down over what happened to the Braves—ahead 3-1 in the Series and they lose it. I don't know how you can be so upbeat."

"Yeah. That was hard to take, but you have to think that there's always next year. They've still got a great team."

"Suppose so. Can't say the same for the Packers, though. They thought that young quarterback Starr would make some difference, but doesn't look like it after the shellacking they took Sunday. They should have the talent, but something's missing."

"Your right. What they need is an inspirational coach. McLean's not the answer." Stan leaned over to open the urn spigot to fill his cup. "You got anything special for me to work on?"

"There's a change of command ceremony at Fort McCoy tomorrow morning at nine. I'd like you to cover that. It wouldn't hurt to go over there today. Talk to the public affairs guy about the setup and make sure you get an interview with the new commander."

"Okay, I'll do that. Anything else?"

"High school homecoming is on Friday. Other than that just the normal stuff."

Stan went back to his desk, wrote up a story from the police report he'd brought in, and was about to leave to go to Fort McCoy when his phone rang.

"Is this Mr. Ellis?"

"Yes, who am I speaking to?"

"This is Helen Grim. Remember me—Lucy's mother."

He took a deep breath, unsure of where this was going. "Sure. How can I help you Mrs. Grim?"

"I know you must have thought you'd heard the last of me after the way Lucy brushed you off last week at the church, but something came up that I just felt I had to talk to you about."

"Okay, Mrs. Grim. I'm listening, but I've done all I can. She needs to see a marriage counselor or an attorney—not a reporter."

"No, they can't help with this. Let me explain. Yesterday Lucy came to me and showed me a diary she found hidden away in a closet in her house. Ray's first wife, Alice, wrote it. You know she died just a short time after George went to prison, don't you?"

"Yes, I knew his wife got sick and died, and then after a short while he married your daughter. What of it?"

"Well, according to the diary, his wife accused him of having an affair with Lucy and wouldn't give him a divorce. Then a couple months later she's dead. I think Ray had something to do with it. I don't know if the police would do anything based on what's in the diary, but I wanted you to look at it and see if there's enough to go to the police. I'm more worried than ever now about Lucy."

This was something entirely new, and Stan took a few moments to catch his thoughts before replying. His first instinct was to tell her to leave him out of it and take it to the police. But something stronger inside told him not to leave it up to somebody else. "All right. I'll take a look at it. I can't come today. Tomorrow evening, after I finish work, I'll drive down there to see you. Is that all right?"

"Yes, that'll be fine Mr. Ellis. Thank you."

.   .   .   .   .

Tuesday's change of command ceremony lasted most of the morning. After dropping his film off at the photo lab, it was already two o'clock by the time he got back to the office. It was a push, but he finished his story by five-thirty and handed it off to Irv who was still at his desk. "Where you rushing off to?"

"I promised I'd meet someone in Elroy. Might be a new story, but I can't talk about it yet."

"Not another wild goose chase is it?" Irv laughed as he watched Stan rush out the door.

When Stan got to Helen Grim's house, she brought him into the living room and sat him down on the sofa. "You want tea or anything?" she asked.

"No. I'm okay," he said as he took off his jacket. "I'd just like to read the diary."

Helen went to a dresser, pulled out the diary, and handed it to him. "I'll let you alone while you read through it. I'll be in the kitchen. Call me when you finish."

He turned on a table lamp next to him, settled back on the sofa, and began reading. After a half-hour Helen came in with a cup of tea and a plate of cookies that she set down beside him. He looked up, thanked her, and continued reading. A half-hour later he closed the book and called out. "I've finished. Let's talk about it."

She came into the living room rubbing her hands together anxiously. "What do you think?"

"I think there's a real possibility that Ray had something to do with his first wife's death. He could have put something in her food—but I could be way off. What was the official cause of death? Do you know?"

"All I know is what Lucy told me. She said Ray told her Alice had a congenital heart defect, and she smoked, and the combination led to her dying."

"I'd like to see the death certificate, but the county will only release that to the police with a warrant. I don't see them going for that." Stan lowered his head to think. "We don't even know for sure it's his wife who wrote this diary. There's no signature."

"I know," said Helen. "But there must be some letters or something that she wrote that would show the same handwriting."

"There may be, but we don't have those letters. Do you know if she has any relatives here in town?"

"I don't know. Maybe Lucy knows. Should I call her?"

Stan leaned forward, trying to work out what he wanted to do. "No, I don't want to get her involved if this isn't going to go anywhere. Do you know when Ray's wife died?"

"Lucy said she died just two or three weeks after the last entry in that diary. It must have been sometime in early March 1955."

"Will you let me keep the diary for a short time? I'd like to check out some things, and I'll need a few days to do it."

"Yes, of course. Take it."

He looked at his watch. It was seven thirty. "I know you have a library off Main Street. Do you think it's open?"

Helen put her left hand to her cheek. "Yes, I think they stay open until nine. Students use it, you know."

"Good. I'll make a stop there before going home." He put on his jacket and looked down at Helen. "Even though I agree with you that the diary creates a lot of suspicion about Ray, other people may not see it the same way. I don't want you to say anything to anyone else about this. Let me look into it some, and I'll let you know what I come up with. It may be nothing."

She looked up at him. "I won't say anything to anyone."

●　　●　　●　　●　　●

The Elroy library was a small stand-alone building with an Andrew Carnegie dedication plaque on the outer wall next to the doorway. An elderly gray-haired woman in a cardigan sweater sat at a desk near the entrance reading a book. He went up to her and asked if they kept copies of the Elroy Gazette on file.

"Yes we do," she said. "What time period are you looking for?"

"March 1955."

"We close at eight-thirty. Is that enough time for you?"

Stan looked up at the clock on the wall. Ten to eight. "Yes, I'll be done by then."

"Just a moment, I'll go look for it." She went to a backroom and came back with a large binder containing the 1955 newspapers. Stan thanked her, took the binder to an empty table, and began scanning through the obituaries starting with March 1. He found what he was looking for in the March 11 issue.

> *Alice Bickle*
> Alice Bickle, 31, passed away at home, after a lengthy illness, on March 8, 1955. Funeral service will be Saturday, March 13 at Talley Funeral Home in Elroy. Burial will follow at Glendale Cemetery in Kendall. Alice is survived by husband Ray Bickle of Kendall, a sister Joyce Banks of Hillsboro, and mother Ruth Cruller, also of Hillsboro.

Stan copied the obituary information onto a sheet of paper, put it in his pocket, and took the binder back to the front desk. When he got back in his car, he was excited about the possibility of talking with Alice's family and finding out what they knew about her cause of death. As he pulled onto Main Street, he did a double-take when he noticed a dark green Plymouth Belvedere with a dent in the trunk parked along the street in front of a bar. He parked a few cars away and started to get out when he saw someone exit the bar and stop to light a cigarette. He waited until the man passed by, got in a car further up the block, and drove away. Then Stan got out to get a closer look at the green car with the dented rear-end. He pulled a notepad from his pocket, walked around the back of the car, and wrote down the license plate number. I'll give this to Glen tomorrow so he can have the license traced. He doubted whether the cops would do anything with the information, but he hoped he would at least find out who had followed him that night and tried to get him killed.

CHAPTER 25

During his lunch break the next day, Stan went to the sheriff's office to see if he could get a trace on the license plate number he'd picked up. He asked for Sergeant Palmer or Glenn, but the desk sergeant told him they were out on the road and he'd see that one of them got the message. It was nearly five when Palmer called Stan at the newsroom. "I got your message that you wanted me to call you concerning the accident report you made last week. Did you come up with something for us?"

"Yes, I did. When I put in the report, you said you couldn't do anything about my complaint unless I could come up with a license plate number. Last night, while I was in Elroy, I saw the same car that was following me."

"How do you know it was the same car?"

"It was a 54 Plymouth Belvedere. The same color, the same dent in the back."

"Okay, give me the number."

Stan had kept the paper with the number on it in his shirt pocket. He pulled it out and read the number: KEG 8641.

"Okay, I got it. We'll check it out."

"Will you let me know who the car belongs to? Whoever was driving that car tried to kill me."

"I understand how you must feel, but it's a long jump from saying a car that looks like one that was following you, was driven by someone who cut your brake line. There's no necessary connection between the two events. In any case, I'll have it run through the system, and I'll have Glenn call you to let you know when we get something back. But don't get your hopes up."

After Palmer hung up, Stan slammed his fist on his desk, causing Rose to jump and hit the wrong key on her typewriter. "What happened?" she asked.

"Nothing. I'm just upset about getting the runaround. I'll be all right."

He picked up the phone again and dialed Operator. "Information. Can I help you?"

"I'd like the information operator for Hillsboro, Wisconsin."

"Just a moment please."

After several clicks in his ear, an operator answered. "This is the operator for Hillsboro. Can I help you?"

"Yes. I'd like to get the number for Ruth Cruller."

He waited several seconds before the operator came back on the line and told him there was no listing for that name. "What about Joyce Banks?"

No listing for that name either. The operator said they had a James Banks, Charles Banks, and Earl Banks. He asked her to connect him to James Banks. A woman answered and told him she didn't know any Alice Bickle. He went back to the Hillsboro operator and asked her to connect him with the Charles Banks number. Again, a woman answered, and this time he got Joyce Banks. He told her he was a reporter for the Sparta Herald and asked if Alice Bickle was her sister. There was a pause on the line before the woman responded.

"Yes. Alice was my sister, but she's been gone for some time. Why are you asking about her?"

"I'm working on a story about the train wreck in Monroe County a few years ago, and I came across a diary she wrote. I wanted to show it to you and ask you some questions about it."

He heard a man's voice in the background, and she interrupted her conversation with Stan to explain that she was talking to a reporter. Then she came back on the line and asked, "How do you know it was written by Alice?"

"I'm not positive. It was found in the house where she lived with Ray Bickle before her death. So I'm pretty sure it's her, but that's one reason I wanted you to look at it. Hopefully, you can confirm that it's written in her handwriting."

"I don't know if I can, but my mother's with us, and she probably can tell if it's Alice's writing—but this is all so strange. What does the diary have to do with the train wreck you mentioned?"

"It may have a lot to do with it, and I think I can explain that to you better if we can meet face to face. Would it be convenient for me to come to your house tomorrow evening to meet with you and your mother?

"I guess that would be all right. Let me ask my husband."

A moment later a man came on the phone. "This is Charles Banks. I understand you're a reporter and want to come here tomorrow night to show my wife some diary her sister wrote. Is that right?

"Yes, it was found in the house where her sister lived before she died."

"How do I know you're a real reporter and not some con artist or something?"

"Oh, I'm a real reporter. I'll bring my press badge with me when I come. You can call my boss, Irv Sloan, at the Herald tomorrow if you want to verify that I work there."

After receiving the office number, Banks said, "Okay. I'm not sure what all this is about, but you've peaked my wife's interest in that diary. If you can get here around seven tomorrow, we'll be here. The address is 336 Water Street."

●　　●　　●　　●　　●

It was mid-morning the next day when Stan got a call from Glenn about the license plate check. "I was wondering when I'd hear from you," he said half-humorously.

"Yeah, it took a while for the DMV to get back with us. We did get an ID on the owner, and it wasn't Ray Bickle."

"That's a relief. Was it a guy named Gibbon?"

"Uh, no. The owner of the vehicle with the license plate number you gave is Frederick Noonan."

"What? That's nuts. Why would he be involved?"

"I can't say. I know it looks odd that it's somebody who we interviewed in connection with Bickle, but there's really no way to connect him to your accident. Maybe it was another car you thought was following you."

Stan shook his head. "No, it was the same car, same dent. Can't you call Noonan in and question him?"

"No," said Glen. "There's no nexus between the car you identified and whoever tampered with your brakes—no fingerprints, no witness. I even talked with Vic about bringing the guy in, but he said we just don't have enough to do anything like that."

"I just wonder if it's going to happen again—or something worse."

"You definitely need to stay alert—at least for a while. If you sense something wrong or find yourself in any kind of trouble, you know you can count on me to do what I can to help. Just don't go looking for trouble."

Stan laughed. "No, I won't."

It was a good hour's drive to Hillsboro, and after work he stopped off at the A&W drive-in for something to eat. Since getting his car back from the repair shop, he hadn't given much thought about the brakes going out again. But as he headed out of town, his mind swirled with questions as to how Noonan could have been involved in cutting his brake line. It couldn't be just a coincidence. He worried whether whoever it was might try again, and at each stop sign he stepped on the brakes cautiously to make sure nothing was amiss. Everything seemed normal. He got to Hillsboro shortly before seven without encountering any mechanical problems and was able to locate the Banks house on a pleasant tree-lined street just a block off the main drag.

Joyce Banks opened the door when he knocked and invited him into the living room where her husband and mother were sitting. After introductions were made, Charles said, "All right Mr. Ellis, you've raised our curiosity about the diary you say you have. Tell us what this is all about and how you're involved."

Stan started off from the beginning with Lucy's call to him and her admission and subsequent recantation about Ray Bickle's involvement with the train wreck. He told them he had all but given up on pursuing the matter until Lucy's mother called him about the diary Lucy had found in the house. "Based on what I've read, Ray Bickle may have had something to do with Alice's death. Maybe I'm reading too much into it. I never knew Alice. That's why I wanted you to see the diary and see what you think."

Charles said, "I only saw Bickle a few times when the family got together on holidays, but he seemed like a normal guy to me, good sense of humor. When he was here we joked, drank beer together, and talked about the railroad. Good horseshoe player, too."

Ruth, Alice's mother, spoke up. "You don't know nothing about him! I never liked him from first time I laid eyes on him. Alice told me some things that made my skin crawl, but she put up with it. I told her she should leave him, but she wouldn't listen."

"What kind of things?" Stan asked.

"Oh, they'd get into nasty arguments, and he'd get physical with her—actually hit her sometimes she said."

"Ma!" interjected Joyce. "Don't go telling such private stuff to strangers." She looked at Stan. "You said you had a diary to show us. Where is it?"

He pulled the diary from his jacket pocket and laid it on the coffee table in front of him. "I put markers in certain places that I thought were especially pertinent. I'd like you to look at those first and tell me what you think."

Joyce picked up the diary and opened it. Charles got up from his chair. "This don't involve me. I'm going to go watch TV.

When she finished reading the pages Stan had marked, Joyce shook her head, handed the book to her mother, and said to Stan, "Alice never told us about the affair Ray was having. We were shocked when she died like that, but we never suspected anything wrong since the doctor didn't find anything out of the ordinary other than she was awful young."

Stan said, "Bickle's current wife, Lucy, said he told her that Alice had a congenital heart problem and she smoked and that aggravated her condition. Do you know if she had any heart defect?"

"She smoked, but I never knew her to have any heart problem when we were growing up." She looked at her mother.

"No. She was an active child. She never had any heart problems I knew about."

Stan narrowed his eyes. "Interesting. You agree then that this was written by your daughter."

"Oh yes," said Ruth. "It's her handwriting."

Stan settled back on the sofa and waited for Ruth to finish reading the highlighted parts. When she did, she shook her head. "How could she have been so blind? Ray must have done something to her."

"I think so, too," said Stan. "Would you have a copy of the death certificate? I'd like to see what it says is the official reason for death."

"I did get a copy," said Ruth. "I'll go to my bedroom and look." She left the room, came back five minutes later, and handed him the document.

He looked over the certificate quickly. The cause of death was given as asphyxia and the manner of death was shown as natural. Primary factors were pulmonary edema combined with instances of cardiac arrhythmia. Contributing factors were listed as pneumonia and smoking. Noting the name Simon Crandall as the certifying physician, he said, "I don't see anything here about a congenital heart problem. Did you talk to this Dr. Crandall at all?"

"No," said Ruth. "Ray took care of everything. I never talked to the doctor."

Joyce said, "I talked to him. I asked him how she could die so young, and he really didn't have any good explanation other than her immunity was down and she wasn't able to ward off the pneumonia."

"I'd like to talk to him. Do you know where he practices?"

"He doesn't anymore. He died last year."

"Ah, not good!" Looking back at the sheet he saw a second signature, that of the county coroner, Clayton Marsh. "Maybe Doctor Marsh can provide some answers," he said. "Would you mind if I kept this certificate for a few days? I'll have a facsimile made and get the original back to you."

Ruth said, "Take it. I want to know the real reason why my daughter died like that. She was always such a healthy girl."

Stan looked again at the certificate that stated "natural" as the manner of death. "I think Ray poisoned her. But the only way we're going to be able to prove that is to have Alice's body exhumed. Are you willing to have that done?"

Joyce looked at her mother and then at Stan. "Yes. We would agree to that."

Stan picked up the diary from the coffee table and got up to go. "I'd like to keep the diary to show some other people. After I talk to the coroner, I'll let you know what I find out."

CHAPTER 26

Friday morning, the first thing Stan did when he got to his office was to make a call to the county coroner's office. It was located in town near the courthouse, an easy walk from the newspaper office. When he called, the office assistant confirmed that Clayton Marsh was still the coroner, and he was able to make an appointment for one o'clock.

While Stan was typing a story on an auto accident that occurred overnight, Irv came up to him and said, "What's happening on that new story you mentioned the other day. You said you were going to Elroy, but then you never mentioned it when you came back. What was that about?"

"Don't laugh, but it's about Bickle, the guy I thought was involved with the train wreck. I got a hold of a diary of his first wife, and in it she accused him of having an affair with Cashman's wife. Then she died under, what seemed to me, suspicious circumstances a few months later."

"I'm not laughing. What I think you're saying is that you believe this Bickle is guilty of outright murder."

Stan nodded his head. "That's right."

"We need to talk to Ed before you go any further. It's too hot to keep to yourself."

"I intend to, but there's something I want to do first. I talked with the woman's mother and sister last night and got a copy of the death certificate from them. It indicates there was no autopsy done. I have an appointment at one with the county coroner. I want to show him the diary and death certificate and see if he agrees with me about the suspicious nature."

"Okay, check in with me when you finish, and we'll go talk to Ed together."

•　　•　　•　　•　　•

The coroner's office was a stand-alone cement block building painted a plain government-gray. There was no one at the front desk when he walked in, but a door, evidently leading to the rear, was slightly ajar. He opened it and went into an open bay room where two men stood with their back to him studying something at a table. One, tall and thin with a full head of untamed white hair, wore a white lab coat. The other was much younger, short and stocky, and also wearing a lab coat. Neither seemed to notice anyone enter the room until Stan coughed to signal his presence.

Both men turned simultaneously. "Who are you?" asked the white-haired man.

"I'm Stan Ellis from the Sparta Herald. I had an appointment to see you at one. Are you Dr. Marsh?"

"Yes, I am. I must have forgot. Unexpected things come up around here, you know." He turned to his assistant. "We can finish working on Mr. Carey after I talk with Mr. Ellis."

The assistant left the room and went out to the front. The coroner removed his gloves and went to a nearby sink to clean his hands. While he was there, Stan glanced at a table in the center of the room where the man he had been tending to was stretched out with a sheet covering him up to his neck. There was an ugly gash in the center of his forehead. Stan's winced at the sight of the body. "Is that someone from this morning's car crash?

Marsh, wiping his hands with a towel, said, "Ah, yes. They brought him in a couple hours ago." Before reaching Stan, Marsh stopped at the table and pulled the sheet over the man's face. "You probably don't want to look at him."

"No. It's not a pleasant sight. If you're busy, I can come back later."

"No. He can wait," he said. "Poor fellow I suspect he drank too much for his own good. I'll know after I get the blood test results. Let's go back to my office."

Marsh taking a seat behind his metal desk said, "So what can I do for you Mr. Ellis?"

Stan pulled the death certificate from a coat pocket. "While working on a story, I've come across some information that makes me think a murder may have been committed. I have a copy of a death certificate of the woman involved. Her name was Alice Bickle. Your name is shown on the death certificate and I thought you might have some recollection of it."

Marsh frowned. "That name doesn't mean anything to me. May I see the death certificate?" Stan handed him the document and Marsh peered down at it. "I see I certified it, but I wasn't the attending physician. That was Doctor Crandall. I routinely certify death certificates like this for our physicians, but I don't personally get involved unless the death occurs as a result of an accident or some violence, that sort of thing. In this case, there was nothing to indicate that, and so I'm not sure why you are questioning the cause of death."

Stan pulled the diary out from another coat pocket. "I was given this diary that was written by Alice Bickle in the months leading up to her death. What she wrote made me think her husband may have poisoned her. He wanted a divorce. She wouldn't give it to him, and she accused him of being involved in causing a train wreck that happened a few months earlier. I've marked some pages that spell out what I'm saying."

Marsh took the diary from Stan, walked back to his microscope table, and sat down and began reading. When Stan coughed to draw his attention, he looked up and pointed to a bench with some magazines stacked on the end. "Oh, I'm sorry. Have a seat over there. I shouldn't take too long."

Stan sat down and sorted through the magazines until he found one he thought looked interesting—an April issue of *Scientific American* with a cover story on Poliomyelitis. After twenty minutes Marsh called Stan to his table and handed the diary back to him. "I do agree that what that woman went through is highly suspicious, but from what I read in the diary, I can't say definitively that her husband poisoned her. There are a lot of complications of pneumonia that can lead to death. Poisoning is probably the least likely possibility."

"But she was so young, barely thirty, and there was no autopsy done. What if the body were exhumed, could you do an autopsy and determine if there was an unnatural cause of death like poisoning?"

"If the body was exhumed, I suppose I could. But disinterment is not a simple thing. It's expensive and there are certain legal procedures that have to be followed. It has to be approved by a judge. It's not something I would do on my own. And as for determining whether a person was poisoned, I would really need to know what kind of poison I was looking for. There are different tests for different things. No—unless the sheriff's office or district attorney were to open an investigation and get a judge to order an exhumation, there's no way to change what's on that death certificate. I'm sorry, but my hands are tied."

Stan gave a disconsolate nod. "I understand. But you do think it looks suspicious?"

"Yes, I do, but that doesn't mean the original determination by Dr. Crandall was wrong. We in medical science have come a long way since Hippocrates, but we don't know everything yet—not even close. I don't begrudge you for asking the question, and if you can convince somebody in authority to take some action, I'd be glad to do my part."

⋅ ⋅ ⋅ ⋅ ⋅

When Stan returned to the office, Irv immediately called him over to his desk. "What'd you find out from the coroner?"

He basically agreed that the diary entries create some suspicion around the woman's death, but he said it's not enough to prove she was murdered. For that they'd have to exhume the body and have it examined, and that would require a judge's order. The only way to do that is to get the sheriff to commit to a new investigation. The sheriff's not going to listen to me, but do you think we could get Ed to push it for us?"

"Let me see that book," said Irv.

Stan went back to his desk to work on something else while Irv browsed through the diary. After a half-hour Irv said, "Let's go in and see the boss."

Ed waved the two of them into his office, and asked Irv, "How was the homecoming parade? Getting everything we need?"

"We got some good shots of the winning floats, and Rose is working up a story on the parade. Stan, here, will get a picture of the king and queen when they announce it at tonight's game. It'll all be ready for tomorrow."

"Good. Is that what you wanted to talk about?"

"Well no," said Irv. "Stan here has come up with some new information about this Ray Bickle who we earlier suspected of framing George Cashman for causing that train wreck."

Ed pursed his lips. "New information? What are you talking about?"

Stan spoke up. "I found a diary written by Bickle's wife. In it she says she refused Bickle when he demanded a divorce, and she accused him of having an affair with Cashman's wife. Shortly after that she started getting sick. A couple months after she died, Bickle married Cashman's ex-wife. Based on what I read, I think he poisoned his wife."

With obvious irritation Ed said, "I suppose you want to write a story and have us publish an accusation that Bickle murdered his wife. We'll be sued before the ink is dry on the paper."

"No, I know we can't do that. But I talked to the coroner, Clayton Marsh. He said that the only way to determine if she was poisoned would be to have the body exhumed and examined. To get that we'd need a judge's order which would probably have to be requested by the sheriff or the DA." He looked at Irv and then back to Ed. "We thought if you talked to the sheriff, he might be willing to—"

Ed held out his hand. "Show me the diary."

Stan and Irv waited silently for several minutes until Ed slammed the book shut. "There's not enough here for me to go to Bascom to ask him for anything, especially after what we already went through with that other woman who claimed she was having an affair with Bickle. After she recanted her story, nothing much you say about Bickle matters. He may be a son-of-a-bitch, but this diary doesn't show me he's a murderer."

Ed leaned forward with his arms stretched out on the desk, "I understand your concern for these women this guy's been involved with. You don't like him, and I don't either, but you're letting your emotions take over your good sense. Tonight you're covering the high school game. Put this aside for now, enjoy the game, and write me up a good story for tomorrow's paper." He leaned back, picked up a half-smoked cigar from his ashtray, and stuck it in the corner of his mouth. "Now get out of here, you got work to do and so do I."

That evening at six, Stan picked up Patty at her apartment, and they drove to the high school athletic field for the football game. On the way he filled Patty in on the events during the week—talking to Lucy's mother, getting the diary, meeting with the coroner, and then getting Ed's cold shoulder.

Patty just shook her head when he'd finished. "Bickle must be a real monster, but it almost seems like he has to be caught doing something else before anyone will pay attention. I don't think there's anything else you can do."

"Maybe you're right. I want to see what Glen thinks when we see him later."

When they got to the field, they met up with Glen and Carol and stopped at a refreshment stand for hot dogs and sodas before going over to the bleachers. Stan went to sit in a reserved seat right behind the home team's bench while the others went up higher.

The four of them met up at Clutter's Bar after the game for a late-night snack and beer. Stan unloaded to Glen about what had happened during the week and how he was almost certain that Bickle murdered his wife. When he finished, Glen said, "You've come up with some good stuff. You've almost convinced me that Bickle may have killed his first wife. But the people you need to convince, the sheriff and the DA, already went out on a limb based on that other woman's story, and it broke when she said she lied about everything. They're not going to go out on another limb without hard proof."

"What are you saying? I just drop the whole thing even though I think the guy tried to kill me by cutting the brake line on my car?"

Glen shrugged. "I just don't think you can get anybody in authority to listen to you, and I'm not in a position to help you either. The only thing I can think of is if you had a private attorney look into the matter, he might be able to push it from some legal angle. But I don't think you want to go paying an attorney."

Stan lowered his head and then looked up. "No, I don't. I guess that leaves me nowhere else to go." He checked his watch and turned to Patty. "I've still got to write up my game story for tomorrow's paper. We'd better get going. I'll drop you off.

CHAPTER 27

It was nearly two o'clock in the morning by the time he finished writing up his recap of the football game. Stan set his alarm clock for six and tried to sleep, but he laid awake for another half-hour thinking about what Glen had said about the possibility of getting a private attorney involved. He certainly couldn't afford to hire one, but there was one person he knew who might be interested enough to do it for free.

It sounded like a jackhammer pounding in his ears. Stan rolled over, saw the clock reading 6:00 a.m., and slammed his palm down on the alarm button. He started to pull the covers back over his head when he remembered he had to turn in his game story by seven. He dragged himself out of bed, went to the bathroom, splashed water on his face, and got dressed.

Although Irv wasn't in when he got to the newsroom, he dropped his story off with Cal for typesetting, and then hurried over to the photo lab next door and waited for the technician to finish developing the film he'd taken during the homecoming half-time. Satisfied that the pictures were front page material, he went back to his office and dropped the photos off on Irv's desk. At 8:30 he picked up the phone and dialed Anson Puller's number. The phone rang three times before someone picked up. "Office of Puller and Kline. May I help you?"

"Good morning. This is Stan Ellis. I'd like to speak to Mr. Puller. Is he in?"

"No, I don't know if he'll be in today. Saturday he doesn't normally see clients."

"I'm not a client, and I really need to see him. I met with Mr. Puller about a month ago concerning the George Cashman case. Mr. Puller told me if I came up with something new related to the case, to let him know. I have new information I think can help free Mr. Cashman. Can you give me his home number?"

"No, I can't do that. He sometimes comes in on Saturday, though, to catch up on work. If you'd like to leave a message, I'll pass it on. You may have to wait until Monday for him to get back to you."

Stan gave her his office and home phone numbers, and after slamming down the receiver, mouthed a silent obscenity that Rose, at the next desk, caught. With a curious smile, she said, "My—did somebody die or what?"

"As a matter-of-fact somebody did. But that's not my problem now." He got up from his desk, went outside, and walked around the block to blow off steam. Returning to the office, he waited impatiently for a return call. Finally at ten o'clock his phone rang. It was Anson Puller.

"My secretary told me you have some new information about the Cashman case."

"That's right," said Stan. "Would it be possible for me to come over and see you this morning?"

"This morning? I'm not sure I can see you today. I was planning on leaving shortly. If this concerns the wife of Cashman and her allegations about her new husband, I don't think there's any point in our discussing it. I talked to John Hamilton about that, and he told me all about how that investigation blew up when she recanted her story. Anything she'd have to say now wouldn't mean anything in court."

"No, it's not that. It's something else. I received a diary of Ray Bickle's first wife that gives evidence that he killed her to keep her quiet and to get her out of the way so he could marry Cashman's wife."

"Really! That's quite an allegation. You say you have a diary. How did you get it?"

"Lucy, Cashman's ex-wife, found it in a closet in Bickle's house."

"How do you know it's something Bickle's first wife wrote?"

"I showed it to the woman's mother, and she confirmed it."

"Sounds like you've done some homework. You got my radar antennae buzzing. Okay, I'll make some time to talk to you. Be here in a half-hour."

When he got to the attorney's office, there was no one in the waiting room except the secretary who told him he could go right in. Puller, wearing an open-neck shirt and casual trousers, was leaning back in his office chair reading a document. When Stan came into the office, he sat up straight, put the document down, and invited Stan to have a seat.

"I appreciate your seeing me this morning, Mr. Puller." He pulled the diary from his jacket pocket and held it up. "This is the diary that Alice Bickle's mother let me have temporarily. I think you'll find it real interesting. I believe what she wrote here implicates Ray Bickle in Alice's death. I believe he killed her to prevent people from discovering his involvement in causing the train wreck."

"How do you think he killed her?"

"I think he was poisoning her—putting something in her food."

"What makes you so convinced he would do something like that?"

"Because he tried to kill me, too. Somebody cut the brake line in my car. I went off the highway. Nearly ran into another vehicle. I'm sure it was him, but I can't prove it. I just know."

"I'm sorry to hear that, but without real proof, in the legal business, you're nowhere."

"Wouldn't you like to see Cashman freed? You said before you thought there was reasonable doubt."

"Sure I would. I was disappointed with the verdict, and especially the severe sentence that Cashman got, but I don't think that's very likely based on what you've told me. I've got paying clients I have to take care of. This guy may be an ass in your opinion, but I don't have time for playing Pin the Tail on the Donkey."

Stan leaned forward on the couch. "I've tried to get somebody in authority to do something about this guy, but nobody'll give me the time of day after what happened in the earlier investigation. You're the only person I could think of that might help me. Won't you at least look at the diary and see what you think."

Puller crossed his arms and looked off to the side. Then he said, "Okay, give me the diary."

Stan raised up and handed it to him, along with the copy of the death certificate. "Do you want me to wait here?"

"No," said Puller. "Wait outside, or go for a walk in the park for a half-hour and then come back. Give me a chance to look this over. Then I'll tell you what I think."

Stan came back from his walk and sat in the waiting room for another thirty minutes until Puller buzzed the secretary for Stan to come back in the office. When he entered, Puller looked up from the diary that was still open on his desk. "We've got a story of a cheating husband and some domestic abuse. Still doesn't prove murder. What is it you want me to do with this?"

"Yesterday I met with the coroner, Clayton Marsh, and showed him the diary. After he read it, he agreed that there was a possibility that the doctor who filled out the death certificate may not have known about all this other stuff, and he could have erred in calling it a natural death with no autopsy. But he said the only way to make sure was to exhume the body and do tests. That, he said, requires a judge's order. As a lawyer, you could initiate that request."

Puller smiled and shook his head. I have to admit, reading that diary raises a lot of questions about this Bickle, and I love a legal challenge, but this—

"I talked to Alice Bickle's mother. She said she would support exhuming the body. She wants to know the answer."

"You're really committed to this aren't you, Ellis."

"Yes sir, I am."

Puller leaned back in his chair and began rubbing his chin thoughtfully. "Say I decided to take this on as a pro bono project. You've been at the Bickle house haven't you?"

"Yes. I went there to meet with his wife Lucy."

"The only way to convince a judge that this Alice Bickle was poisoned is if there's evidence that he kept certain kinds of poisons in the house. Do you think you could get back into the house? I'm not talking about breaking and entering, but you seemed to have some kind of relationship with the new wife. Maybe she'd let you in to look around."

"She did trust me before, but I don't know about now."

He pushed the diary to the front of the desk. "Unless you can get me some evidence that shows Bickle had the means, as well as the motive, to poison his wife, there's nothing I can do. It's up to you."

Stan got up from the couch, walked up to the desk, and picked up the diary. "Okay. I need to think how I should do this. I'll let you know when I come up with something."

·   ·   ·   ·   ·

After work Stan picked up Patty at her apartment around six o'clock for a dinner date at Hoffman's. He was bursting to tell her about his meeting with Puller, but he wasn't sure how she would react. He wasn't even sure he should tell her anything at all about what he intended to do. He didn't want to spoil the mood for supper, and so he avoided talking about it while they were at the restaurant.

Later that evening, when they returned to her apartment, Patty took out some snacks from the pantry, opened a can of beer for Stan and a Coke for herself, and brought them to the living room where Stan was obviously mulling over something. She went to turn on the television, and he said, "Wait, I need to talk to you about something."

She came back to the couch and sat next to him. "Must be important to miss *Gunsmoke*."

"It is. I talked to Anson Puller today about helping me to get an exhumation order for Alice Bickle. He said he would."

Her eyes became silver dollars. "Really! Just like that?"

"He had one condition. I have to go to Bickle's house and find the poisons that he could have used to kill his wife."

"You can't do that! I won't let you."

"You gotta let me do this. I could call her mother. I think Lucy would let me in her house when Bickle isn't around if her mother explains to her that I've talked to Alice's family and I'm working with an attorney."

"This is too dangerous, Stan. You can't do it."

"I have to get to the bottom of this. I've gone too far to stop now. At least I can call Lucy's mother to see what she thinks."

"It's too late. It's nine o'clock."

"I'm sure she's still up. She won't mind."

"Stan, I think you're crazy. If I didn't love you so much, I'd have you admitted to the asylum."

"I love you too, Patty." He smiled, took her hand, and gently squeezed it. "Now I need to use your phone." He got up and went to the kitchen phone, pulled a notepad from his pocket, and flipped back pages until he came to the one with Helen Grim's name and phone number. He dialed the number, and after three rings, she picked up.

"Hello?"

"Hello Mrs. Grim? This is Stan Ellis. From the Sparta Herald."

"I was just thinking about you and wondering what you'd done with the diary. Are the police going to do more investigating?"

"At this point they're not, but I showed it to Alice Bickle's mother who lives in Hillsboro, and I've talked with the county coroner who thinks there's a possibility she was poisoned, but it would require the body to be exhumed and examined."

"Oh my lands. That's a drastic step. Is that even possible?"

"It is, but a judge has to authorize it. I talked to a local attorney who said he might take on the case, but he said I'd have to find him some evidence of poison that Bickle might have been keeping in his house. I can't go there when Bickle is home, and I'm not sure Lucy wants me to call, so I'm asking you if you would call Lucy to find out when Bickle will be away and if she even wants me in her house."

"I think I can get her to agree to that. Actually, I'd like you to go check on her anyway, because when I talked to her on the phone yesterday she said she's been having stomach upsets and headaches again—and even some trouble breathing like she's coming down with pneumonia or something. I don't want to bother her tonight, but I'll call tomorrow morning and let you know."

He gave her both his and Patty's telephone numbers and thanked her. As he hung up the phone, Patty was standing by the couch staring at him with her arms crossed. "What did she say?"

"She's going to call Lucy and let me know when Bickle is out of the house. She was actually glad I called. She said Lucy's been having some stomach problems and wanted me to check on her. So as soon as she calls and gives me the go-ahead, I'll drive down there and see what I can find."

"I don't like it. Especially you going alone. If you go, I'm going with you."

"That's not necessary."

"I think it is."

"Oh, all right. Come along if you want."

"I want. Besides, if she's having some health problems, you may be glad to have a nurse with you."

CHAPTER 28

Stan was relaxing in an armchair reading the Sunday Journal's sports page when Helen Grim called. "I just got off the phone with Lucy," she said. "She agreed to have you come by, but Ray is home today, so you have to wait. He's supposed to go to work tomorrow morning, not sure exactly when, and he won't be back until Wednesday evening. She said he's taking the car, so if the driveway is empty you should be okay."

"All right. I'll go over there tomorrow evening. I have a friend who's a nurse who'll be coming with me."

"Oh, I'm glad to hear that. Lucy said she's still feeling under the weather, ever since last week."

• • • • •

Monday afternoon, Stan stopped by the hospital to pick up Patty as she was getting off work. It was raining and Patty came running to the car with her jacket draped over her head. As she got in the car, he asked, "What's that you have with you?" He pointed to a leather case she was holding in her lap."

"It's my medical kit. I thought it might be useful since you said Lucy's been sick. I brought along a syringe and vial to take a blood sample if we need it."

"I hadn't thought of that. Brilliant idea Watson."

It began raining soon after they left and was still pouring down when they arrived at Bickle's house forty minutes later. Before getting out of the car Stan took off his jacket and gave it to Patty to put over her head, then they both rushed thirty feet to the covered porch. Stan knocked on the door, and after a few seconds a young boy's voice came from the other side, "Who's there?"

"It's Stan Ellis. Are you Billy? Your mother's expecting me."

He heard the deadbolt lock release, and the door slowly opened to show a blonde-headed boy about five feet tall in blue jeans and a tee shirt staring up at him. Stan held out his hand. "Hi, I'm Stan. This is my friend Patty. Can we come in?"

"Sure," he said without smiling. "My mom's not feeling good. She's lying down in the living room."

Stan gave Patty a worried look. He took off his soaked shoes at the entrance and Patty did the same. When they went into the living room, Lucy was wearing a bathrobe and getting into a sitting position on the couch. "I'm sorry you have to see me this way, but I just didn't feel like getting dressed today." She started coughing and then added, "I called in sick for work today. I don't think I have a fever, just nausea, body aches, and some shortness of breath at night."

"Don't apologize," Stan said. "I'm glad we came when we did," said Stan. "This is a friend of mine, Patty McGowan. She's a nurse, and maybe she can help diagnose what's happening with you."

Patty smiled and said, "Have you seen a doctor since starting to feel this way?"

Lucy nodded. "Yes, Dr. Bradford came over a couple days ago. He couldn't see anything particularly wrong with me, other than possibly getting some bronchitis. He gave me some antibiotic, and I'm taking it. I think it's helped some."

Stan said, "Since you let us in, I'm presuming your mother filled you in on why I wanted to come see you."

"Yes, she told me you think Ray murdered Alice and you want to see if there are any kinds of poisons lying around that he could have used. If you'd come to me with that idea a couple weeks ago I would have kicked you out of my house. But after some of the things Ray's said since, I want to find out myself."

"Do you think he could have put something in your food to make you sick?"

"I've tried to think. We've got cleaning supplies that are marked poison, and we've got iodine in the medicine cabinet."

"What about the things growing in the yard?" Patty asked.

Lucy shrugged. "There's lots of different flowers, bushes, vegetables."

"Do you know their names? Some could be poisonous."

"I never thought of flowers being poisonous. I know we have hydrangea and forsythia. And there's lily of the valley along the side of the house. When they're in bloom, they make a nice table setting. I told Mr. Ellis before that my husband's the gardener, and he spends a lot of time in the yard taking care of everything. I help him some with canning pickles and vegetables, but I don't know much what he does other than that."

"If you don't mind," said Patty, "I'd like to take a sample of your blood to have tested to see if there's any evidence of any poisonous substance in your body."

She shrunk away from Patty, crossing her arms tightly against her chest. "Is that necessary?"

"I really think it is."

She let her arms relax to her sides. "Okay, if you think so."

Stan got up from his chair. "While Patty checks you out, I'm going to go around the house and see if I can find anything that looks suspicious."

He went to the kitchen and looked under the sink and found no obvious poisons other than a can of drain cleaner that contained lye. He took out his notepad and wrote it down, even though he doubted that Bickle would use that for food poisoning. Seeing nothing else of interest on the first floor, he went up to the second floor bathrooms. He looked through the medicine cabinets, but the only potentially dangerous things he found there were bottles of aspirin and iodine. He went back downstairs to the living room where Lucy was watching television with Billy. When he came in the room, she turned and said, "Did you find what you were looking for?"

Stan shook his head. "No, not yet, but I'm not finished. You said you helped your husband can vegetables. Where does he keep the canned goods?"

"He keeps all that stuff on racks in the basement."

"How do I get down there?"

Billy jumped up off the couch. "I'll show you. I know where things are."

Stan smiled. "Great, I could use a helping hand." As they walked down the steps to the basement, he said, "Last time I was here, you had a black and white cat. You like animals?"

"Yeah, but we don't have it anymore."

"What happened?"

"We think it ran away. It was my mom's cat, and she was really upset, but Ray said he'd get her another one."

When they got to the bottom of the stairs, he flicked a wall switch to cast a dim light from an overhead bulb. An oil furnace and water heater, both looking quite new, were in the center of the large open space separated by supportive I-beams. Old furniture was stacked up here and there. Off to one side was a ringer washing machine next to a deep sink set against the wall. A workbench with a variety of hand tools hanging from wall hooks was on the far side of the basement. "I don't see any jars of canned goods. Where does he keep it?"

"Back there," said Billy, pointing to an enclosed room toward the rear of the basement.

As they entered the room Billy pointed to a light chain above, and Stan reached up and turned on the light revealing a room about eight-foot square. A wooden worktable was set against the back wall and six-foot high wooden shelving stood on the two side walls. An open toolbox was sitting on one side of the table next to an electric mixer. There was a tiny scale and a Bunsen burner with a hose running off the side of the table. He looked underneath the workbench and saw a propane gas tank. Next to the gas tank was a small bag of cat food. Curious place to keep cat food, he thought. Wonder if it has anything to do with the cat going missing?

He eyed the shelving on the left side. The lower shelves had empty jars, tin containers, and floral vases. The two upper shelves were filled with quart and pint jars labeled with their contents including sweet pickles, dill pickles, pickled beets, corn, and stewed tomatoes. On the other wall, a row of books filled a lower shelf. The bindings were visible, and he scanned the titles. The first few were on gardening and landscaping. A thick volume titled *Encyclopedia of Plants* anchored the little library. He pulled it from the shelf and opened it. The cover was worn, and the pages were beginning to yellow. He looked at the publication date—1928. Too old to be something Bickle bought for himself. The last two books on the shelf caught his attention. One was titled *Botanical Guide to Toxic Plants* by Dr. Edward Glazer. The other was titled *Plant and Herbal Pharmacology* by Hans Drubeck. He took it off the shelf, glanced through the table of contents and checked the publication date—1950. A simple gardener wouldn't need those kinds of books, he thought while writing the titles and authors down on his notepad.

Above the books were more jars. But these were filled with dried materials, and marked with a single letter, T, S, B, A, D, C. He opened the top of the first one with "T" on the label. It had a familiar smell, but couldn't quite place it. He opened the one on the other end, "C". The purplish powdered material didn't seem to have any smell. He put the jars back and looked at the upper shelf. There were six cardboard boxes on the upper shelf. Each had something written on the side. He took the first box down. It was very light. He read what it said on the side: Thymus. He opened the box and found dried, crushed herbs. He bent down and smelled. It was thyme, the same as the powder in the first bottle. He closed the box and put it back on the shelf and took down the end box that was labeled Convallaria. It contained more dried and crush plant material, but was mixed with little pearl-white balls. He leaned close and smelled a pleasantly sweet fragrance, but he couldn't identify it with anything. He looked in the other two boxes. They too contained dried and crushed plant material. One was marked with the words Digitale Purpurea. The other hand was labeled Aconitum. The words must be Latin, he thought, and each box must match up with one of those bottles of powder. He didn't know what it all meant, but he thought Dr. Marsh might be able to tell him. He drew three small paper envelopes from his pocket, picked out a sample from each box, wrote the Latin name on each, and stuffed them back into his pocket.

He put the boxes back on the shelf where he found them, turned around to go, and saw Billy still standing there watching him intently. "I forgot you were here. You've been so quiet. Do you have any idea what Ray was doing down here with all these dried plants and stuff?"

Billy shook his head. "He never let me come in this room when he was here. He told me to stay away."

"Let's go upstairs and talk with your mother."

When Stan and Billy entered the living room, Patty was just putting some instruments back into her bag. "Did you find anything of interest?" she asked.

"I think I did," said Stan. "He's got a workroom down there that raises a few questions in my mind." He looked at Lucy. "I know you said that Ray was into gardening, but from what I saw in his workshop, it looks like it's more like a biology lab than just a casual hobby. It doesn't fit my image of him. How'd he get so interested?"

Lucy thought for a moment. "It was his grandfather I'm sure. He was a biology teacher at the high school. Ray grew up here with his grandparents."

"Yes, your mother told me."

"The big garden and the flowers you saw in the backyard—that's all what his grandfather made. He and Ray were very close. Ray told me more than once that his grandfather taught him everything he knew about gardening, and he wanted to keep the place just like he did."

"That explains some of the books in his workshop, but why does a gardener need a book on pharmacology and toxic plants? Why does he have dried crushed plant material in boxes with Latin descriptions? Why does he need a Bunsen burner and electric mixer in his garden shop?"

She shook her head. "I don't know what he had down there. He told me to stay out of his workshop area. He said it was his special place."

"It looked to be a *very* special place," said Stan. He turned back to Patty. "Were you able to tell what's ailing Lucy?"

"No, I couldn't find anything definite. She doesn't have a fever. I took a blood sample and told her I'd get it tested and let her know the results."

"Good. We've got what we came for." He put his hand on Billy's shoulder and addressed Lucy. "You've got a very bright son here. He was a big help to me. I'm going to talk to the county coroner about what I found, and we'll have to see what transpires from that. I'm concerned about whether you'll be safe when Ray comes back home."

"We'll be okay. He sometimes flies off the handle, but I don't believe he'll do anything to harm us."

"All right. I'll be back in touch—if not direct, then through your mother."

He bent down to shake Billy's hand, and the two of them left. Not until they started driving back to Sparta was Stan able to tell Patty what he'd discovered in the basement.

It looks to me like Bickle has toxic plant material in his basement workshop. I found a bag of cat food there too."

Patty looked puzzled. "Why is cat food a problem?"

"I don't think it belongs there. Billy told me when we were going downstairs that the cat turned up missing not too long ago. He said his step-dad told him it ran away. I'm thinking maybe Bickle was using the cat to experiment with his poisons."

"Do you really think so?"

"Could be." He pulled the envelopes containing the plant samples from his pocket and handed them to Patty. "Do you recognize the names?" She glanced at what he'd written and shook her head. "No, I don't know what they are, but I can ask at work."

"I'll show what I have to Dr. Marsh. I'm sure he'll know. What are you going to do with the blood sample?"

"I'll ask Mary Pierson in the medical lab if she'll do some tests for me."

"If this shows that he's poisoning Lucy, then that should be enough to get him arrested."

"I just hope we're in time. I'm worried about what her husband will be doing between now and when we can find out the test results."

"I worry about that too, but she seems confident she'll be okay."

CHAPTER 29

"Patty called you and wants you to call her back," said Rose. Stan, just returning from an interview with the county commissioner, hung up his jacket and cap, went to his desk, and dialed Patty's office number. "What's up?"

"I talked to Mary about doing the blood test. She was going to do it, but when Dr. Reynolds found out, he said we couldn't do it unless there was an order for a lab test from the coroner."

"That'll take more time. I was going to go and talk to Dr. Marsh after lunch anyway. I wanted to show him what I collected and, hopefully, get confirmation that it contains poison. If it is, I'm sure he'll order the tests."

Stan had called the coroner's office to make an appointment at one, but when he got there, the coroner's assistant at the front desk told him that Dr. Marsh had been called away because of a drowning at Perch Lake, and he didn't know when to expect him back.

"When did he leave?"

"He left about two hours ago."

"I'll wait," he said, but after an hour, Stan decided he needed to get back to work, and told the assistant he'd check back later. At five thirty he left his office and drove back to the coroner's office. There was one car, a black Chrysler, in the parking lot. He grabbed the paper bag he'd brought along and went to the front door. When he tried it, it was locked, and there was no light visible in the lobby. He went around to the side of the building where there was another door, and there was a light coming from a window in the back. He knocked on the door, and after a few moments Clayton Marsh, his white hair askew, opened the door. "Mr. Ellis! What are you doing here at this hour?"

"A couple days ago I talked to you about Alice Bickle and what it would take to exhume her body and do an autopsy. You said you'd need to have some kind of evidence that she'd been poisoned. I think I found it."

Marsh's eyes brightened. "Come in. Let's go back to my office." He walked Stan past the examining table where the body of a young man in his teens was laid, a sheet covering his lower half. The body looked serene and unmarked, as if the boy were sleeping. "Is that the drowning victim?"

"Yes," said Marsh. "Poor boy evidently tried to swim across the lake with another boy. The other one made it, but he didn't."

In the office Stan sat down on the faux leather couch opposite Marsh's desk and waited for him to finish filling and lighting his pipe. Marsh took two strong drags, blew out a puff of smoke, then leaned back in his chair. "What have you come up with Mr. Ellis?"

After talking with you, I met with Anson Puller, he's an attorney. Do you know him?"

"Yes I do. Good man."

"Well, he suggested I try to talk to Bickle's current wife, Lucy, to let me in the house when Bickle's not around to see if I could find any kind of poisons. I did that yesterday, and I found a workshop he had in the basement where he had bottles of ground up plant material and several boxes of dried flowers and leaves—all of them labeled." He opened the paper bag at his side, pulled out three small packets, and laid them on the desk in front of Marsh. "Some of what he had is ordinary garden herbs such as thyme and sage. These three I don't know exactly what they are, but I believe they contain some type of poison and that Bickle was adding small amounts to his wife's food. I wrote the name on each packet. I thought you would be able to identify them."

Marsh leaned forward and looked at the envelopes. "Yes, its taxonomic nomenclature. He opened the envelope marked 'Digitale." took a pinch of the contents between his thumb and forefinger and smelled. "Not sure what the common name is," he said. "Digitale is a substance often used in cardiac-related drugs, but it can be dangerous, causing cardiac arrhythmia, if applied in the wrong doses." He turned around in his chair and picked out a book from a shelf behind him and began reading. After a moment, he said, "Ah! Foxglove is the common name." After reading further, and jotting down some notes on a writing pad, he closed the book, laid his pipe in an ashtray, and picked up the envelope marked Convallaria and began flipping pages in the book. "This one is lily of the valley," he said, holding up the envelope. "It says here the flowers as well as the leaves and root contain toxic glycosides. Some of the early symptoms of ingestion include nausea, headaches, blurry vision, and diarrhea that can lead to cardiac arrhythmia, respiratory difficulty, and death if left untreated." He picked up the third envelope marked Aconitum and flipped through more pages. "Ah! This is the real baddie. Its common name is monk's hood, and it says here, it contains both neuro toxins and cardio toxins that will cause paralysis of the heart and respiratory system. It wouldn't take much. If somebody was trying to poison another person, this would do it quickly." He closed the book and held both hands to his cheeks without looking up.

Stan slapped his hands together. "I knew it! He was poisoning his first wife."

Marsh jerked his head up and raised both his arms in the air. "Hold on just a minute. Just because there were poisonous substances found in the home, doesn't, by itself, give us the authority to disinter a body. After combining this with what was in that diary, there is more than circumstantial evidence of some misdoings, but I'm not in a position to ask a judge to order exhumation—not yet. Now you said you've been talking with Anson Puller. If he wants to initiate a request through the DA— "

Stan flapped his long arms as if he wanted to ask a question of his schoolteacher. "But Dr. Marsh, I don't think it's just Bickle's first wife. I think he may be trying to do something to Lucy, his current wife, too."

"What?"

"Yes, Lucy's been experiencing some of those symptoms you've mentioned over the last couple weeks—nausea, dizziness, weakness, heart palpitations. They sound similar to what Alice Bickle wrote in her diary."

Marsh scratched his chin. "Do you think she'd be willing to come in to give me a blood sample?"

"No need," said Stan. "My girlfriend who's a nurse at Memorial Hospital went with me to see Lucy and she got a blood sample. She took it to the hospital lab, but she said Dr. Reynolds told her they couldn't do it without an order from you identifying what he has to look for."

"Reynolds? Yes, he's the head pathologist there. I'll talk to him in the morning and put in an order for the tests. It may take a few days to get the results."

When Stan left the coroner's office, he drove directly to Patty's apartment. He was almost breathless with excitement when he sat down on her couch. "Dr. Marsh is going to put in a request in the morning for your lab to do tests on Lucy's blood. He said it might take a few days."

Patty sat down beside him. "Even if they rush, it'll probably take at least three days. This is Tuesday. So maybe Friday, Thursday at the earliest."

"I wish it were sooner. I hope nothing happens to Lucy in the meantime. I'm going to call Anson Puller tomorrow morning to see if I can get in to talk to him, let him know what we've done, and see if he can pull any strings."

"I'm glad you're getting somebody else involved with this. I don't want you doing anything more on your own."

"I won't."

"Take your jacket off and relax. Jackie Gleason's on tonight. You could use a little humor to get your mind off that Bickle business."

"No, I've gotta get going. I just wanted to let you know about my meeting with the coroner. I've got something I need to finish up for tomorrow's paper. I know you have to go to work tomorrow early too, so I'll get out of your hair."

"All right. I'll let you go." She started up from the couch. "Oh, I almost forgot. My parents invited both of us to their house for Sunday dinner. You don't have anything else planned do you?"

"No. Sunday sounds good. Maybe by then this thing with Bickle will be over and the cops will have him arrested. I'll bet anything that he was the one who messed with my brakes."

"I hope it's over too, but things don't usually work that quickly."

She walked him to the door and gave him a long kiss to see him off.

At one o'clock the next afternoon, Stan walked into the Puller and Kline Law Office and told the secretary he was there to see Mr. Puller. "He's expecting you. You can go right in." He smiled to himself. How things had changed. When he entered the inner office, Puller got up from behind his desk and greeted him with a handshake.

"Good to see you Stan." He pointed to the leather sofa along the wall "Have a seat I understand you found something at Bickle's place."

"That's right. I found several boxes of crushed plant material in his basement. Each one was labeled with its biologic name. Last night I took some samples to Dr. Marsh. Although he didn't do any tests right then, he said three of the plants shown on the labels were highly toxic. Bickle also had several jars of powders. It looked like he'd ground up the plants like you'd use for seasoning food. But Dr. Marsh said he'd need to examine Bickle's wife's body in order to determine if she'd actually been poisoned."

Puller leaned back in this chair and nodded. "I'll give a call to Dr. Marsh and see if he's done any testing on the plant material and see what direction he plans to go regarding any exhumation. Anything else you find?"

"Bickle's current wife, Lucy, has been sick and I think he's been poisoning her too. Patty, my girlfriend, was with me. She's a nurse, and she took a blood sample for testing at the hospital. They won't test it without a physician's order, but Dr. Marsh said that he would do that today. Hopefully, that's been done."

Puller nodded, a look of concern on his face. "When you went to Bickle's house, who was there?"

"Just Lucy and her eleven-year-old son Billy."

"You said she was sick. How sick?"

"She took off work. Seemed more like flu symptoms."

"What about the boy?"

"He's okay, but she said she normally gives him something other than what she eats. I think she's being more cautious now. But I'd like to get those lab results back so we can know for sure. Is there anything you can do to speed up the process?"

"No, the docs are not going to be swayed by an attorney." He patted a thick file folder on his desktop "I've been reviewing the Cashman case, and I think if what you found pans out, I may be able to convince a judge to order a retrial."

"That would be great. But Cashman probably won't be able to pay you. You're okay with that?"

"If he's proven not guilty and released because of a false conviction, the state will be on the hook for quite a bit. I'll get something out of that, but that's not why I'm willing to take this on. I felt there was enough reasonable doubt in the first place for a not guilty verdict, and I don't like losing."

"If the lab results show poison, will that be enough to arrest Bickle? Lucy wants so much to get away, but she's afraid, and for good reason."

"If that proves out, I'll go directly to John Hamilton and show him what we've got. I'm pretty sure he'll have the sheriff pick him up. Now as to getting a judge to agree to an exhumation, that's another process that will take time. Then getting this to trial is another hurdle, and I can't even guarantee it'll get to trial. But if the blood tests prove out, it should be enough to get him arrested, and then your Lucy friend will be free to get away."

"It's got to go to a trial. A guy like Bickle is a danger to society."

CHAPTER 30

Friday came, and Stan still hadn't any word on the test results. Chatting with Irv during a coffee break, he asked, "Did you see the AP story yesterday about Ike's agreement to meet with the Soviets and Britain to ban nuclear testing?"

"I didn't," said Irv, "But it's about time they did something. Just about every month it seems the Soviets are doing some test in Siberia and then the U.S. follows with a bigger one in the Pacific. Eventually they'll get one that can blow up the whole damn earth in one shot."

Esther, the office bookkeeper, interrupted their conversation. "The phone's ringing on your desk, Stan."

He went over and picked it up. It was Helen Grim. He'd called her the day after going to Lucy's house to let her know what they'd found, but he hadn't talked to her since.

"Hi Helen. I'm sorry I haven't called you all week. You're probably wondering about the lab results..."

"Yes," she said in a wavering voice. "I do want to know about that, but I'm calling because I'm worried about Lucy."

Stan's heart began beating faster. "Why? Has anything happened?"

"I'm not sure. I've tried to call Lucy twice this morning, but she hasn't answered. I called where she works, and they said Ray called in to say she's sick. I'd go over there and check myself, but I don't drive, and the friend I usually rely on is out of town today. I wasn't sure who else to call except you."

"It sounds like Ray's home. I don't think it'd be a good idea for me to go there. Did you call the police in Kendall?"

"I haven't. Do you think I should?"

"Yes. Call them and ask them to check on her. If you run into any problem, call me back. I'm still waiting on the blood test results. The hospital's working on it, and I'll let you know when I find out something."

Waiting for the test results was unnerving, and five minutes after getting off the phone with Helen, he made a call to the hospital to talk to Patty. He had to leave a message and waited another fifteen minutes before she returned his call.

"Any news yet on the test results?"

Sounding a bit annoyed, she said, "I told you I'd let you know as soon as I found out anything. I know it's important, but the hospital has other things going on too. Just be patient, and I'll call you."

He hung up and tried to concentrate on finishing up a story on local fishermen who competed in The Angler's Choice Tournament at Lake Geneva over the weekend. After getting half-way through, he stopped typing, and told Irv, "I'm going to go over to the courthouse and check on this week's court docket."

The courthouse was an excuse to get away from the office. He wanted to meet with Dr. Marsh to see if he'd found anything more. As he got in his car he failed to notice a dark green Plymouth parked across the street. He stopped at the courthouse as he said he would, and after collecting information that he needed, he drove on to the county mortuary. When he got there, the mortuary assistant at the front desk told him that Dr. Marsh was out on a case, but should be back soon. It was a half-hour before the doctor returned. When he entered the lobby, Stan got up to greet him, but Marsh spoke first. "I haven't got any news yet on the test results if that's what you're here for."

"I know I'm being impatient," said Stan. "I just wanted to check with you."

"These things take time. There's a chance we could get something back from the lab by the end of the day, but it may be longer."

. . . . .

Stan left the coroner's office with an empty feeling in his stomach. He wanted to do something, but there was nothing he could do. When he got back to the office, he sat down at his desk and was about to get back into the fishing story, when Esther walked up to his desk, and said with a hushed voice and a slight grin. "You had a call while you were out. Some woman—she didn't give her name—said that her husband has left, and won't be back until tomorrow. She said she needed to show you something she found at the house. Sounds exciting."

He looked at her with a pained look on his face and pushed his chair back from his desk. "No, it's not what you're thinking. I'm not having an affair with somebody's wife. It's a domestic abuse case I've been working on. Irv and Ed know all about it."

He pondered what it could mean. What else could she have found? He opened up his desk drawer and drew out a memo pad where he'd written down her telephone number. He dialed the number, but after four rings there was no answer. Maybe she's outside doing something. Helen never called me back, so everything must be okay, he thought. He put the memo pad back in his desk and worked through his lunch hour on his article. When he finished and turned the story into Irv he said, "I'd like to take the afternoon off and go to Kendall to do some follow-up on Lucy Bickle."

He looked up from the copy on his desk. "Is this related to what you've been talking to the coroner about? Possible poisoning?"

"Yes, it is. Lucy called and said she found something and wanted me to come and look at it while her husband is gone. I'll just go there, see what she has, and be out of there."

"Don't you think you ought to leave it to the police at this point?"

"So far they haven't been willing to do anything. The coroner is waiting on some lab tests that will give the cops a reason to arrest Bickle, but not sure when that'll come."

"Okay. Go, but be careful."

Before leaving, he stopped at his desk and called the hospital to talk to Patty. She wasn't happy when she answered the phone. "I told you I'd call you when the results came back. They're not here yet."

"No," he said. "I'm not calling about that. I got a call from Lucy that she found something else and wants me to come to her house so she can show it to me."

"Let the police handle it. I don't want you going near that place alone."

"I've been in this thing from the start, and I need to see it through. Bickle's not home, she said, so there's no danger. But I'll stop at the local police station in Kendall and check in with them."

"I'm going to call Glenn and tell him he needs to meet you at the police station. Don't go to the house until he gets there."

Stan chuckled. "You think they're going to dispatch Glen to Kendall to babysit me. I doubt it. But okay I'll wait there at the police station. I love you." After hearing her say, "Me too," he hung up.

.   .   .   .   .

It was quarter to two by the time he reached Kendall. The police station was a small office tucked inside the village hall on Main Street that included two or three other administrative offices, a small library, and a gymnasium that doubled as a public meeting place. When he walked in the office, he saw a lone figure in a khaki shirt and pants sitting at a desk looking at a magazine. He appeared to be in his twenties, with blonde, longish hair that grew untidily over his ears and down the nape of his neck. "I'm looking for Chief Chapman," he said.

The young officer dropped the magazine, spun around in his chair, and looked up with an easy-going smile. "He's not here today. He went hunting up north. I'm his deputy. Anything I can do for you?"

"Maybe. I'm Stan Ellis. I'm a reporter with the Sparta Herald. I came down this way to talk to Lucy Bickle about a story I'd been working on with her. Her mother called me early today and said she couldn't get a hold of her. I told her she should call you to check on her. Did she do that?"

"Yep. About nine o'clock. I went out there and talked to her husband Ray. I didn't see her. He said she was sleeping late because she hadn't been feeling so good, but he got some medicine from the doctor, and she should be better."

"Oh, so her husband was there? Her mother was very worried about her. Don't you think you should've gone in and checked her yourself?"

The officer shrugged his shoulders. "No reason to question him. I've known Ray for years. He's a little older than me, but my brother used to hang out with him quite a bit. An okay guy in my book. I don't know if he's still home. He said he had to go to work sometime today."

Stan crossed his arms and looked away while the deputy continued talking. This guy's going to be no help, he thought. Got to be careful what I say to him.

"I read in our local paper a couple weeks ago about someone looking into Lucy Bickle's ex-husband and whether he should get a new trial or something. Were you working on that?"

"Yeah, I was."

"So, anything come of that? I hadn't heard anything lately."

"It kind of all fell apart. But I got a call from Mrs. Bickle that she had some new information, and so that's why I came down today."

"I hope you find what you're looking for. I know Ray works on the railroad and probably knew her ex. He might be a good source for you."

"Yeah, possibly. I'll be sure to talk to him if he's still there." Stan leaned his chin into the palm of one hand, wondering if Patty had been able to reach Glen, and if he was on his way. "Would you mind if I used your phone to make a call back to Sparta?"

"Well, we normally want to keep it open for official calls, but if you don't take too long, I guess it'd be okay."

Stan picked up the receiver, dialed the number to the hospital switchboard, and was transferred to Patty's nurses' station. The nurse who answered said that Patty was with a patient. She didn't know how long she would be and asked if he wanted to leave a message. "That's all right," he said. "I'll call back later."

He put down the phone and said, "I was expecting a friend to meet me here, but I'm not sure when he's going to show. I'm going over to the Bickle place now. If my friend shows up tell him where I went, will you?"

"Sure will," said the deputy.

. . . . .

Stan turned onto Hardy Road. As he drew near the house, he slowed down and looked to make sure the driveway was empty before pulling in and parking. Even though Lucy's message had said Ray had gone, he didn't want to take a chance that he was still there. He parked the car, went up on the porch, and knocked on the door, once, twice, three times. No answer. He tried the doorknob, and it was unlocked. He opened it and went in. It was quiet. He called out, "Lucy are you home? This is Stan Ellis." No answer.

He walked slowly through the living room, peeked into the kitchen, and then walked down the hallway to where he thought the master bedroom was. The door was closed, and he opened it slowly. It was three in the afternoon, but the shades were pulled down and the room was dark. He could see someone lying in the bed, and walked over and saw it was Lucy, covered up to her chin with a light blanket. Her chest rose and fell gently under the cover, but her breathing sounded wheezy. He touched her arms and shook her lightly. "Lucy, wake up."

Lucy moved her head slightly and let out a low groan. Her eyes flickered open. Who? Who are you?"

"Stan Ellis. You called me a couple hours ago. Said you had some information."

"I... I didn't call," she said groggily.

"Who called me then?"

"I dunno."

"Where's Ray?"

She moved her head slowly from side to side and coughed. "Last thing I remember he gave me some pills to help me sleep. I was sick last night."

"Can you get up?"

She pushed back the covers and tried to rise up, but she fell back. "I can't. I feel so weak. I'm dizzy. I have a headache." She took in a deep breath and coughed again. "I can't breathe so well."

"He's poisoning you. We didn't get any results back yet from the hospital, but I'm sure of it. Have you called a doctor at all?"

"No."

"I need to get you away from here before he comes back."

"What time is it?"

He looked at his watch. "It's three fifteen."

"Billy will be home soon. I have to get Billy."

"Is he at school? We can pick him up there. I'll take you both to your mother's house, and we can call a doctor from there."

"Don't want my mother involved. He'll kill her too."

Stan took a step back. He must have threatened the entire family. "The police are on the way. You'll be safe." He reached over to pull back the blanket. "Let me help you get up and get dressed. I'll call your mother to let her know we're on the way."

Lucy slowly rose again and tried to move her legs over the edge of the bed, and Stan turned to go to the phone in the kitchen when he heard the crunching of tires on gravel in the driveway. He went to the window, raised the shade up half-way, and looked out. A dark green Plymouth was parked behind his car.

CHAPTER 31

Stan pulled the shade down and looked at Lucy, uncertain of what to do. Her hands trembled as she bit into her lower lip. No sense to hide, he thought. He knows my car. He stood still next to the bed, watching the bedroom door, and waited. He heard the front door open, then footsteps coming slowly down the hallway. Bickle appeared in the doorway holding a paper bag in one hand. Although he was three or four inches shorter than Stan, he probably outweighed Stan by thirty pounds—all muscle. He had a thick torso with broad shoulders and powerfully thick forearms, just as Helen had described.

Bickle smiled. "Caught you in the act! Mr. Ellis, I presume."

Standing up straight and as imposing as he could, Stan said, "Yes, I'm Stan Ellis. I came here because I got a call that your wife wanted to talk to me. I didn't know she was so ill." He started to move towards the door. "I'll leave now, and if she wants to call me later..."

Blocking the doorway, Bickle held both arms out straight. "Not so fast friend." His smile became a sneer. "My wife didn't call you. You know that now, and I know it."

"I... I was wondering. It was a woman, though. Who called?"

"Who called? Oh, that was my old friend Betty Mullin. We used to date. You met her once at Libby's when you went there to meet with Lucy. Remember? She thinks you're having an affair with my wife, and she wanted to do me a favor."

Stan scoffed. "You know I'm not having an affair with your wife. You know I'm a reporter, and I was doing a story that implicated you in causing that train wreck."

"I don't know any such thing. All I know is that you've been seeing my wife for the past several weeks, and people are beginning to talk. I know you were here in this house earlier this week doing whatever you do with my innocent wife. You wouldn't tolerate that. As the aggrieved husband, I can't either. I have to do something about it." He gave a smug smile.

Stan felt anger building in his chest. "Was it you, or did you put somebody else up to follow me last week and cut the brake hose on my car? I tracked down the license plate and found it belonged to a friend of yours. How'd you get him involved?"

"Yeah, it was Freddie's car. I figured you knew what my car looked like. So I asked him to lend me his. We been friends since our army days, and he was happy to do me the favor after I told him you'd been fucking around with my wife. I thought I'd put a scare into you, and you'd be smart enough to back off. I guess I was wrong. You ain't that smart."

"Why are you telling me this? You know I'm going to go to the police."

He shook his head slowly. "You aren't going to tell anybody anything."

"Yes I am. I know you've been poisoning Lucy, and I think you poisoned your first wife. I took samples of some of the stuff you got downstairs. Got a blood sample of Lucy too, and the hospital is testing it right now. When it comes back, the police will have what they need to arrest you."

Bickle shook his head. "I don't believe you, but got to hand it to you Ellis. You're persistent. As you can see Lucy is okay—maybe not exactly well, but she's alive. Just been a little sick. I had a doc here three days ago, and he couldn't find anything more wrong with her than a flu bug and maybe a touch of pneumonia. They ain't going to prove anything, because you've given me the perfect excuse for what's going to happen."

"What do you mean?"

"Your affair with Lucy. She's already lied to the cops about the train wreck thing. She told them we were having marriage trouble, and she wanted to get back at me. She took up with me when she was tired of Cashman, and now she's doing the same thing all over again. At least that's what people will think. After that telephone call to your office today, even the people you work with are going to believe you've been screwing my wife."

Stan's face turned red, and he clenched his fists. "I'm leaving." Stan took a step toward the door, and Bickle blocked the way. He tried to push him aside, but Bickle didn't budge, and instead drove him backward hard enough that he fell onto the bed, landing on Lucy who let out a scream. Stan quickly sat up on the edge of the bed, while Lucy wriggled to the other side with her back against the headboard and a sheet pulled up to her neck.

"What's that?" Stan asked, as Bickle emptied the contents of the bag he was carrying onto the floor—a coil of hemp rope, a roll of black electrical tape, and a box cutter. "What's that for?" he asked shakily.

"It's for you and my dear wife. We're going on a short trip."

"What do you mean a short trip?" Stan's eyes focused on the rope and the tape. *Where's Glen? Is he even coming?*

"A fishing trip. You like to fish?" Bickle snickered. "I know a perfect spot just a few miles from here—Powell's Pond. Ever hear of it? It's not very big. Only about seven feet deep but lots of soft gooey mud on the bottom. Just right for burying things so they'll never be found."

"You've gone crazy! If you try to do anything to Lucy or me, the cops will know it's you. You won't get away."

Bickle picked up the coil of rope. "Like I said before, people around here already know you and Lucy have been having a little thing going on for some time. It won't be hard to convince the cops that you and her took off to parts unknown, leaving poor old me to have to continue on alone."

"But there's the boy."

"Yeah, the boy. I'll have to tell him the sad story about his momma and you, and he'll have to adjust. Probably send him to his grandma to live. That's not so bad. That's what I had to do, and I turned out all right." He let out a chuckle.

Stan leaped up from the bed and took a wild swing at Bickle that landed on the side of his head, but only momentarily stunned him. As Stan tried to move around him, Bickle grabbed him by the waist, wrestled him to the floor and began punching. Stan flailed helplessly as the heavier man crouched over him, his knees in his ribs. He felt a blow to the nose and thought he heard a bone crack. Next a blow to the mouth, and then the taste of blood. He was losing consciousness. Then Bickle got off, pulled him to his feet, and threw him back on the bed. Bickle rolled him over on his stomach, pulled Stan's arms behind his back and began tying his wrists together. As he laid there, Stan said, "I know you caused the train derailment. Lucy told me you admitted it. But I still haven't figured out how you got the liquor bottle in the engine cab."

Bickle stopped tying and laughed. "I told you I had friends. Old Ty Gibbon was the one who did that. He's a brakeman like me, and we worked together a lot on that same train route. About the time I started to think about how to get rid of Cashman, he told me how he hated the man for turning him in to the trainmaster and getting him suspended for some minor incident. I told him I knew a way he could get back at him by putting a bottle of his own whiskey in the cab. Then when the Division inspectors come through, tell them Cashman's been drinking on the job and have them check the tool box. I gave him the bottle in a paper bag, and he put it in the engine cab just like I told him. He never knew what I intended to do to derail the train. He thought he was just gonna get Cashman suspended. It worked out great. Pretty smart, huh?"

"You're good at using people. One of these days it's going to catch up with you, and you'll pay for what you've done."

He yanked on the knot as he finished tying up the wrists, then cut off a foot-long piece of tape and wrapped it around his wrist and over the knot to make it more secure. "Well, you won't be around to see what happens Mr. Reporter." Letting him lie there face down, Bickle went to a dresser and pulled a gun, a snub-nosed .38, from the top drawer, checked to see it was loaded, and stuck it in his jacket pocket.

While Bickle was concentrating on Stan, Lucy sat terrified on the other side of the bed. Next to her was a nightstand with a table lamp along with a pencil and a book she'd been reading. She managed to reach over, pick up the pencil, and pull a scrap of paper she'd inserted in the book as a bookmark without Bickle noticing. She quickly jotted something down, and hid the paper and pencil under the pillow.

Bickle returned to Stan, grabbed the rope between Stan's wrists and jerked him off the bed and to his feet. "Let's go" he said.

Stan didn't move. "Why should I? You're just going to take me somewhere to kill me. You got the gun. Do it here, if you're gonna do it."

Bickle smirked. "Can't do that Stanley. Don't won't to leave any telltale evidence around the house." He pulled up with such force on his wrists that Stan thought his shoulder was being dislocated. Bickle punched him in his lower back and ordered, "Now let's go." As he pushed Stan out of the bedroom, he turned his head back toward his wife. "You wait here, hon, while I take your boyfriend out to the car. Be back for you in a jiffy."

As Bickle pushed him outside and led him over to the green car, Stan wondered why Bickle was driving Freddie's car and not his own Chevy. Then, as he watched him open the trunk lid, it hit him. He didn't want the cops to be able to trace anything to his own car. He tensed as Bickle grabbed the front of his shirt with two hands and stuffed him unceremoniously inside the trunk, then pushed his body around to fit into the cramped space.

When he finished, Stan was lying in a fetal position, his hands tied together as if in prayer and his knees nearly touching his chest. Bickle looked down with feigned sympathy. "It'll be a little tight I'm afraid. Those chains take up quite a bit of room. I know you'd like to cozy up to Lucy, but no room. I'll have to put her in the back seat. She won't be any problem the way she's feeling." He reached one hand up to grab the trunk lid. "Hope you're not afraid of the dark. You'll need to get used to it anyway where you're going." He shut the trunk lid with a THUNK.

CHAPTER 32

It was one thirty in the afternoon, and Glen was on a routine patrol in the western portion of the county when he received a call from dispatch. The sheriff was at a farmhouse south of Clifton initiating a search for a missing four-year-old boy. The dispatcher gave him the address and said he was to meet the sheriff there and give assistance. When he got to the farmhouse, he found the sheriff on the back porch looking over a map with Vic Palmer and Deputy Dave Lucas. Glen walked up onto the porch and stood by until the sheriff looked over at him. "You got here fast. That's good. I'm going over there to talk to those volunteers." He pointed out to the yard where about thirty people milled around. "I'll divide them up into three groups, and you'll each take one."

A few minutes later, while the sheriff was speaking to the volunteers in the yard, another deputy, Bill Porter, came up beside Glen, pulled him aside and said, "Just got a call on my radio. Your wife called dispatch. Said she has an emergency and needs you to come home right away."

Glen blanched. "It must be something to do with her pregnancy. She's not due yet. I need to get back there." But he couldn't leave without getting the sheriff's okay, and he couldn't interrupt him while he was speaking to the volunteers. He waited anxiously for ten minutes while the sheriff went through his instructions for the volunteers and answered questions. When he finished, Bascom turned toward the deputies standing to his rear, and Glen quickly stepped forward. "Sheriff, I hate to ask it, but my wife called and said she has an emergency. She's pregnant, and I really need to go to her."

The sheriff frowned, looked at Porter and then back at Glen. "You need to be with your wife. Go." He looked back at the other deputy. "You've just been drafted Porter."

Glen jogged back to his vehicle and sped to Sparta with his flashers on. When he entered his house, he shouted. "I'm home."

When she didn't answer right away, he started to panic, but calmed down when he heard the toilet flush and then saw her come out of the bathroom with no apparent distress. "Are you okay? They said it was an emergency."

"I'm okay. I called because Patty called me. She said Stan needs your help, and she wasn't able to get a hold of you. The dispatcher told her they would only contact you for a family emergency, and so that's what I told her we had."

"Carol! That's false pretense. You can't do that."

"Well, I did it. Are they going to hang me for it?"

"No, but it could mean my job. We were about to start searching for a missing boy."

"That's important, I know. But so is what Patty called about. They have other people who can help with the search. Patty really seemed frantic about Stan's safety, and right now they need our help."

"It's about Bickle, I'll bet. What kind of scrape has he got himself into?"

"He was going to Bickle's house to check on Lucy. Her mother called him and told him she couldn't reach her, and she asked Stan to help. Patty told him to let the police do it, but he wouldn't wait. He said he was going to stop at the Kendall police station and check in with them first."

"That damn fool. He's—.

The phone was ringing, and Carol picked up the receiver. "Yes, he's here. What! The results came back? Oh no! She's in real danger. I'll tell him." She hung up the phone and turned to Glen with a worried look on her face.

Patty says results of the blood test on Bickle's wife came back. It showed traces of cyanide and digitalis. That was from several days ago. No telling what condition she's in now. She needs to be taken to a hospital."

Glen held his arms out straight, motioning to her to calm down. "Okay, okay, no need to get excited. You said he was going to stop at the Kendall police station. I'm sure I've got a directory around somewhere. I'll call them and see if he's still there."

"Bickle is trying to poison that woman, and Stan is going to Bickle's house by himself. You need to get down there and make sure he's okay."

"I will," he said as he started looking through his top desk drawer. Finding the county directory, he dialed the number for the Kendall Police Station, and Officer Canfield answered the phone.

"This is Deputy Horner with the sheriff's office. I'm trying to locate a Stan Ellis, a reporter with the Sparta newspaper, who said he was going to stop in at your station. Have you seen him?"

"Yep, he was here. But he left about forty-five minutes ago."

"Did he say where he was going?"

"Ray Bickle's place. Said he wanted to check on his wife. Not sure why. I went over there earlier and talked to Ray, and she was okay."

Glen put one hand to his forehead. "Is Chief Chapman there?"

"No, he's on vacation this week. Anything you need me to do?"

Had the chief been in, he would have asked him to go to Bickle's house to save time, but this guy sounded like a dunce. He wasn't going to put his faith in him. "No, thanks for the info."

Glen put down the receiver and looked at Carol. "I'd better get going. Once this lab report gets to the DA, I'm sure we'll be taking action, but I think you're right. The woman could be in immediate danger."

"Aren't you going to call in to get someone to meet you there?"

"No. If Bickle's not there, there shouldn't be any problem I can't handle. If I call the lieutenant, he'll probably tell me it's the village's responsibility. He'll want me to wait till the sheriff gets back. That's too long. If I see I might run into a problem, I'll radio for help."

"Call me as soon as you can to let me know what's happening."

$$\cdot \quad \cdot \quad \cdot \quad \cdot \quad \cdot$$

It was a little after four when Glen got to the Bickle house. There was one car in the driveway. It was Stan's gray Ford. He got out of the car, went to the front door, and knocked. When there was no answer, he tried the door, and it opened. He stepped inside and hollered out, "This is Deputy Horner with the sheriff's office. Is anyone here?"

He walked through the living room and went straight to the master bedroom at the rear of the house. The bed was mussed up, the bed stand on one side was out of place and the lampshade on top was askew. He looked down at the carpet and saw spots of blood. There was blood too on the sheets—and somebody's tooth. Was it Stan's? There'd obviously been a fight. But where could they have gone? He opened the closet and saw a partially used roll of black tape and a length of rope on the floor. He didn't touch it, but closed the door and began looking around the floor of the bedroom. Near the door was a crumpled up scrap of paper. He picked it up and unwrapped it. The word "Powells" was written on it. What did it mean? He put it in his pocket and began checking the rest of the house, including the basement. He found the workroom in the basement and inspected the bottles of crushed plant material. Not finding anything else of interest, he exited the house intending to call in a 10-78 request for assistance to the sheriff's dispatcher, but when he got to the porch, he saw someone walking up the driveway—a young boy carrying a lunch pail in one hand and a book satchel in the other.

Glen stepped down from the porch and met the boy in the front yard. "Do you live here?"

The boy nodded his head.

"What's your name?"

"Billy. Billy Cashman."

Glen bent over to look the boy in the eyes. He was sure that Bickle had taken both Stan and Lucy somewhere, but he didn't want to frighten him. "I'm Deputy Horner. I came here looking for your parents. No one's home. Do you have any idea where they went?"

"I...I don't know. I was at school all day. My step-dad was here when I left home this morning. My mom was in bed. She's been kinda sick."

"When did you go to school?"

"It was a little before eight. That's when my school bus comes."

"Did your step-dad say he was taking your mom anyplace?"

"No. My mom was sleeping when I left, and he didn't say anything to me."

"What kind of car does your dad have?"

"It's a blue and white Chevy."

"I'm going to have to put out a search for your dad and mom. But first I need to get you someplace where you'll be safe. You have any relatives here in town?"

"No. My grandma lives in Elroy. She's my only relative around here."

"Okay, I'll drop you off at the police station in town, and they can get you to your grandma's."

Sensing from the tone of Glen's voice that something was very wrong, Billy said, "I don't want to go to my grandma's. I want to help."

Glen rubbed the side of his face with his right hand and thought of the scrap of paper with the word "Powells" on it. "Maybe there is a way you could help." He pulled the paper from his pocket, unfolded it, and showed it to Billy. "Do you have any idea what this name means? I think your mother dropped it on the floor before she left trying to leave you a message. Do you know anyone by the name of Powell?"

Billy shook his head. "No. Don't know anyone with that name."

"What about a place? Any place with that name?"

Billy frowned and thought hard. "There was a place a little way from here called Powell's Pond. Ray took me fishing there a few times after he married my mom. But I haven't been there in a long time."

Glen's eyes lit up. "That's it! How big was the pond?"

"Not real big."

"I mean was it wider than from here to the end of the driveway?"

"Yeah, maybe to the end of the driveway. That's how big."

Glen estimated it was about forty yards. Just a small pond, and probably wouldn't show up on the map. "Go sit on the porch while I check my map to see if it's on there." Glen went to his patrol car and as he opened the passenger door, he noticed a dark red spatter, apparently blood, on the gravel where Bickle would have been parked. He bent down and touched it. Still wet. Further evidence of some kind of struggle. Must have missed them by only a few minutes. He opened the car's glove compartment, took out a regional map, and unfolded it on the hood of the vehicle. He had never heard of Powell's Pond and had no idea where to focus on the map. The larger lakes were identified by name, but he could find nothing that said "Powell."

Glen folded up the map and went to the porch where Billy was sitting with his chin in his hands. "Do you think you can find where your step-dad took you fishing on this map?"

Billy shrugged his shoulders. "I don't know. I can try."

With the two-foot square map spread on the floor, both Glen and Billy knelt on hands and knees peering down. "Here's where we are now," said Glen pointing. "Which direction did you go from here when you went fishing?"

Billy swiveled his head around to look at the driveway and then pointed off to the right. "We went that way."

"Okay, that's east. So how long did it take you to get to the fishing place? Fifteen minutes, a half-hour, an hour?"

Billy thought for a moment. "Maybe a half-hour. I can't remember exactly."

Glen put a hand to his forehead and tried to imagine where Bickle might be headed. If he was going to a small lake a half-hour away, he'd likely be traveling mostly on gravel roads. So he wouldn't be driving over forty-five. That means the pond should be within a twenty-mile radius of the house. It might be in the next county, but he couldn't worry about that. He drew an imaginary arc on the map with his hand to identify the area where the pond might be and looked at Billy. "Can you see any spot in the area I've circled that might be Powell's Pond?"

"I... I can't tell."

Glen straightened up. "I need to call an APB to my office and get you over to your grandma's."

Billy pounded the porch floorboards with his fists. "No! I can find it if you'll take me in your car."

Glen looked down at him. "You really think you can?" He knew he shouldn't take a chance on endangering a kid, but time was crucial.

Billy gave an emphatic nod. "I'm pretty sure."

"Okay," said Glen. "Get in the patrol car and let's go. Whatever happens, stay in the car."

CHAPTER 33

Stan blinked his eyes. Everything was black—totally black. He tried to take a breath, and it was difficult with his body curled up so. He cursed himself for not waiting for Glen. There was no chance he could escape. He was going to die. His mind turned to thoughts of what drowning would be like. How long would it take? He tried to roll over and felt something cold and hard against his cheek—it was a heavy iron chain. He heard a car door open, and he heard Lucy cry out. He felt the car rock gently underneath him as her body was dumped in the back seat. A door slammed shut. He thought about his parents and wondered how they would react when they learned of his death. He thought of Patty and how he'd been planning to ask her to marry him when this thing was over. Now it would never happen. He thought of how the Herald would report it in the newspaper. It would probably even be in the Milwaukee Journal. Would they say he had disappeared along with Lucy and that they had been having an affair? Would Patty believe that? No, never!

The car vibrated as the engine started up, and he felt it backing out of the driveway. If he were Houdini, he could escape from these knots. Even if he were tied up in chains and dropped in the water, he could escape. But he wasn't Houdini. He started to cry, and then stopped himself. He couldn't just give up—not when he thought of Patty. Maybe he wasn't Houdini, but he'd learned to tie knots in the Boy Scouts. Maybe he could untie himself, and at least try to escape when they got to wherever Bickle was taking him. As he felt the car turn onto the paved road, he started to twist his wrists in an attempt to loosen the tape so he could get at the rope. The tape didn't adhere to the rope fibers and he was quickly able to push it clear of the knot with a thumb and index finger. Then he began scraping at the knot fibers with a fingernail. It was a double knot, but after a difficult four or five minutes he was able to untie the first one and start on the next. Another couple of minutes and the second knot was undone.

He wiggled his wrists back and forth to further loosen the tape and rope hanging around his wrists and was able to slip one hand out. Finally, his hands were free, but now what? There was little room to maneuver. He couldn't win in a hand-to-hand fight with Bickle. Was there anything in the trunk he could use? This wasn't Bickle's car. Maybe he overlooked something. He felt around and touched the chain and shuddered. He felt along the edge of the trunk. Above his head his hand found a canvas tarp covering something hard. His fingers crawled underneath the tarp and touched something cylindrical. His first thought was a metal thermos bottle. He let his hand slide over it and realized it was a tire jack, and it was resting on something else. He stretched his arm further and felt another metal object—something with multiple arms. His fingers ran along the outer edges of the object. It was a lug wrench. Bickle hadn't thought to take it out of the trunk. It was a possible weapon.

Stan sensed the car veer off the paved road unto gravel. As he was being bounced and jostled over the gravel back-road, he concentrated on how to surprise Bickle when he opened the trunk. His concentration was broken when he felt the car leave the gravel road and go onto what seemed like a rutted dirt track. They were getting close. He reached for the lug wrench with his right hand and brought it behind his butt so that when he rolled over to get out, it wouldn't be immediately visible to Bickle. After only a couple minutes the vehicle stopped, and he tightened his grip on the wrench and waited.

He heard a car door open and slam shut. Then another door open and the car bounced. He heard Lucy shout something and Bickle respond.as he was apparently taking her out of the car. Their voices began to fade as they moved away. He was taking her somewhere first before he dealt with Stan. The minutes ticked off until he heard footsteps nearing the car. He heard a key turn in the trunk's keyhole. The trunk lifted and Bickle stood staring down at him with one hand on the trunk lid and the other with the .38 revolver pointed at him. "Get out." Bickle ordered.

"I can't move my legs. No circulation. You got to help me get my legs out of the trunk first."

Bickle put the gun in his pocket, bent over and pulled his legs straight so they hung over the edge of the trunk. While he was still bent over, Stan sprung straight up and swung the lug wrench with all his might at his head. It wasn't a direct hit, but it was enough to stagger Bickle and gave Stan an opportunity. He leaped out of the trunk, and as Bickle started to pull the gun from his pocket, he threw the wrench at him. Bickle raised his arm to deflect the wrench and Stan dove for his legs, tackled him and drove him to the ground. Lying on top of Bickle, Stan wrestled for the gun, and they rolled over the ground struggling to gain control of it. Bickle's strength eventually was too much. Stan, lying on his back, found the trigger of the gun with his index finger and pulled. It fired, but the shot went into the air. Bickle ripped the gun away from Stan's hand and rapped him hard against the side of the head with the butt of the gun.

Stan was out for only a brief time, but when he opened his eyes, he was again laying on his stomach with his hands being tied behind his back. Blades of grass poked him in the eyes, and his whole head was throbbing. Feeling some solid object loose in his mouth, he spat, and a bloody tooth dribbled off his swollen lower lip onto the grass. When he tried to turn his head to get some air, it felt like a jolt of lightning had struck him square in the jaw. Tears welled up in his eyes and he tried to scream, but the only thing that came out of his mouth was a piteous mewl.

"You had your chance buddy boy," said Bickle. "Gotta hand it to you. I didn't think you had that kind of guts. But that was your last chance. As he was being pulled to his feet, Stan heard the sound of a car engine. He and Bickle turned at the same time to see a county sheriff's car stop thirty yards away. Nothing happened for two minutes as Bickle positioned himself behind Stan, gripping him tightly by the back of his shirt collar and holding the gun to his back.

The driver's door to the patrol car opened, and he saw an officer get out and maintain protective cover behind the open door. Then he heard Glen's voice. "Throw down your gun and lay down on the ground Bickle. You're under arrest for kidnapping."

"I think we've got a Mexican standoff deputy. I'm not dropping my gun. You drop yours, or I shoot Mr. Ellis here."

"I called in the location and I've got help coming. You need to give it up now. Release your hostage and drop your gun."

"I don't know how you tracked me, but I know this place isn't on any map and by the time anyone finds it here I'll be long gone. I don't think you'll take a chance on shooting an innocent man. But I've no qualms about shooting. He fired his pistol and Glen ducked his head behind the driver's door as a bullet shattered the window above him.

Stan, being taller, was a perfect shield for Bickle. He knew that Glen would be reluctant to try to shoot Bickle for fear of hitting him. After firing the first shot, Bickle pushed Stan forward to where they were only about twenty-five yards from the patrol car. He knew Bickle was going to keep moving him forward until he could get an unimpeded shot at Glen. His jaw felt like one giant toothache. The pain was almost more than he could stand, and every time he tried to take a breath he felt a stabbing pain in his side. He felt Bickle's fingernails digging into the back of his neck and knew it wouldn't be easy, but somehow he had to twist away at the right moment to give Glen a chance at a clean shot. Otherwise, they were both dead men.

Bickle pushed Stan another five yards forward, being careful to keep Stan's body between him and Glen's possible line of fire. They were twenty yards from the patrol car when Bickle fired again. This time he aimed for Glen's lower legs visible below the car door. Glen let out a yell and he returned a shot that went high and wide in an apparent attempt to get Bickle to back away. "Not even close," hollered Bickle. Your time's running out. Throw your gun away. Give me the vehicle, and I'll let both of you go. I don't want to have to kill you."

Bickle started pushing Stan again, not noticing a small figure with an iron lug wrench in his right hand quietly approaching from behind. Glen, evidently hit in the leg or foot, had maneuvered himself partially back into the driver's seat, drew the driver's door half-way closed and aimed his long-barreled .38 at Bickle. Stan knew the standoff was coming to an end one way or another, and he had to be ready to move. The next time Bickle shot, Glen would also have to shoot—this time to kill. Now about fifteen yards from the patrol car, Stan felt Bickle remove the pistol from his back. His body tensed as he prepared to drop, when he heard a heavy THUMP, felt the grip on his neck loosen, and heard the crack of a gun going off. All in the space of two seconds he dropped to the ground, heard two more quick shots, and saw Bickle fall to the ground beside him.

A moment later Glen came hobbling over, kicked away the pistol that was still in Bickle's hand, and turned him over. "He's still breathing. Not sure if he'll make it to the hospital." He rolled him on his side and cuffed him, then looked at Stan with a big grin, "You ducked just in time. You knew just what I was thinking." He pointed behind Stan and said loudly. "The real hero, though, is our little buddy over there. He threw that tire wrench at Bickle and hit him. Threw his shot off. Saved both our lives."

Stan got to a sitting position, turned his head, fighting the intense pain, and saw Billy standing ten feet away with his hands to his sides and a frown on his face. Stan couldn't open his mouth to talk, but he simply clasped his hands together prayerfully and rocked back and forth. Billy pointed toward a rowboat at the edge of the pond. "My mom's over there. She needs help."

Glen raced over to the boat, with Billy following close behind, and found Lucy curled up in the rowboat, her hands and ankles tied, a coil of chain wrapped around her torso. She was conscious, but barely. He got her out of the boat, untied her on the bank and carried her back to where Stan was, laying her down on the grass. After checking her over quickly, he saw her vital signs were weak, and her words weren't making sense. He took off his jacket and laid it across her upper body. Then he went to the patrol car to radio in the situation and to request ambulances. He pulled a first-aid kit from the car and went back to do what he could to save Bickle who had bullet wounds in his stomach and his right shoulder. He looked at Stan who was in obvious agony. "Just a few more minutes. Help is on the way. As he attempted to staunch Bickle's bleeding, the sound of sirens could be heard drawing near.

CHAPTER 34

Stan had been running relay laps over and over, practicing for tonight's track meet, but every time he tried to pass the baton, he couldn't quite reach Glen's outstretched hand. When he got close, his legs felt like wet logs, and he ended up falling face-first onto the cinder track. We can't fail, cried Glen. "People are depending on us. Just once more."

"I don't know if I can," said Stan. "But I'll try."

Somewhere in the distance Stan heard the voice of his mother saying something. He realized he was dreaming and wondered if she was here to see him run in tonight's track meet. He forced his eyes open, expecting to be in the familiar surroundings of his old bedroom in the house he grew up in. As his blurry eyes focused on his surroundings, he saw he wasn't in his own bed, and realized he wasn't still a high school senior. An IV tube was stuck in one arm, his chest wrapped with tight bandaging, and a monitoring machine chirped ominously on a shelf above his bed. He touched his face and felt some type of tubing hanging from his nose. Then it dawned on him what had happened.

He turned his head to the left and saw his mother in a chair with a book in her lap and his dad next to her dozing with his chin on his chest. There was a vase with a bouquet of flowers sitting on a table between them. He was about to say something when Patty, who'd been sitting in a chair at the end of the bed, stood up and said, "He's awake!"

Immediately his mother put down her book, jumped up from her chair, came over, and put her hand on his free arm. His dad roused himself from his nap, snorted, and came to stand beside his wife. Stan tried to say "Mom," but he couldn't open his mouth.

"Don't try to talk," she said. "The doctors had to wire your mouth after doing surgery to fix your jaw. It's broken. We were just waiting for you to wake up."

His father leaned over the bed. "Your mother and I were worried out of our skin when the sheriff's office called last night to tell us there was a shooting and you were hurt. Didn't know what to think, but the doctor says you'll be okay. You'll just have to put up with that contraption in your mouth for a while."

Stan couldn't tell if it was day or night and didn't know how long he'd been there. He patted his wrist where his watch would normally be, and Patty came to the side of the bed with a pad and pencil. When he saw her, his eyes brightened, and he reflexively tried to open his mouth to speak, but only an anguished "UUUH" came out.

She raised one hand to signal he shouldn't try to talk, and with the other laid a small writing pad and a pencil into his open hand. "Just write what you want to say."

"He wrote a question. "How long I been here?"

"Two days. They brought you here Friday evening at seven. It's ten o'clock Sunday morning now. Doctor Shaw performed surgery on your jaw and nose yesterday. You've been sedated pretty heavily since you came out of surgery, so I'm not surprised you don't remember. You also had two fractured ribs, but that didn't require surgery. They just wrapped you up."

He picked up the pencil again. "How long do I stay here?"

"I'm not sure," said Patty. The doctor should be here soon, and he can give you some idea, but you'll probably be here three or four days anyway. I'm supposed to be on duty over in B Wing, but Mary, my supervisor, told me I could sit here with you until you wake up. She put her hand on his. "I'll be back to check on you when my shifts over at five."

A few minutes later Doctor Shaw came into Stan's partitioned-off space, greeted his parents, and then asked them to step outside while he examined Stan. After they left, he picked up a chart hanging on a rail at the end of the bed. When he finished reading it over, he went to the bedside and introduced himself.

He removed the stethoscope from around his neck and said, "I know you're not feeling very chipper after what you've been through, but your surgery went well, and I don't expect any complications. I see you have a pad and pencil handy. I'm sure you have a number of questions, but first I need to check how you're doing. It'll take just a few minutes."

After he'd finished with his examining protocol, Stan wrote out, "Do you have a mirror?"

The doctor went over to a cabinet and pulled a hand mirror from a drawer and handed it to him. When he looked into it, he didn't recognize the image as a human being. He looked like a chimpanzee who'd stuck his nose into a beehive. His lips, parted slightly to reveal bits of shiny steel braces, were swollen in the shape of two Oscar Mayer hotdogs lying one atop the other. His whole lower face was puffed up like a party balloon. Blue-black rings circled his eyes, a plastic feeding apparatus hung from his nostrils, and the bridge of his nose was covered with a broad white bandage. If he didn't know it was actually him, he would have laughed out loud at the sight. He put down the mirror, and wrote, "When can I eat and talk?"

The doctor explained the surgical procedures that he'd performed and told him he would have to keep the mouth wired for at least four weeks. He added, "After the wires are removed, you'll be able to talk, but you'll need to ease into eating normal food. You'll also need to arrange with a dentist to have dentures fitted."

Stan pointed to his nose. "We can probably remove the bandage from your nose when you leave, but you're going to look like a boxer that's just gone a few rounds with Rocky Marciano." The doctor then pointed to his own nose. "We'll probably be able to remove the feeding tube from your nose tomorrow, but you'll be using a straw and be on a liquid diet until the wires are removed."

Stan grimaced and placed a hand on his midsection that was tightly bandaged.

"The ribs will heal themselves," said the doctor. "You just need to keep it bandaged for another week. We'll schedule you for a follow-up visit in the office.

Stan nodded and wrote, "When can I go home?"

The doctor smiled. "That's always an important question. We need to keep you here for a few days. Let's see how you're doing after three or four days. We need to be sure everything is okay before we let you go.

That wasn't the news he wanted to hear, but at least it was a date to look forward to. The doctor said, "You're on pain medication that's going to keep you sleepy. If the pain gets too great, you can buzz for the nurse and we may be able to increase the dosage. She'll be in to check on you periodically. Any more questions?"

Stan shook his head.

When the doctor left, Stan's parents returned to his bedside and remained for another fifteen minutes until his father got up from his chair, looked to his wife and said, "We have to get going Nell. The cows still need to be fed, and I got hay to put up." Stan knew his father, who farmed 250 acres on the north side of Tomah, was not the sentimental type, and he was actually surprised that he'd spent this much time sitting here with his mother.

Before they left, his mother leaned over and gave him a kiss on the forehead. "I'll be back tomorrow, but your dad might not be able to make it. Once they release you, you'll be coming home to stay with us until you get that thing out of your mouth."

He hadn't had time to consider how he'd be able to take care of himself when he left the hospital, but his mother had just solved that problem for him, and he didn't argue. He just squeezed her hand and said, "Mmmm."

After his parents left, he heard talking on the other side of the curtains surrounding his bed and realized there was at least one other patient in the room. He laid back and thought about what he'd been through. The last thing he remembered was hearing the sirens, and then somebody looming over him, picking him up, and then putting him in an ambulance. What happened to Bickle? What about Lucy? Just as he started to drift off, he heard a rustle of the curtain and saw a head poke through. It was Glen. "How you doing pal? You got time for me."

Stan raised his hands and tried to part his lips to no avail. Glen, hobbling on crutches, came up alongside, reached out his hand, and Stan grabbed it and held it tight. "I know. It was a close call. But it came out all right," said Glen. "If it hadn't been for Patty calling Carol and getting her to call me in the field, I wouldn't have known anything about what you were doing."

Glen pulled up a chair, laid his crutches down, and sat next to the bed. Stan pointed at the crutches.

"Yeah, Bickle got me in the foot," said Glen. "It could have been a lot worse. The doc says I'll be able to walk without a limp in a few weeks. In the meantime I'm assigned to office duty, which I'm okay with, at least for a while."

Stan nodded and wrote, "What happened to Bickle?"

"The bastard's going to live. I shot him twice, but the docs were able to save him. He's still in recovery and under guard now, but as soon as he's well enough he'll be going to county to wait for trial. I'm pretty sure the judge won't let him out on bail. The important thing is we got him cold now for attempted murder and kidnapping. He's not going to escape that."

"What about Lucy?"

"Ah, Lucy. After I shot Bickle, her son showed me she was over by the pond, in a rowboat, her hands and feet all tied up. He even had an iron chain wrapped around her. She was conscious but not making much sense. I untied her and carried her over to where you were and waited for an ambulance. She's a sick girl, but they tell me she's going to make it. When they brought her into the hospital Friday, she was in bad shape. Luckily the lab results on her blood came back Friday afternoon identifying the poisons in her system."

Stan frowned and held out his hands, palms up, asking him to explain.

"Yeah, it was just like you thought. They found evidence of toxins that matched up with the plant material you found in Bickle's basement. Patty was in the emergency room when the ambulance arrived with Lucy, and she let the doctor on duty know about the lab results. He knew right away what he needed to do to counteract the poison. I don't think she's entirely out of the woods. They still have to do tests to find out what lasting damage the poison may have done to her. I imagine she'll be in the hospital for a while."

Stan picked up his pencil and wrote, "What about Billy?"

"Hah!" Glen exclaimed. "That's one brave boy. I brought him along because he said he knew the way to get to Powell's Pond. I told him he'd have to stay in the vehicle. Thank God he didn't listen. I couldn't believe my eyes when I saw him creeping up behind Bickle. Up to that point I thought I was a dead man. I was just hoping I'd be able to take out Bickle without hitting you. Then, just as he started to take aim at me, the kid flung that lug wrench like a boomerang, hitting Bickel square in the back and causing him to jerk his arm up. His shot went up in the air, and when you dropped to the ground, I was able to get my shots off. Like I said, Billy was the hero, and the sheriff told me he was going to talk to the mayor about having a special recognition ceremony for him."

Stan went back to his pad. "Hooray!"

He noticed that Stan appeared to be getting drowsy, and he tapped his arm. "I don't want to keep you up from your beauty sleep. You need to get your rest. I'll call tomorrow to see how you're doing."

It didn't take long for Stan to fall into a fitful sleep with the events of the preceding days running through his mind. At some point he started dreaming of Patty and him going to Bickle's house to look for evidence of poison. Lucy wasn't home, but her husband was. Bickle greeted them at the door, told them Lucy was in bed, and invited them into the house to see her. Bickle led them to the bedroom and allowed them to go in first. What they saw caused Patty to cry out. Lucy was dead, lying on the bed with a sheet covering her body up to her chest. Her eyelids were open, and she stared blankly at the ceiling. Her face and shoulders were as white as the sheet covering her. Before either of them could react, Bickle grabbed Patty, put a gun to her head, and marched both of them outside to the car. He ordered Stan into the trunk and shut the lid. He heard Bickle scuffling with Patty, a scream, and then silence. As the car started to move, he felt around the pitch-black trunk for the wrench. There was no tarp, no tire jack, no wrench. There was nothing but the steel chain. He and Patty were going to die. He imagined himself and Patty wrapped in iron chains, sinking to the bottom of a lake. He tried to shout, but nothing came out. He thrashed and kicked futilely at the trunk lid.

"Wake up! Wake up!" Stan sensed someone shaking him by the arm. He opened his eyes. He was back in the hospital, and Patty was standing over him, her hand on his arm, with a worried look on her face. He stared up at her, took her hand in his and squeezed tight. "You were having a bad dream," she said. "What was it?"

He tried to speak but was immediately reminded his mouth was wired shut. Tears began to form in the corners of his eyes as he let out a plaintive moan.

She pressed his hand tighter. "You've been through a lot. I'm not surprised you're having nightmares. Maybe you need to see a counselor to help you get your mind straight again."

He let go of her hand, picked up the pencil and paper, and wrote, "Don't need counselor. Need you. Marry me?"

She opened her mouth and raised her arms in surprise and then leaned over and kissed him on the forehead. She picked up the notepad and wrote, "YES!"

CHAPTER 35

December 8, 1958

Stan stomped the snow off his boots before entering the newspaper office. It was his first day back at work after he'd had the wires removed from his mouth. He could hardly wait to get back to work full-time after almost six weeks staying at home. He hadn't been completely idle during that time. Having his mouth wired shut hadn't stopped him from doing some writing for the Herald. Just the week before they'd published a lengthy personal story he'd written covering his investigation into the train wreck, the subsequent adventure involving Ray Bickle, and his close encounter with death.

Normally he would be at work by seven thirty, but he told Irv he'd be in a little late because he had to stop by Dr. Shaw's office to get some stitches out before coming to work. When he walked into the newsroom at nine, he saw a banner hanging from the ceiling above his desk with the words "Welcome Back Stan" written on it. As soon as he came in, the staff, including the guys from the press room in the back, gathered around him telling him how much they missed him. He noticed Rose and Esther raise their eyebrows in surprise when he first opened his mouth revealing the huge gap where his two front teeth had once been. He feigned embarrassment and briefly covered his mouth with one hand. "Sorry ladies for scaring you so. My girlfriend, Patty, had a similar reaction when she first saw it. I've got an appointment with Dr. Wilcox on Wednesday to get some dentures, so you won't have to put up with this face too long.

Even Ed Malloy came out of his office to pat him on the back. After things settled down, and everyone headed back to their desks or machines, Ed asked

Stan to see him in his office once he had a chance to have his coffee. After filling his coffee mug and picking up one of the glazed doughnuts from the box someone had brought in for the celebration, he went and sat down next to Irv's desk.

"I hear you're getting married. Congratulations," said Irv.

"Yeah. We got together with both our parents last Friday and set a date for April 11. It'll be a big change in my life, but it won't change what I love to do, and that's working on the paper. I know you've been doing a lot of double duty while I've been out. I felt bad about leaving you in the lurch like that."

Irv shook his head. "You needn't have worried. We all were just hoping for your full recovery, and from the looks of you, it seems like you're pretty much there—except for those teeth." Irv smiled and cocked his head to examine Stan's profile. "Actually, the surgery you had may have done you some good—more mature, tough guy look. Now if you could just grow a mustache, you'd fit in anywhere as an investigative reporter."

Stan laughed. "Maybe I'll try growing one." Changing the subject, he asked, "With my mouth wired shut these past several weeks, I haven't been able to talk to anyone about what's happening on the legal front with Bickle. Any talk of a trial date yet?"

"Not yet. There's still a lot going on with his case. Right now he's still being held in the county jail on attempted murder charges and kidnapping, but I talked to the coroner Saturday. I'm sure you read that they exhumed Alice Bickle's body a couple weeks ago."

Stan nodded. "I was so glad to see that. Any results yet?"

"The sheriff's going to make an announcement today. I talked to Doctor Marsh on Saturday and he said the results of her autopsy came back positive for poisoning, and he's going to revise the cause of death as homicide. I'm sure the district attorney will be adding murder one to the charges already filed against Bickle. I wrote up a piece for today's edition."

Stan punched the air with his fist. "That bastard Bickle! He's such a manipulator of people. You know he convinced some of his friends I was having an affair with his wife. There was that woman who called here and left a message for me saying she was Lucy and wanted me to come see her because her husband was away."

"Yeah, there was some whispering in the office after you left that day."

"That was a waitress friend of his he convinced. And then there was that guy he borrowed the green car from to disguise the fact that it was him who cut the brake hose on my car. If Bickle had succeeded in killing Lucy and me, he was going to try to convince the police that Lucy and I had run off together and he was the jilted victim. You wouldn't have believed that, would you?"

"Not me. Not for a minute. But it's difficult to say what others might have thought if you'd disappeared, and they couldn't find any bodies. Thankfully, it never got to that point. The next time you see Bickle, I expect will be in a courtroom. That probably won't be easy for you."

"No, I'm looking forward to that. I'll be ready. I want to be sure he's put away for good. It sounds like there could be a second trial as well. I heard on the radio over the weekend that they arrested Ty Gibbon on conspiracy charges."

"Yep, that's right. According to the information I picked up at the sheriff's office on Saturday, Bickle turned on Gibbon. Claims the two of them conspired to have Gibbon hide the liquor bottle in the engine cab in order to frame Cashman and make it look like he'd been drinking on the job. I'm not sure whether Gibbon knew what Bickle's plans were as far as derailing the train, but maybe we'll find out when he goes to trial."

Stan started to get up but then had another thought. "What about George Cashman? Anything new there?"

"As a matter-of-fact there is. You lawyer friend, Anson Puller, has taken Cashman on as a client and has filed a petition with the state appeals court for a retrial based on the new evidence. Because of all the publicity the Bickle story has created, they're expected to rush a decision. If all goes as I expect, Cashman will be freed eventually. Maybe they won't even have to have a jury trial. We could use an in-depth on him. You want to take it?"

"You bet I do. I already have an appointment to meet with Cashman up at Waupon tomorrow. I think I'll go see Anson Puller this afternoon to see if he can fill me in on what's involved with the new appeal and any other option he's considering if that fails."

Irv raised his eyebrows. "Not wasting any time. That's good. I'm sure Cashman will appreciate your going to see him."

"It's something I've been planning for a while. When I met with Cashman back in October, he said he hadn't laid eyes on his son in nearly four years and just wanted to see him before he died. I don't want him to have to wait any longer. I asked his ex-wife to go with me and bring her son. She said she's not yet ready to face him, but she agreed to let me take Billy. I'm going to take him and his grandmother with me tomorrow. It should be quite a reunion."

Irv clapped him on the back. "You've got a big heart Stan Ellis. No rush on the story, but I'd like to get something by the end of next week. Now you better go see Ed before he comes out looking for you. He seemed in a good mood, so let's keep it that way."

Stan finished off his doughnut and stopped back at his desk to leave his coffee cup before going in to see the boss. He knocked on the side of the door, and Ed waved him in. Stan took a seat in front of the desk and waited for his boss to speak.

Ed, an unlit cigar tucked into the side of his mouth, sat looking at him intently for several seconds, then leaned forward, putting the cigar aside. "I've been running this newspaper a long time, just as my father did before me, and I've prided myself on making good business decisions. There were times I wondered whether I made a good decision on hiring you. I don't think I've been wrong much over the years." He slapped the table hard with one hand. "But I've got to admit I was wrong in trying to hold you back on the Bickle story." His face brightened into a warm smile. "You took a hell of a chance in pursuing this story, but it paid off big time—both for our little newspaper and for the community as a whole. But even more than that, you've proven you've got what it takes to be a newsman."

Stan reddened. "Thank you Mr. Malloy."

Ed leaned back in his chair and picked up the cigar again. "I'd like to keep you around here working for a long time, but I'm not sure I can compete with some of the people who are going to be coming after you."

Stan looked puzzled. "What people are you talking about?"

"That feature story you wrote got picked up by papers all over the state— the Milwaukee Journal, the State Journal, the LaCrosse Tribune—and I've got calls from their editors. Early this morning Cliff Hanover at the Milwaukee Journal called me. I've known him for years. We went to college together. He asked me to have you call him. He said he's got an opening he wants to consider you for and asked me what I thought. You want to know what I told him?"

Stan gave a nod of his head.

"I told him he'd be a fool not to hire you."

Ed tore a page from a notepad that had the telephone number on it and gave it to Stan. He looked down at the paper, feeling unsure how to respond. He was thrilled that there was interest from a big paper, but didn't want to appear overeager to leave the Herald. "I... I've always hoped to get an opportunity like this. It isn't that I'm unhappy here, but if I get a chance like this..."

"If he makes you an offer, take it," said Ed. "Don't worry about us. This paper has been around for nearly a hundred years and we'll be around another hundred whether you're here or not. Now go make that call."

NOTE FROM THE AUTHOR

Word-of-mouth is crucial for any author to succeed. If you enjoyed *Going Off the Rails*, please leave a review online—anywhere you are able. Even if it's just a sentence or two. It would make all the difference and would be very much appreciated.

Thanks!
Richard

ABOUT THE AUTHOR

Richard S. Brown was born in Elgin, Illinois, but moved to Wisconsin at age 8 when his father began working for the Chicago & Northwestern Railroad. After high school, he served in the U.S. Navy for three years, then attended Northern Illinois University where he majored in political science. After completing graduate school, he began a thirty-year civilian career with the U.S. Army. Richard and his wife live in Overland Park, Kansas.

Thank you so much for reading one of our **Mystery** novels.
If you enjoyed our book, please check out our recommendation
for your next great read!

K-Town Confidential by Brad Chisholm and Claire Kim

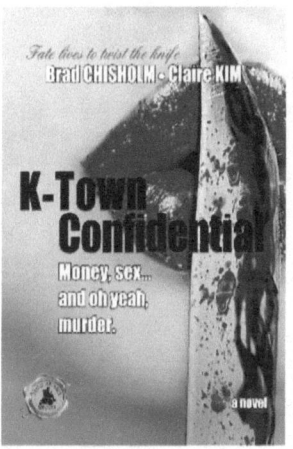

"An enjoyable zigzagging plot."
-Kirkus Reviews

"If you are a fan of crime stories and legal dramas that have a noir
flavor, you won't be disappointed with *K-Town Confidential*."
-Authors Reading